# EIGHT ARMS
# TO HOLD ME

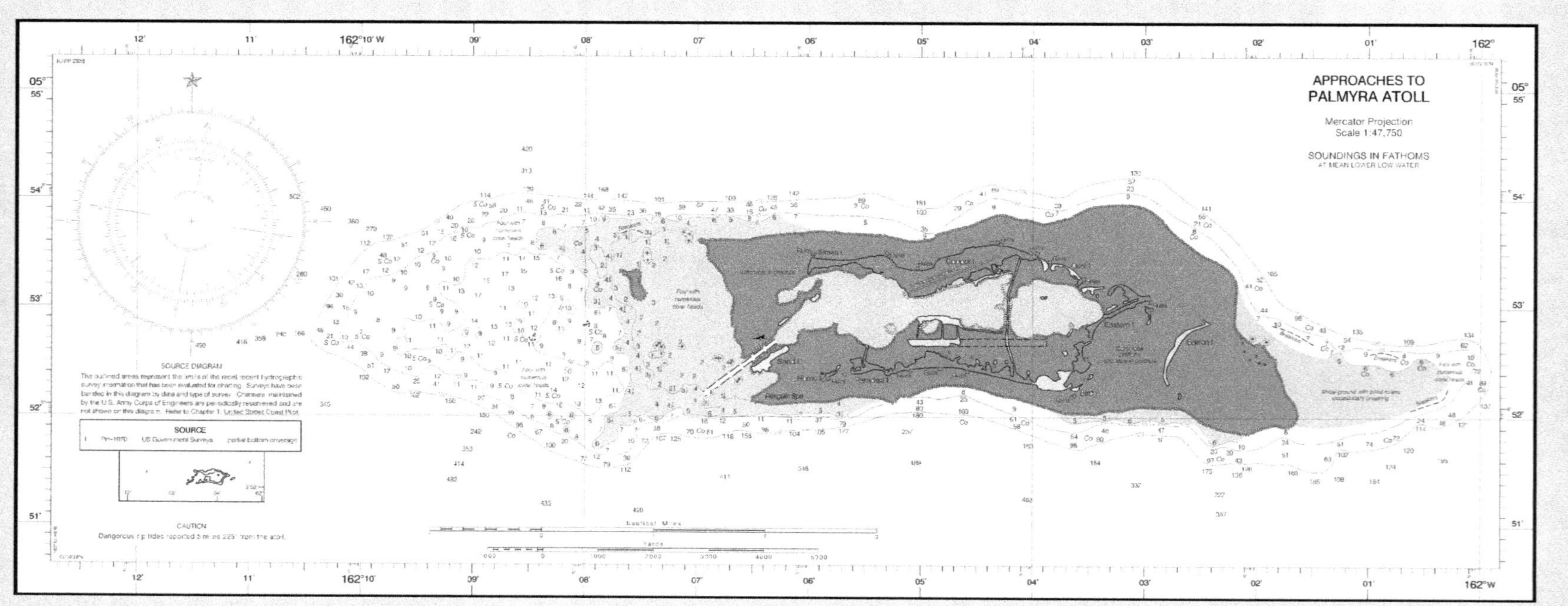

APPROACHES TO
PALMYRA ATOLL
Mercator Projection
Scale 1:47,750
SOUNDINGS IN FATHOMS
AT MEAN LOWER LOW WATER
SOURCE DIAGRAM
The outlined areas represent the limits of the most recent hydrographic survey information that has been evaluated for charting. Surveys have been bounded in this diagram by date and type of survey. Channels maintained by the U.S. Army Corps of Engineers are periodically resurveyed and are not shown on this diagram. Refer to Chapter 1, United States Coast Pilot.
SOURCE
Pre-1970    US Government Surveys    partial bottom coverage
CAUTION
Dangerous rip tides reported 5 miles 225° from the atoll.
Nautical Miles
Yards

# EIGHT ARMS TO HOLD ME

## AN OLIVER THE OCTOPUS ADVENTURE

### BY JOSHUA MERTZ

ISBN: 979-8-9906575-1-9
Ebook ISBN: 979-8-9906575-2-6

Manufactured in the United States of America.

Cover illustration by Cash Chapman | circuscaash@gmail.com
Title font by Jake Clark | Jake Clark @ Reedsy
Octopus art by Michael Schropp | @schropptheartist
Octopus silhouette art by Ron LaFond | z.ronlafond@gmail.com

Book design by Maureen Forys, Happenstance Type-O-Rama

10 9 8 7 6 5 4 3 2 1

*For my mother,*
*who gifted me with*
*her love of words.*

# PROLOGUE

*The dark side of the moon is battered and pockmarked from the millennia of meteorites it has diverted away from Earth. The dark side of the moon is mysterious; in art it represents a troubled mind, deep secrets, or madness. If you wished to hide anything, the dark side of the moon would be a good place, a jumble of confusion in which you could hide, for instance, your spaceship if you were a spacefaring civilization.*

*On the night of the new moon a rock formation pushed itself loose from the hidden face of the lunar surface and drifted silently away from Earth's satellite. It was a very regularly shaped rock formation. One that was invisible to radar and moved with strange energies. It fell toward the blue planet below.*

## GERSHON OCEANOGRAPHIC INSTITUTE ASSET PROFILE

| | |
|---|---|
| **SPECIES** | Giant Pacific Octopus (augmented) <br> *Enteroctopus dofleini schreinerii* |
| **NAME** | Oliver |
| **HEIGHT** | —n.a.— |
| **LENGTH** | Variable; arm span up to 17 feet / 5.18 meters |
| **WEIGHT** | 58 pounds / 26.3 kilograms |
| **COLORING** | Extremely variable; see Augmentations below |
| **HANDLER** | John Rauchenberg, M.S. Marine Biology, OSU |
| **AUGMENTATIONS** | Total neuron mass increased by 40%, distributed: main brain 33%, throughout eight arms 66%; lifespan increased from 4 years to 60 years; chromatophore coloration adopted from a spectrum of genus Octopoda species |
| **LANGUAGE SKILLS** | English via keyboard; overall skill medium; word recognition high; vocabulary medium; cohesive expression low to medium |
| **COMMUNICATION TOOLS** | **Input:** Submersible speakers (Strategic Design) <br> **Output:** Submersible keyboard and external non-submersible speakers (Strategic Design) |
| **READING LEVEL** | 4th grade skill and comprehension (approx.) |
| **SKILLS** | Dexterity very high; problem solving very high |
| **INTERESTS** | Chess; darts; specific television programs; toys; Rubik's Cube |
| **COMMENTS** | Oliver is highly intelligent. He is playful and curious, is very good with tools, and displays moods and emotions. Be aware that his mind is not a human mind. He is, for all intents and purposes, an alien intelligence. |

FORM GOI/AP 7469.2

# PART ONE
# IN THE LAB

# CHAPTER ONE

*I hate this octopus,* John Rauchenberg said to himself. He shouldn't have, but he did. The octopus, a genetically enhanced Giant Pacific Octopus, was named Oliver. His brain size had been enlarged by forty percent and his life span increased from four years to sixty. Oliver was John's life's work, the reason he got out of bed in the morning, and the most fascinating individual he had ever known. Oliver was five years old when John's master's thesis on cephalopod intelligence brought them together. It had been fourteen years since the Institute had hired him, which made Oliver nineteen. John and the octopus had bonded over the years, but right then John couldn't stand him. Not only had Oliver taken John's queen, both bishops and both his knights plus most of his pawns, but he was gloating and had just squirted John with cold water. Checkmate in three.

In desperation, John castled, feeling that it was his doom. And it was. Oliver rose up out of his tank and fixed his right eye on the marine biologist as he tapped his underwater voice synthesis keyboard. The artificial voice said, "Ahhh. What Oliver wants." He manipulated the pitch and envelope of the voice synthesis unit to make it sound sarcastic. John shouldn't have let it get to him, but it did. The octopus snaked a dripping tentacle out of the tank and moved his queen to a diagonal attack. "Check," the speaker intoned. His skin turned green with purple circles: the color of gloating.

John pushed his king around evasively for the next couple of moves, but Oliver trapped it with a queen and a knight. "Checkmate!" he exulted, then played a throaty, evil laugh. Oliver may or may not have had a sense of humor the way humans do, but he delighted in using the evil laugh. He waved three of his tentacles above the glass and sent a squirt of water John's way. John managed to duck the soaking.

"OK, time for bed," John told Oliver.

Oliver turned a sullen ocher and slouched lower into the water. Even when he was a pissed-off blob of brown John still found Oliver beautiful: the silky body, skin like wheat in the wind, the lyrical curl of tentacles. John rolled the sulking octopus's traveling tank over to the expansive main tank. Oliver's tentacles flashed over his keyboard and a petulant voice came from the speaker. "Oliver won. Why cannot Oliver stay out longer? We can play checkers or darts." He was a dead shot at darts.

"It was a good game and you played very well," John said, putting a smile in his voice. Oliver's chromatophores dotted his skin with happy magenta freckles. He was a sucker for praise.

John put the back of his hand to his lips, the sign for 'kisses,' then plunged his arms into the octopus's tank. Oliver flowed over to the glass and wrapped two tentacles around each of John's arms. The octopus's color warmed to a light whitish blue, the color of a happy, relaxed state. They did kisses at the beginning and ending of every session; it was their way of bonding, like holding hands or hugging. John was leery of a full-on hug, though. Oliver weighed just under sixty pounds and his tentacles, which could stretch out to a span of almost seventeen feet, could pull a locked door off its hinges. This from an animal that fit comfortably in a ten gallon bucket.

John's arms were cold in the chill water of the octopus's tank, but he was used to it. Oliver gripped his arms loosely and dark flecks of doubt flowed across the octopus's skin. An octopus senses your chemistry with their sucker cups and skin. They can read your palm better than any fortune teller.

Oliver reached out a tentacle, darkened with concern, to his keyboard. "You are angry at Oliver," he said.

"I'm not mad at you," John said. "You're my friend."

A wave of blue flowed up the tentacles that gripped John's arms, but Oliver's mantle remained dark. "You are angry you lost chess." The tentacles tightened.

"I'm not angry that I lost at chess," John said to him. Waves of color washed across the cephalopod's body; green, dull red, blue, mottled brown. Never lie to an octopus.

"Yes, you are."

"OK, so I don't like losing at chess. Neither do you." John tried to move his arms but they were held tight. "You can gloat if you want."

This seemed to mollify the mollusk. Oliver's skin went green with purple circles again. He tapped at his keyboard. "Oliver won chess."

"Yes, you did. You are very smart," John replied. "And I love you for it." At this Oliver went full sky blue. Waves of darker blue rippled across his skin and up his tentacles. It was his way of saying "I love you too."

"Let's go, Oliver." The octopus let go of John's arms. Tentacles rose like writhing snakes and attached to the smooth glass of the larger tank. Oliver crawled in his undulating way up the side of the tank and over the top, lowering himself into the water without a splash. Once in the water he dropped to the bottom, watching his human companion intently. He knew what would happen next.

John unlocked a small aquarium nearby and used tongs to extract a crab. Oliver turned a mottled brown, his hunting color. John dropped the crab into the tank and human and cephalopod watched it drift down to the bottom. The crab tried to scurry away but Oliver flowed onto the hapless crustacean and wrapped himself around the crunchy treat.

"Good night, Oliver," John said. "We had a very good day."

A single tentacle unwound and tapped the keyboard. "Good night."

John knew in his heart of hearts that he didn't really hate Oliver; in fact, he loved the octopus very much. He just found him aggravating at times. Like a teenager. He sighed inwardly at the prospect of another microwave dinner alone while watching re-runs of *Star Trek,* and wiped his damp hands on his lab coat.

By the time John had gathered his stuff and cleaned up, Oliver, the smartest octopus on Earth, had finished his bedtime snack and retreated into his private den of coral and rock. The light of the television came on. John figured he was probably watching The Cartoon Network.

The mind of an octopus is a curious thing.

John Rauchenberg, marine biology tech and octopus nanny, ordered a hamburger and french fries at the cafeteria. A skinny nerd with black horn rim glasses would be the cruel description of him—slim, shy and sporting classic couture would be kinder. He saw a woman sitting down at a table nearby and felt his breath catch. His face felt warm and he was suddenly aware of his heartbeat. This had been his reaction since the first time he had seen her. He knew nothing about her except that she worked in the dolphin intelligence unit. John found that intriguing.

At least half the Gershon Oceanographic Institute's employees were women, but this one radiated intelligence and intensity. She was the kind of woman who drew men's eyes: raven hair over a face that needed no make-up, full lips, perfect cheekbones, and hints of curves under her shapeless lab coat; in other words, the kind of woman with whom John knew he had zero chance. But a glimmer of hope nibbled at him; they both worked with augmented oceanic species, so there was the possibility that conversation might ensue. Summoning every ounce of courage, John picked up his tray and walked over to where she was sitting.

"Is this seat taken?"

"It is now," she replied.

"Hi. My name's John," he said, sliding into the seat across from her and did his best to smile.

"Gina."

"You're the porpoise girl, right?"

Fire ignited in her eyes. "Porpoise girl, eh?" She scrutinized his name tag. "And you must be the octopus *boy*."

John had never heard the word 'boy' spoken with such vitriol. He did his best to stand his ground. How had he managed to mess up so quickly? "Yeah, I guess so."

Gina beetled her brow and flamed him with her gaze. "Well just keep your tentacles off me."

John attempted a light-hearted laugh. "Ha ha! Good one!" He picked up his hamburger and gazed at it wistfully. "I didn't mean to insult you. I'm sorry."

"That you are," she replied. "In the Southern sense."

She ignored him and John sat silently for a bit. "Excuse me," he said, then got up and took three steps away from the table. He squared his shoulders, turned around, and approached Gina again.

"Pardon me," he said. "I'm sorry to disturb your lunch, but have you seen a man about my height, horn rim glasses, lab coat, shaggy hair, sometimes says stupid things?"

Gina gave him a half-smile. "I think he was just here."

"Oh dear," said John. "He's on the lam. He's not all that bad, you know. But his social skills are rather, um..."

"Abysmal?" she offered.

"I was going to say 'rusty.'" John sat down across from her and looked her in the eye for several seconds. "Can we start over? Hi, my name's John and I work with a very intelligent sea creature. I thought we might have something to talk about."

"I don't know about that, John. I work with augmented oceanic mammals that have a lot in common with humans, whereas you work with a spineless bottom dweller with blue blood."

"I know that my octopus sounds like he should be a lawyer—" This brought another wisp of a smile to Gina's lips. "But intelligence is intelligence. And kind of hard to define, don't you think?" Having lobbed the ball into her court, he knew enough to shut up. He took a bite of his sandwich.

"Intelligence is pretty hard to define, I'll give you that," she mused. "My guys play a lot of games, but getting them to settle down and do stuff like reading and cognitive differentiation is tough."

"Oliver can be pretty rebellious, too."

Gina gave a snort of laughter. "Rebellious doesn't even come close with my guys. Sometimes it's like trying to teach a bunch of second graders on crack."

"Oliver can focus pretty well. He's a good chess player and can use tools. But he likes to watch TV. Not sure how intelligent that is."

"What does he like to watch?"

"Guess."

"*Spongebob Squarepants.*"

"How did you know?"

"C'mon. That's a gimme."

"Fair enough," John replied. "He also likes *Teletubbies* and is a serious *Game of Thrones* addict. The porpoises get TV, too, don't they?"

"Of course they do. Part of the overall normalization metric. And they're dolphins, not porpoises, you idiot. I thought you were a marine biologist. Dolphins are incredibly social animals. And as far as TV goes, they are completely hooked on all the *Housewives of Wherever* shows." She took a leisurely last bite of salad and looked straight at John. "And they watch a lot of porn."

Flustered, John didn't know what to say. He felt himself flushing. "You're messing with me."

Gina laughed, a tinkling merriment that under any other circumstance would have delighted John. "Maybe just a little bit. You're red as a beet, by the way." She stood to leave, holding her tray in one hand. She looked down at John. "Nice talking to you."

"Uh, yeah. It's been a pleasure." He tried to hide his embarrassment by looking her in the eyes. "Let's do it again some time. Gina."

"We'll see." She turned and strode away.

John watched her go, berating himself for being so clumsy and trying not to be entranced by the sway of her walk.

From: fws.gov/tarleysimon
To: usgs.gov/phelpsrobert
Re: Palmyra Research Station

Hi Bob,

Got a call from Diane Johnson at the Palmyra Research Station about twenty minutes ago. Two AM her time. She said something about a meteor lighting up the sky and then the line went dead. Probably just a blown fuse, but I worry that something might have happened. Do you have anything on your seismographs at about 8AM EDT? Haven't told Wasserman about the call yet. Thought I'd check with you first..

Thanks, Simon

-----------------------------------------------------------------------------------------

From: usgs.gov/phelpsrobert
To: fws.gov/tarleysimon
Re: Palmyra Research Station

Yo Simon—

Nothing on the seismo from the Pacific at or near 8AM EDT. A little shaker in the Atlantic up near Iceland but that's it. Quiet planet. I queried NASA and tapped Ray over at the Weather Service to check and see if they had anything. Nothingburger. Speaking of which, I sure hope the taco truck shows up soon.

—Bob

Back from lunch and John was still flustered by his conversation with Gina. He tapped on the glass of the big tank and made the kisses gesture. Oliver flowed like smoke over to the clear wall and John plunged his arms into the frigid water. The octopus wrapped each of John's arms in a tentacle. Oliver's soft and gentle touch was an alien embrace that John looked forward to and enjoyed. Oliver's skin, beige with relaxation, became dotted with red blotches. A tentacle reached out to his voice keyboard.

"Hamburger and french fries."

"Lucky guess, my little friend,"

"No guess. Ketchup stinks."

John's gelatinous buddy hated the "smell" of ketchup. "Would bleu cheese dressing be better?" John said.

Oliver found bleu cheese dressing even more repulsive than ketchup. His skin darkened through violet to dull red and rivulets of sickly green ran down his body and up his tentacles. His grip tightened ever so slightly.

"Just kidding," John said calmly. The large cephalopod could snap John's arms like toothpicks if he got too wound up. "I don't even like bleu cheese." This was a lie and Oliver knew it. They had played this game before.

The octopus tapped at his keyboard. "May you choke on bleu cheese."

"I love you, Oliver. You know that." Oliver smelled the love on John's skin and his color calmed to bluish white. "Oliver loves John," the octopus replied. The human and his boneless friend bonded silently for a while.

Red blotches started flashing on Oliver's skin. "You cannot get your crab."

John was puzzled by the reference. "What do you mean?"

"You cannot open the bottle." The red stars began to dance across his skin.

"I don't understand." And he didn't. But then again, verbal communication is a pretty alien concept to an octopus. John was surprised Oliver did as well as he did. "Explain."

Oliver hesitated a few seconds before tapping at his keyboard. "You cannot have the crab. The crab does not hamburger. The crab has vinegar."

John's arms were getting numb from the cold water. He was about to give up and end the session when it dawned on him. "I had lunch with a woman named Gina. She had a salad with a vinegar dressing. Is that what you mean?"

Oliver turned sky blue but the red blotches remained. "Crab Gee-nah is a happy place. You are buggabugga." 'Buggabugga' was a term Oliver and John had invented to indicate that an idea or word combination was outside Oliver's area of understanding or ability to express. *Things* he could name; he had a harder time with expressing ideas.

"Gina is very nice," John said.

"Gee-nah is buggabugga," said Oliver. The red blotches on his skin changed to black and grey blobs.

"Yes, Gina is buggabugga." John was more than a little bit uncomfortable with a blue-blooded alien intelligence delving into his emotional life. "That's enough about Gina," he said.

"Gee-nah is tasty crab," said Oliver.

Time to change the subject. "OK!" John declared. "Let's get to work."

Gina suited up with an almost autonomic efficiency. As a business-man was with twirling his tie into a Windsor, so was Gina Martinelli with her diving gear. She went underwater at least forty percent of her working hours and today was no different.

While she slipped into her swimsuit and donned her scuba gear, she thought about the skinny guy with the glasses who had been bold enough to sit at her table at lunch. She smiled to herself at how easy it had been to embarrass him. A little too easy, maybe a bit cruel, but guys had been hitting on her since she was thirteen. Shutting men down had become sort of a hobby for her.

The guy at lunch hadn't seemed all that bad, really. What was his name again? Jacob…Jason…no, John. The octopus boy. But he hadn't tried the standard routes to try to weasel his way into her good graces: no asking her what her favorite movie or TV show was, no mention of his car or what sports teams he was into, and no sexual innuendoes. Did guys really think that sort of approach was endearing? This John guy talked about animal intelligence, hadn't tried to touch her, and had looked her in the eye. Mostly. She had felt him scanning her, of course. Not the worst man she had encountered, but definitely male. He seemed to have a sense of humor, though, and listened to what she had to say. And he had looked her in the eye.

She picked up her fins, all thoughts of intrusive men fading from her consciousness, and went to meet with her dolphins.

The radio room at Pearl Harbor Naval Air Base was a secure facility in an air-conditioned windowless bunker. The senior watch officer sat at his desk watching a football game. The mood was relaxed. Two of the radio operators were monitoring supply transports headed for the China Sea and watched the game when they could.

The third radio operator was in contact with a Navy jet on a reconnaissance mission out over the South Pacific. The pilot and co-pilot needed to make their quota of hours, and a milk run out to a remote atoll a thousand miles from Hawaii to check on a bunch of scientists fit the bill quite nicely. Fish and Wildlife had lost radio contact with their research station and asked the Navy to look in on them. The radio operator turned to his superior officer. "They're almost in range, sir."

The watch officer turned the sound on the TV down and walked over to stand behind the radio operator. "When he checks in remind him that he needs to drop the bird." The 'bird' was an experimental drone from Strategic Design.

The radio crackled to life. "Zero foxtrot five, we are thirty-five and closing," the pilot reported.

"Roger that, Seven bravo niner," the operator replied. "Command reminds you to deploy your drone."

"Already on it. Hank, drop the bird!" Another voice came on the channel. "Bird's away," followed by a distant clunk. "Ye haw!" the first voice crowed.

"Tell him to cut the crap and treat this exercise seriously," the watch officer growled.

"Yes, sir," the radio operator said. He turned to his equipment just as the jet pilot's voice again came from the speaker.

"Island is in sight. We are twelve..."

The line went dead.

A second of shocked silence, then the radio operator's training came into play and he went into emergency mode. "Seven bravo niner, do you read?" he calmly spoke into the microphone, repeating it after several seconds. All the while he checked his equipment for any anomalies. "Diagnostic," the watch commander said. The operator turned to his computer and brought up a screenful of bars and numbers. "All good, sir," he said, then called again to the crew of the jet.

The officer leaned in. "Grab the drone," he commanded, pointing at the computer screen. The operator brought up the drone program. The splash screen indicated the drone was active, but there was no picture from its camera. The radio operator tapped the 'capture' button and a green dot came on next to the icon. Still no picture.

"What's wrong with the camera?" the watch officer asked.

The radio operator studied his computer screen. "Video is labeled 'eyes only,' sir. It's being routed to a secure server."

The watch officer pursed his lips and picked up the phone.

The engineering and marine science departments at MIT had come up with a project they called "Spatial and Polyappendage Construction and Attendant Chromatophoric Mentation." The key word here was "construction." Oliver got to build something while the video recorded his competency and color changes. Oliver enjoyed such projects, but this time he was to do it with minimal help. Oliver had mastered the screwdriver a few years ago and was damn good with a crescent wrench. Watching him use a socket set, though, was amazing. He felt the nut with the sensitive tip of one tentacle, selected the correct socket with another tentacle, and used two more to handle the ratchet part. Smooth, like dance. It took John months to teach Oliver the tools, each one learned a little faster, but once he got it, he got it completely. With two thirds of his neurons in his tentacles, Oliver's muscle memory was phenomenal. The Mozart of the socket set, John called him. Oliver didn't get it.

John trained a video camera on the tank, then lowered a basket of parts and tools into the water. "There you go, little buddy."

Ripples of red and blue cascaded across Oliver's skin, indicating definite interest. "What is it?"

"You get to build a car."

"What is a car?"

"A car is a toy that you get to make."

Flashes of yellow joined the red and blue ripples on the octopus's skin. "Oliver likes a toy. Oliver likes to build a car."

"This time it will be a little different," John said. "This time I will not show you how to do it. You will look at pictures and read instructions and do it on your own. Without my help."

"Read," Oliver said, the synthetic voice flat and emotionless. His coloration retreated to a dull brown.

"Yes," John said. "You will have to read the instructions to make your car toy."

"Oliver likes a car toy."

John was watching Oliver lay out the pieces and arrange the tools when Mr. Harris—that's Dennis "The Menace" Harris, Director of the Gershon Oceanographic Institute—strolled into the lab. Harris was a stocky, balding man with an unruly mustache and a face cast in a perpetual scowl. He stopped well away from Oliver's tank. The octopus disliked the director and squirted him with water whenever he had the chance.

"Ah. The MIT project," Harris said. "How's it going?"

"We're just starting, so I don't have anything to report yet."

"I hope you appreciate how important this MIT contract is."

"I know that, sir."

"It means a lot to us here at Gershon. Having MIT on the roster does a lot for our fundraising efforts. How long do you think it will take that calamari of yours to complete the project?"

"Oliver's an octopus, sir, not a squid."

"Same family. 'Calamari' is a more melodious word."

"Oliver's very good with tools, so maybe a week or two. We'll have to see how well he catches on to this particular project. It's an autonomous approach, as you know, so…"

"I need something I can show the board," Harris scowled.

"Yes sir. I'm putting it on video, so it should be…"

"They'd rather see the dolphins," said Harris. "Dolphins are cute. Octopuses are weird."

"He's mighty smart, though," John countered, miffed at being cut off.

"True," Harris said. "But I'm willing to bet the dolphins are smarter."

John could not hold back the snark. "When they learn how to use a socket set, let me know."

Director Harris fixed him with a cold stare. "You're developing an attitude, Rauchenberg. I have a stack of resumes on my desk a foot high of extremely qualified people who would love your job."

"Sorry, sir." John squinched his feet on the floor, waiting for Harris to leave. The director took a last look around the lab and stalked off. Oliver slapped at his keyboard and the speaker made a rude noise.

"Stop it," John said under his breath. The cephalopod draped himself over the pile of parts and tools and regarded John with unblinking eyes. His chromatophores pulsed black and red. John stared at the door Harris had exited through, his mind churning with dark thoughts. Oliver tapped on the glass, pulling him out of his reverie.

John sighed wearily. "OK, let's get back to the project."

The office was understated; not small, not big, grey walls. A table with a scattering of maps sat to one side. In front of another wall decorated with photographs and awards, beside large windows that looked out onto the bright Hawaiian sunshine, sat a desk with a name plaque that read "Adm. Phillip Westminster, Cmdr. Pacific Fleet Command." Behind the desk sat the man himself, with four stars on the shoulders of his crisply ironed khaki blouse. On the other side of the desk stood a second man, similarly attired save for only two stars on each shoulder. Rear Admiral Hector Diaz held himself rigidly at attention, his face a mask of control. Between the two men hung a palpable tension.

"Have a seat," said Westminster. Diaz hesitated. "Sit," Westminster said again. Diaz sat.

"Why did you come to me, Hector?" the admiral asked. "You should have taken this up with the 7th Fleet. Anderson would have told you what I'm going to tell you and what you should already know: that requisitioning a ship in under four days is damn near impossible. Plus your proposal is way out in left field."

Rear Admiral Diaz struggled to control his features. "I must respectfully disagree, sir. This is an urgent matter. A Navy fighter jet with my son onboard has been shot down twelve miles from Palmyra Atoll."

"'Shot down' is wild speculation. And in any case, we're taking care of it."

Diaz looked scornful. "With what…an aging rescue plane? This is serious, sir."

Westminster clasped his hands on the desk. "Yes, this is serious. And we're following protocol. We have two of our newest radar planes flying a grid pattern." He looked down at his hands, then back up. "We sometimes lose pilots, Hector. I'm sorry."

Admiral Diaz leaned forward slightly, his features intense. "Respectfully, Phil, my son was not 'lost.' He was shot down. Whatever's out there, it kills planes."

Admiral Westminster leaned slightly forward as well. "You need to calm down, Admiral. We can't just give you a ship to go look for your son."

Diaz was still intense. "It's more than that, sir. Have you seen the video? I have."

Westminster leaned back in his chair, turning to look out the window. After a long moment he turned back. "Yes, I've seen the video." The admiral sighed. "It's a fake, Hector."

"And what happens when another one of our planes gets shot down?"

Admiral Westminster frowned. "Listen, we've been experiencing an uptick in hostile electronic activity. We're not even sure if it's the Russians or the Chinese, but between you and me, it's bad. What you saw was manufactured, a deep fake. The radio operator who got the plane's last message…we found marijuana and pills in his quarters and we're looking into him and his friends. We've got the electronics guys from Intelligence dissecting the video, but it's some kind of new format or something. For all we know, what got the plane could have been some sort of malfunction in deploying the drone. Whatever happened, we'll find out." After a pause the admiral continued. "What it boils down to is I cannot authorize a ship for you."

"The video is real, sir," Diaz continued. "It's real."

The four star admiral sighed. "You're my friend, Hector, but we already have two planes searching the area. We take the loss of a Navy pilot very seriously. Especially your son."

"But the video…

"Take some time off, Hector. You've been through a lot. Carmen needs you."

An urgent knock came at the door. "Come," Admiral Westminster called out. A young ensign came in and stood at attention in front of the desk. He seemed agitated as he snapped a salute.

"Sir!"

The admiral gave a perfunctory salute back. "What is it, ensign? I'm in the middle of something."

"It's about the rescue planes looking for the downed pilot, sir. They went off the radar."

The admiral's brow knitted. Diaz turned around in his chair and looked at the ensign. "What do you mean 'went off the radar?'"

"They just...disappeared. One minute they were there and the next they weren't. Radio was in the middle of getting a status report when their line went dead."

Both admirals stared at the ensign for several seconds. Westminster spoke first. "You're telling me that two of our newest search aircraft just up and disappeared."

The ensign was on the verge of stammering. "Yes, sir."

"I assume you have thoroughly checked your equipment."

"Very thoroughly, sir."

Westminster looked at the ceiling, lost in thought. He lowered his gaze to the ensign. "Thank you, ensign. Dismissed."

After the ensign left, Westminster looked into the distance. "Jesus," he said softly. His gaze came back into focus and he gave Rear Admiral Diaz the slightest of smiles. "Looks like your cockamamy idea might have some traction after all."

John Rauchenberg needed two days to work up the gumption to sit at Gina's table again. It was a four seater and an older gentleman studiously reading a magazine was in one of the seats. John did not bother to ask permission; he sat down across from Gina and smiled.

"Hi, Gina." John ventured.

"Hi yourself."

"I'm John," he said. "We met the other day."

She looked at him with cool blue eyes. "I remember."

"I shouldn't have called you porpoise girl."

"That again?" she replied, becoming annoyed.

"Humor me," John said. "Because, one: you're a woman, not a girl and two: you work with bottlenose dolphins, *Tursiops truncatus.* Family *Delphinidae.* They're not porpoises."

"Look at you getting all scientific."

"Well I do have a masters degree in marine biology. Did my thesis on cephalopod intelligence. So yeah, I'm scientific."

"I have a masters in marine biology, too, octopus boy."

"Man."

"Octopus man. My thesis was on deep social interchange in cetacean pods."

"I know. *Crosscultural and Interspecies Content Interpretation.* I read it."

Gina looked at John askance. "Are you stalking me?"

"No. Of course not," John replied. "I read everything I can find on animal intelligence. I read your thesis a couple of years ago, long before I knew you worked here." Gina met his gaze with a raised eyebrow. "So I guess we can't out-master each other," he continued. "Dolphin woman."

Gina smiled for real. "Looks like it. Octopus man."

John ventured a mouthful of salad while Gina nibbled at her sandwich, both eyeing the other without actually looking. John broke the silence. "So why does everybody call dolphins porpoises?" he asked.

Gina's brow furrowed. "It's a plot by mad marine scientists to confuse the public."

"No, really."

"Yes, really! They do it on porpoise!" She worked to suppress her grin.

John chortled. "And here I thought it was just a fluke."

It was Gina's turn to laugh. The same tinkling merriment he had heard a few days previously but without the derision. "I bet you think you're clever."

"I try to keep it hidden." He munched another bite of salad.

The older gentleman closed his magazine and rose from his seat. "Stay clever, young man. It helps you get through life." He picked up his tray, nodded politely to Gina, and left.

"Clever can only get you so far," said Gina.

"Tell that to Oliver."

"I gather Ollie is pretty intelligent. For a mollusk."

"He prefers Oliver. And yeah, he's mighty smart. And clever. For a mollusk. But I'm dying to hear about your dolphins. What smart things do they do?"

She shrugged. "All sorts of things. But not that hokey SeaWorld stuff. My guys are very smart, especially at group problem-solving. Interactive input leading to universal cognition. That sort of thing."

"Can they read?"

"Of course they can read. The trick is getting them to do it. Reading is a solitary activity. Dolphins are all about the pod and interacting. They like it when I read to them."

John smiled. "I can see you in a lounge chair at the bottom of the tank reading to the dolphins through your scuba gear." He held his fist up to his mouth and made bubbling sounds while holding an imaginary book in front of him.

Gina rolled her eyes. "I sit at a desk outside the tank. They hear me through underwater speakers, which I'm sure you have for your octopus."

"What do you read to a pod of dolphins?"

"Children's books mostly. The words are simple and they love the illustrations. We put the page I'm reading on their flatscreen. They were crazy for *Where The Wild Things Are*. I had to read it every day for two weeks."

"Do you love it? Working with the dolphins?"

She looked him in the eye. "It's my life."

"Me too. Only octopuses."

"Does Ollie read?" she asked.

"At about a fourth grade level. Right now I've got him on Winnie the Pooh, and he's struggling with it. The environment, the Hundred Acre Wood, throws him. Also, human wit and octopus wit are very different."

She smiled. "So give me an example of octopus wit."

At that moment both their cell phones buzzed simultaneously, stopping the conversation. They whipped their phones out and frowned at the screens. "They want me at the director's office," said Gina. "Like right now."

John looked at her, puzzled. "Me too. Weird."

"What's this about?"

"Beats me," he replied. "Maybe there's an emergency."

"Or we're all getting fired."

"They can't fire us," he scoffed.

"Well, if it was an emergency there would be alarms."

"Only one way to find out." He rose and picked up his tray.

Gina followed suit. "Yup. Direct experiential observation."

The conference room was packed to the gills. The table and chairs had been moved out to create space. John recognized his friend Hank, the main guy in crustaceans, and several administrators and project managers whose names he could never remember. Larry and Barry, fellow nerds who worked with the Institute's submarine, were across the crowded room. John stood as close to Gina as he dared, which wasn't all that close. She had seen people from her department and immediately gone to them. He opted not to intrude.

The door opened and Director Harris came in, his shirt sleeves rolled up and the usual grumble on his face. He closed the door and swept the room with his steely glare. The crowd muttered down to silence.

"I'll get right to the point. The Department of Defense, the Navy specifically, called and said they might need what they called an 'inquiry unit.' They said they might—notice I have used that word twice now— might be in need of underwater observation and interpretive experts. Basically everything we have at the drop of a hat."

"But why us? What do they want us to do?" asked one of the elder scientists.

"That's on a need-to-know basis, Gary. And I'm one of those who doesn't need to know, which means you don't need to know either. I'm just following orders. I suspect being near San Diego influenced the Navy contacting us. I get the impression that it is pretty much a go. And they made it clear that this is not a request. It's an order."

John raised his hand. "What does the Department of Defense want with an octopus?"

The Director shook his head. "Your guess is as good as mine, Mr. Rauchenberg. Strangely enough, they requested you by name. And your octopus."

"What if I refuse?"

"You don't want to do that."

John crossed his arms over his chest. "Why not?"

"Because your octopus goes whether you do or not," Harris growled. John opened his mouth to reply and Harris overrode him. "I would remind you—and I'm sure our legal team would be glad to remind you as well—that when you were hired you signed an iron-clad contract with both the Institute and the federal government agency that funds us." There was an electric tension between Director Harris and John.

Gina raised her hand and piped up. "I'll go. My pod needs me to be with them."

Harris looked at her. "Thank you, Ms. Martinelli." He turned his scowl back to John.

John glanced at Gina but couldn't get a read on her expression. "OK," he said to Director Harris. "Oliver needs me to be with him. I'll go."

"How very gracious of you," Harris replied. He looked around the room. "One other thing," he said. "Everyone in this room is required to sign a non-disclosure form." A stunned silence hung in the air. "The secretaries will be handing them out as you leave. Any questions?"

There were no questions.

# CHAPTER TWO

– 25 –

Oliver was all aflutter when John got back from the meeting. He picked up on the worried vibe as John paced and fretted in front of his tank. *What is this about?* John wondered. *Why me? Why Oliver?* Pace, pace, pace.

The octopus in question was crawling back and forth on the glass, frantically making the kisses sign. John could not refuse. He rolled up his sleeves and plunged his arms into the cold water. Oliver flowed over and wrapped tentacles around the human's arms. John marveled again at how gentle his touch was. Innocent. Open. Calm. Man and mollusk communed silently for a few minutes. Eventually John's arms began to go numb and he tugged gently at the tentacles. Oliver's grip tightened ever so slightly.

"Something is wrong." The flat voice of the synthesizer betrayed no emotion.

"Something came up. You wouldn't understand."

Oliver flashed purple zig zags across an otherwise relaxed beige. "Something is wrong," he repeated. Oliver could smell a lie, or even a half truth, a mile away.

"There's a new, uh…project."

Oliver turned bright red behind the purple zig zags. He was worked up. "Tell Oliver."

John was well enough versed in cephalopod psychology to know that Oliver really needed to know what was going on. He chose his words carefully.

"My boss wants me to be ready to leave at any time. He has not told me where he wants me to go. I am upset because I do not know why. Also…he wants to take you." John paused and added for good measure, "Our cave is not safe." It was an octopus phrase Oliver sometimes used to indicate uncertainty or danger.

Oliver's chromatophores calmed to a dull maroon. Not quite relaxed, but feeling better. They held the silence for a bit. His tentacles on John's arms pulsed a few times, then relaxed.

"Oliver understands," the synthesizer intoned. "Maybe play chess?"

John pulled his arms from the water. "You're very good at chess, my friend, but we don't have time for that right now." He dried his arms and flexed his fingers to get some feeling back. "How is your car coming along?"

Oliver jetted over to the MIT construction project, his skin a light ocher with waves of purple running up his tentacles. John could tell that Oliver was pleased with himself. Two tentacles danced across his synthesizer keyboard. "Oliver is very good at making."

"Yes, you are very good."

Oliver had been busy while John was gone. The platform had been assembled and the tools were neatly arranged within tentacle reach. He had turned the contraption upside down in order work on the axle and drive train gears. *Damn impressive*, John commented to himself. Better than expected. "Very nice, Oliver." John nodded and smiled; Oliver was a whiz at reading facial expressions.

Red fireworks coursed across the octopus's skin. "Oliver is tools," he tapped out on his keyboard.

John looked more closely at what Oliver had put together. Something seemed wrong. He consulted his copy of the plans. Sure enough, Oliver had put the drive gear in the middle of the axle, not the starboard side as depicted.

"Oliver, look at the axle. The gear is in the wrong place. It is not correct."

Now red and green stripes rippled across the octopus's skin. John had seen this color only a few times before. "Toy car is correct," Oliver said.

John pressed the diagram of the axle drivetrain up against the tank. "It is not the same as the plan."

Oliver paused, holding his bright stripes. "Plan is not correct."
"But..."

Oliver spoke over John. "Oliver sees lose a bishop. Oliver moves a knight."

John found that this damn cephalopod could be irritatingly oblique at times. He would try to use things he knew to depict a thought he had could not quite verbalize. Like the weird crab-in-a-bottle observation about Gina the other day.

"So the chess move means that you think the diagram has a flaw?"

"Yes," said the octopus.

"No, it doesn't" said John. "This thing has been put together and taken apart and put together again countless times by a swarm of incredibly smart MIT graduate students. There is no design flaw."

"Oliver fixes flaw," said the octopus stubbornly.

John was about to argue further but caught himself. Experience had taught him that there would be no talking Oliver out of it. Better to indulge him and include some notes to the MIT folks about the pig-headedness of a certain cephalopod. Honestly, he should have expected something like this. Enhanced DNA or not, Oliver was still an octopus, and octopuses just thought differently.

Dr. Schreiner's genetic tinkering had led to many failures on the way to engineering a smarter octopus that didn't die in four years. Out of thousands of eggs, Schreiner's team produced only ten viable augmented octopuses. Of those ten, three had died of disease and two had committed suicide, leaving five super-smart octopuses scattered around the world. Two were in America—Oliver at the Gershon Oceanographic Institute on the West Coast, and Octavia at the Smithsonian on the East Coast—plus Ochiko-san in Japan, Otto in Germany, and Odysseus in Athens. Oliver was the most intelligent of the five and John was honored to be his friend.

Giving an octopus more brain power had been very challenging. An octopus's main brain is wrapped around its throat but two thirds of its neurons are in its arms; like having nine brains all doing their own thing but acting together. As John was fond of saying, the mind of an octopus is a curious thing.

John's favorite example of that statement was when he had given Oliver a Rubik's Cube. He was about eleven at the time and well acclimated to manipulating human objects. An octopus's dexterity compared to a human's is Ferrari versus bicycle. When John dropped the toy into Oliver's tank, the octopus was immediately fascinated. John showed him how the puzzle worked, showed him how to make each side a solid color, then ran him through a bunch of exercises.

The next day John came in and found the Rubik's Cube carefully balanced atop a piece of coral. Each side was mottled with two or more colors in a seemingly random pattern. John drew Oliver's attention to the cube and told him, "Let's make the cube correct."

Oliver slid closer to the cube and looked up at it. "Rubik Cube is correct."

"The sides are not solid colors," John told him.

"Rubik Cube is correct," the octopus repeated.

"But the sides are not solid colors." John didn't know what else to say.

Oliver's skin had turned bright red with green stripes, the same chromatic reaction he was having to the supposed flaw in MIT's design. He had stared at the cube for a long minute, then went to his keyboard. He had hovered over it as if lost for words, then hit a single key and the synthesizer said one word: "octopus." He then went into his den and would not come out for the rest of the day. John thought he might be saying, "I'm an octopus, dude, and I think like an octopus and I'm upset that you can't see my point of view."

*So what the heck*, the marine biologist mused. *This MIT thing is about octopus mentation.* He decided to give Oliver all the leeway he wanted and see how badly he botched the project. "OK, Oliver," he said. "Do what you want."

Oliver curled his tentacles under him and turned brick red, his content and excited pose. A tentacle shot out and tapped the keyboard. "Thank you," the artificial voice said.

John watched Oliver tinkering with his tools and his mind began to wander. What in the world did the military want with an octopus?

John went back to the cafeteria to finish his interrupted lunch and saw Gina at her usual table. He plopped down in the chair opposite her. "That was the weirdest meeting," he said. "What do you suppose is going on?"

"I haven't the slightest," said Gina.

"I think it's a top-secret military attack team. I think it's aliens from Mars or Arcturus or somewhere bent on enslaving and devouring all life on Earth, starting with us. And we here at the Gershon Oceanographic Institute, we are the Aquanauts, Mighty Defenders of the Planet." He paused and nodded with mock solemnity. "That's what I think."

Gina made a disgusted sound. "No, really."

He grew more serious. "Really I have no idea. But I know it's military, and that kinda scares me."

"Yeah, me too."

They munched their sandwiches in silence for a while. John spoke up. "So do we just carry on as usual until we hear something further?"

"What else can we do? But I'd still like to know what the hell's going on."

John screwed up his courage and asked her the question he'd been formulating all day. "While we wait to hear what the hell's going on … would you like to meet Oliver?"

Gina's eyebrows went up a tick. "I'd love to meet your octopus."

"Well, he's not technically mine. He belongs to the Institute. I'm just his caretaker."

She fixed John with her smoky gaze. "He's your octopus."

"Kinda, I guess. We're more on a friendship level." John chuckled nervously. "That must sound weird. An octopus as my friend. Definitely weird."

"Not weird at all." She smiled—her real smile, John realized, something he suspected she did not share with just anyone. It lit up her entire face, and John's only thought was that he would do anything to make her smile like that again. "I think of my dolphins as friends" she continued. "They all have such personalities. I'm part of their pod. I believe there is a cognizant bond between intelligences. I imagine you have a bond like that with Ollie."

"Come see for yourself. I think you'll like him. And he prefers Oliver." When she did not respond immediately, he rambled on. "You know, I'd like to meet your dolphins."

"Are you dive certified?"

"DAN certified, rescue rated."

"Well I'm dive master rated, so I outrank you."

John snapped a flashy salute. "Yes sir, ma'am!"

"You got a wet suit?"

"Somewhere."

She curled her lips into a wry smile. "Been a while since you went under, eh?"

"Coupla weeks." He avoided her eyes. "Maybe more."

"You funny guy. Tell you what…how does tomorrow around eleven sound?"

John felt tingly and flushed. "Is there a place for me to suit up?"

"I meant me meeting Ollie. We can do a dolphin encounter Thursday. Does that fit into your schedule?"

John decided not to correct her again over Oliver's name, and gazed blankly into space, seeing his calendar. "Tomorrow sounds good. And Thursday sounds good, too. It's a date."

"Don't get ahead of yourself, octopus dude." Gina bit off the end her pickle. "It's not a date, it's a chance to meet another intelligent mind." She paused to let the moment breathe. "Present company excepted."

John smiled. "OK then, it's a, uh, professional encounter."

When John got to the lab the next morning, Oliver was driving around his aquarium on the finished project car. John was floored.

"You finished the car!" John exclaimed. "I thought it would take longer! You are very good!"

Still driving, Oliver dragged a tentacle across keys on his keyboard as he passed by. This produced only nonsense sounds. "Gah! Bloop!" Oliver rolled on.

John stepped up to get a better look at the machine that Oliver had finished. It was mostly what the MIT engineers had designed. Mostly. The deck and the axles and the basic structure were the same, but the steering was subtly different. Oliver perched in the center of the platform, four tentacles on the steering bar, two turning the crank that made the wheels go, and two holding him to the car. He was bright blue with red splotches and appeared quite proud of himself. As he passed by his keyboard again he slapped at a couple more keys. "Foo! Glem!"

John tapped on the glass. "Time for kisses! Kisses!"

Oliver raised one tentacle and made a feeble kisses gesture. His concentration was entirely on driving his new toy car. John noticed that the design of the crank had been altered, moved behind the axle and lowered so that it better fit Oliver's tentacles. Clever. Oliver cranked harder as he banked into a turn at the end of the tank, sending up a spray of sand and gravel, thrashing at the keyboard as he went by. "Zob! Feh!"

John was fascinated that Oliver had not only finished the project so quickly, but that he had figured out how to use the little car and was now stunt driving it. As fascinating as this was, though, it was growing tiresome. John tapped on the glass again. "Come over for kisses and I'll give you a crab." It worked. The octopus would do pretty much anything for a crab. Oliver made another circuit of his tank, then carefully parked the vehicle by the door to his den. Like a kid with his first car, John thought to himself. Except this kid has three hearts and no bones.

John lowered his arms into the water. When the tentacles embraced him, he could feel Oliver's excitement; a tension and electricity coming through the octopus's arms. "The car is amazing!" John told him. "Oliver can make things."

Oliver's skin rippled blue and purple as tentacles danced across his keyboard. "Oliver makes a car!" Octopus and scientist talked cars for a few minutes, like any two guys would, until John's arms got numb. John fetched a crab and dropped it into Oliver's tank. The octopus flowed onto it.

John toweled his arms back to life and watched his friend eat the snack. "We're going to have a visitor this morning," he said. Oliver stared blankly at John. Without a face to paint emotions on, staring blankly was about all he could do. Coloration was a different matter. Oliver went all beige, with little patches of brick red forming and dissolving in a random pattern on his skin. John knew the pattern: Oliver was moderately curious.

"It's Gina, the girl from lunch. She's coming over to meet you."

No reaction from the cephalopod.

"You'll like her."

Oliver undulated over to his keyboard. "Will she give Oliver a crab?"

"Maybe. We'll see how it goes."

They began their daily tasks: stretches, photos, an abbreviated game of catch. Oliver was eager to show off his handiwork on the MIT underwater car. John took extensive videos and photographs, composing a report in his head.

A knock at the open door made John jump. Gina strode into the room and stopped well clear of the main tank. "Nice place you have here. Looks like a lab."

"Thanks."

"I didn't think an octopus would need such a big tank."

"Oliver is a big guy and we need a lot of room for all the stuff we do. Five meters by ten gives us lots of room."

At the mention of his name, Oliver approached the front glass, his skin rippling with red and blue bands that indicated curiosity.

John gestured for Gina to step up on the observation platform beside him. "Come on up. I'll introduce you."

She did so and smiled down at Oliver. "He's very cute."

So far, so good, John thought. He ventured a noncommittal smile. "Dennis the Menace thinks he's weird."

"Dennis the Menace," she countered, "is an ass."

John looked around conspiratorially and put his finger to his lips. "Shhh. I suspect microphones," he whispered.

"And I suspect he has heard the truth many times," Gina whispered back. She nodded at Oliver's tank. "Introduce me."

"OK. You're gonna get your arms wet." He made the "kisses" sign and the octopus flowed over to the glass.

Gina had on a short-sleeved blouse. She held her bare arms before her like a surgeon after scrubbing in. "What do I do now?"

"Just stick your arms into the water. It's pretty cold, so be ready." John raised a finger of caution. "Fair warning. He might squirt you."

"My guys splash me all the time. I'm used to it."

They both lowered their arms into the chill water and Oliver wrapped tentacles around them. Gina jumped a little at the first touch, but relaxed right into the experience, much to John's delight. She smiled a smile of true enjoyment. "It's like velvet," she said softly.

"Oliver," John said, "this is Gina. Say hello."

A couple of tentacles tapped at the keyboard. "Hello, Gee-nah."

"I told her how smart Oliver is."

She smiled at the cephalopod holding her arms. "Hello, you beautiful octopus," she said. "Do you mind if I call you Ollie?"

Oliver turned light blue with shades of sky swirling up and down the tentacles holding her arms. After a pause, he tapped at his keyboard. "Yes. Oliver loves Ollie," the synthetic voice enthused.

She cocked her head at John. "If that's OK with you."

"That's between you and Oliver," he said, trying to keep the resignation out of his voice.

"Good." She turned back to the tank. "You are absolutely beautiful, Ollie."

"Oliver is beautiful and smart," the octopus's synthetic voice said with a hint of pride.

"Yes, you are," she said softly. Oliver's skin calmed to a milky beige, and the odd trio settled into a comfortable silence. It was nice, the kind of moment with Gina that John had hoped for.

Then Oliver tapped at his keyboard and his voice broke the quiet. "John wants Gee-nah to be crab."

She looked at John questioningly, brow furrowed. "What does he mean by that?"

John could feel himself blushing. "He, uh, just says weird stuff sometimes. You know, random associations."

"Ooooh kaaay," she said dubiously, then turned back to the octopus holding her arms. "Tell me more, Ollie."

"John likes horrible ketchup." Oliver's tentacles danced on the keyboard. "John sees Gee-nah delicious crab. John thinks Gee-nah is buggabugga."

Gina frowned at John. "Buggabugga?"

"It's just a nonsense phrase we, uh…you see, sometimes there's something he can't say…"

Her eyes narrowed. "Can't say?"

John could feel his heart in his throat. He attempted to pull his arms from the water, but the large glob of intelligent jelly held him tight. "No, it's not like that. I mean, it's hard for him to say stuff sometimes because…"

"Because why?"

John got the feeling that she was enjoying his discomfort. "It's a, uh, code word we use to indicate an idea or concept that Oliver can't grasp."

"Your little octopus pal here just told me that I'm a concept you can't grasp, right?"

John was frantically trying to figure out what to say when Oliver's synthesized voice cut in. "John wants to grasp Gee-nah."

John grinned nervously and tried to keep his voice calm while not looking at her. "I think kisses are over, Oliver. Kisses are over."

The voice of director Dennis Harris came from the doorway. "Who is kissing who here?"

Oliver released his grip on the two humans and zipped into his den. Gina and John pulled their arms out of the chill water and rubbed them with towels. Harris watched from the doorway, arms akimbo. But there was an extra aura of tension on him today.

"You two should know better than to fraternize on company time. And you picked a pretty weird place to do your kissing."

Gina spoke before John could. "It was nothing like that, Mr. Harris."

"I've been looking all over for you, Miss Martinelli. Never thought I'd find you here."

"Sorry about that."

"Both of you need to report to the administration offices to get your orders. We're shipping out tomorrow."

"Our orders?" John asked.

"Yes, orders. Dry your hands and get your asses up to administration. Now." He turned on his heel and left.

They watched him go, holding the silence for a few heartbeats, neither one knowing what to say. "Is Harris 'buggabugga?'" Gina ventured.

"Yeah," John replied. "But not in a good way." John looked Gina in the eye. "Sometimes there's an idea that Oliver can't express or a concept that he simply cannot grasp. So 'bugga-bugga' became a code word for that…state of mind." He looked away from her gaze. "I guess it kinda sounds off-color, so I apologize for all that."

Gina gave John a thin smile. "You're a lot of fun to torment."

"I resemble that remark."

"Plus you do John Lennon quotes." She crossed her arms and regarded him with half-lidded eyes. "You're not all bad. And you take abuse readily."

"Maybe I think you don't mean it," John replied.

Gina held his gaze for several seconds, a wry grin on her lips. "That was a fascinating experience communing with Ollie. I think I should say goodbye to him."

But Oliver would not come out of his den, which John took as a bad sign.

# PART TWO
# AT SEA

# CHAPTER THREE

Octopuses do not get seasick because they live underwater and have no inner ear. Octopuses "hear" the same way they "smell"—through their skin. It is similar to how a rock music fan experiences a loud concert while wearing ear plugs: they feel the bass in their bones and the treble on their skin. Same thing with octopuses, only far more sensitive. The underwater speaker in Oliver's tank dropped the outside voice down about an octave and tweaked the treble. John once stuck an ear into Oliver's tank and spoke into the mic. His voice sounded like Orson Welles on helium.

John, however, did have an inner ear and did not live underwater, so for the first couple of days aboard ship he felt like a water balloon about to pop. He puked only once and stayed away from the beef stroganoff after that. Director Dennis "The Menace" Harris made sure there was no goofing off on his ship, in his wonkish way haranguing his people to stay busy, while Oliver constantly bugged John to play a game, preferably chess. John kept himself active, miniaturizing his cephalopod lab in a small, grey metal room with a floor that could not make up its mind as to what was level. At least he was not bored. Queasy, but not bored.

*Darwin's Dream*, the institute's oceangoing research vessel was, at three hundred eighty feet, a mighty big boat, but it felt small and cramped with all the personnel and equipment onboard. John found the bunk they had assigned him to, in a room with three other men, cramped and stinky. So he set up a cot in his lab and slept with Oliver. Cephalopods don't snore.

Gina's dolphin lab was in a converted storage hold a few decks down. The area had been cleared by consolidating supplies and equipment into other quarters. A large tank held three dolphins who were racing back and forth, testing the confines of their habitat. Gina was struggling with hooking up a water filtration system when there came a polite tap at the door.

The woman in the doorway was tall, with a braid of hair as black as night. She stood rigidly, hands clasped behind her back. "Virginia Martinelli? I'm Lieutenant JG Ellison."

Gina turned and faced her visitor. "Is something wrong?"

Ellison smiled and relaxed. "Goodness, no! I'm a linguistics nerd and when I heard you were on board I just had to come meet you."

"Linguistics nerd?"

Lieutenant Ellison stepped into the room. "It's what my degree's in. I read your paper on *Crosscultural and Interspecies Content Interpretation*. Really impressive. The tonal shadings of dolphin song took me back to my Mandarin Chinese studies."

"Thanks!" Gina smiled, at a loss for words.

"Yeah," Ellison continued. "And I thought I might, uh, you know ... get a chance to talk to the dolphins. If that's OK."

"My guys aren't all that talkative after being sloshed around in cramped quarters for the past couple of days," Gina replied. "And right now I'm trying to get this damn filter assembly to work."

"Can I help?"

"Sure. A girl needs all the help she can get stuck out here on the ocean in a tin can full of men. You got a first name?"

"Norma. Norma Ellison." She crouched down beside Gina and laid a wrench to a brass fitting.

"I thought your initials were J.G. First name Julia or Jenny or something," Gina said.

"Hah!" Ellison snorted. "Lieutenant JG. Stands for Junior Grade. Next step up from ensign. Pass me that half-inch."

"Pleased to meet you, Norma. Thanks for dropping by. What do you do here?"

"I run the communications division. Study linguistics in my spare time."

"So what's your favorite language?"

"Probably Plains Indian Sign." Ellison tucked a new washer into the brass fitting. "Learned it from my grandma. She was full blood Lakota Sioux. Used to call me Mika." She smiled in remembrance. "It means 'clever racoon.' Grandma was my inspiration to learn languages. In Plains Indian Sign the gestures change with region and context. It's tougher than you think. Like the way German mashes words together to express a complex idea."

"That's the way dolphins do it," Gina said.

Norma gestured at the tool box. "Pass me the pliers, please." She began to tighten the brass fitting. "The study of language is the study of the human mind." She smiled at Gina. "Or any other intelligent creature."

"Keeps the men from being all over you too, I guess." Gina measured off a length of plastic tubing and slid a couple of clamps onto it.

"I don't mind the guys," Norma said. "They're almost always polite. I've certainly been around worse."

Gina frowned. "That's a mighty low bar, Lieutenant."

Ellison gave a rueful smile. "I find with men it's best to grade on a curve."

Gina laughed for the first time in days. "Ain't it the truth! Tell you what ... after we finish with the filter, I'll teach you how to say 'hello' in dolphin."

As the afternoon was on the verge of fading to sunset, John went topside to breathe some healing tropical air and try to quell his rebellious stomach. He sought out his favorite spot back by where the *Beagle*, the Institute's research submarine, sat in its cradle. Larry and Barry, the two techs who operated the sub, were leaning on the railing. They were a classic pair: Mutt and Jeff, Abbot and

Costello, R2D2 and C3PO. Larry was tall and skinny with a goatee and Barry was short and round with a head of unruly red hair. John joined them and the two wordlessly nodded at him. Fellow nerds and old friends.

John took a deep breath of the warm, humid air and let it out with a sigh of contentment. "So nice to be out on the ocean," he said.

"I suppose," Barry replied. His voice held no joy.

"We're off on an adventure in the South Pacific!" said John.

"Please don't sing anything from the musical," Larry pleaded.

"I bet he does his "Some Enchanted Evening" schtick," Barry said to no one in particular.

John looked up at the sky and sang in a quavering tenor, "Sam and Janet evening, you will meet a stranger..." He dropped into a Groucho twang. "And they don't make 'em any stranger than me!" he quipped.

Larry cracked a weak smile. "I'll grant you that."

John surveyed the scene, taking in the shimmering light on the water, the billowing clouds glowing with afternoon light, and the large, grey Navy ship escorting them. "That looks like quite a boat. The Navy must think we're pretty special."

Barry shook his head. "The Navy doesn't give a rat's patootie about this expedition."

"Why do you say that?" John asked.

"That, my friend, is a *Spruance*-class destroyer, built in the 1970s," Barry said. "It's so old they probably have dinosaurs down in the engine room. I thought they had all been decommissioned, but I guess I was wrong."

"It's the *Shanklin*," Larry threw in. "But I don't recognize the number."

"They're still sweeping the mothballs off it," Barry continued. "Outdated armaments, probably stripped the missiles. It's a sad old tub. Kinda tells you what the Navy thinks about us and our mysterious mission."

"Not much," Larry said softly.

"Maybe it's to make this expedition look more stealth," John said. "Maybe it has more teeth than you think."

"Maybe it has warp drive and photon torpedoes," Larry said in his best deadpan. "But I wouldn't hold my breath."

The plates had been cleared in the officers mess of the *USS Shanklin* and four well-fed people relaxed over coffee: Rear Admiral Diaz, practicing geniality for the occasion; Lieutenant Commander Amundsen, a lean, poker-faced woman; Captain Janet Murphy, the *Shanklin's* commanding officer, a compact woman with salt and pepper hair; and Kyle Montgomery, a slight, stylishly dressed man. He was the only one not in uniform.

Montgomery was smiling and dramatically finishing off a joke. "...so the guy says, 'I took them to the zoo like you said, officer. They loved it! We're going to the movies!'"

The other three laughed, relaxed in camaraderie. "Nice thing is," Montgomery continued, "it's clean enough to tell to an eight-year-old. If you know any eight-year-olds."

"Hell, my grandkids are in their twenties by now!" Captain Murphy chortled. Kyle Montgomery was the only one to laugh with her. A silence settled over the table, eating into the relaxed atmosphere.

Diaz raised his cup. "To the *USS Shanklin*, may she get us there and back!"

"She is a beautiful old lady," Captain Murphy said, smiling proudly. "Creaky in places, I'll admit, but still afloat."

Four cups clinked and coffee was sipped. "She is a beautiful old lady indeed," said Diaz. "Last of the *Spruance* destroyers."

Murphy nodded with mock dignity. "Thank you, Admiral. But I must correct you. There is one other: the *Nicholson* is on permanent museum patrol at Norfolk."

This got a chortle from Diaz. "The veal was excellent, by the way. My compliments to your cook."

Murphy beamed. "Kyle here had it flown in from Seattle before we left." She put a hand on his arm.

"Do you two know each other?" Amundsen asked.

Montgomery grinned. "Her daughter married my sister. Or the other way around."

The captain nodded and sipped at her coffee.

Lieutenant Commander Amundsen frowned slightly. "You brought your brother-in-law?"

"He's the Strategic Design rep. We have a lot of their equipment on board."

"I'm just here to babysit the stuff," Kyle explained. "An observer, if you will. There's a lot of experimental and proprietary stuff onboard. Besides," he grinned, "how could I turn down a vacation in the South Pacific?"

"I don't know how much of a vacation this is going to be," Amundsen commented.

"Lieutenant Commander Amundsen and I will bunk over on the Institute's ship once we drop anchor," Admiral Diaz said. "Stay out of your hair."

Captain Murphy waved her hand dismissively. "You're not in our hair at all, Admiral. Honored to have you aboard." She sat silently for a few seconds before speaking. "Anything you can tell me about this big rush-rush, hush-hush mission, Hector? I got only the briefest of briefings."

Diaz shook his head. "I'm afraid not, Janet. We drop anchor tomorrow morning and Lieutenant Commander Amundsen and I will give a very thorough briefing at that time."

"I don't know how much help the *Shanklin* can be," Murphy lamented. "We have zero missiles, not much in the way of ammunition for the big guns, and I'm running on a lean crew. Some strings got pulled to get us on this detail, but I guess they missed a few."

"Don't you worry. I'm sure the *Shanklin* is a tough old dame," Diaz said. "I had to pull my share of strings, too. The brass thinks

I'm crazy. No offense, but I was hoping for one or two *Arleigh Burke* class destroyers."

Murphy tilted her head. "Why does the brass think you're crazy?"

Diaz waved her away. "Briefing. Tomorrow."

A tired air settled on the table. "I heard about your son," Murphy said solemnly. "My deepest condolences, sir."

Diaz cleared his throat and looked down at the empty plate before him. "Thank you, Captain. You are most kind."

"I heard he went down somewhere out here in the South Pacific," Murphy continued. "Does this mission have anything to do with his disappearance?"

Diaz fixed Captain Murphy with an implacable gaze, holding it for a few seconds. "Like I said, there will be a comprehensive briefing tomorrow."

Diaz and Amundsen strode down a metal corridor on the way to their respective cabins. "Permission to speak frankly, sir," Amundsen said.

"You always do, so why stop now?"

"Why wasn't this mission sent out with a couple of *Arleigh Burke* class ships?"

Admiral Diaz frowned. "The top brass thinks the video is a deep fake."

"What about the missing planes?"

"They put them down to mechanical failure."

It was Amundsen's turn to frown. "That doesn't make sense, sir."

"I thought you worked in the Pentagon, Gladys. Not everything makes sense there."

"Mmm. Point taken."

They walked a few steps more in silence. Amundsen turned slightly toward the admiral and spoke in a low voice.

"He's lying, you know. That Kyle guy."

"He's a company man," Diaz said.

"I don't trust him."

"You don't trust anybody," the admiral retorted. "I like that about you."

"He wants something," she insisted.

"What do you think he wants?"

"You know as well as I do what he wants," Amundsen said. "Strategic Designs is making strategic moves."

# CHAPTER FOUR

The two ships dropped anchor the next morning. "Dropped anchor" was a figure of speech since the seabed was thousands of feet below them. The ships' engines kept them in position, their thrumming giving the hulls a subtle vibration.

The briefing was held at ten o'clock. An excited group of scientists, technicians, and Navy personnel were present in the mess hall, the largest room on *Darwin's Dream*. John brought Oliver to the meeting in his portable aquarium. It had been an effort to get the cart through two hatchways and into the elevator, but since the military had demanded the presence of an octopus on this mysterious foray, John thought that Oliver deserved to see what it was all about.

John got one of the aqueous spectrometry guys to scoot over so he could have an aisle seat. He rolled Oliver's aquarium up close and draped his hand into the water, smiling as the octopus softly wrapped a tentacle around his finger. Several rows of folding chairs faced the front of the room where a large flatscreen was bolted to the bulkhead. John looked around the room, recognizing many of the people from the Institute. Lab coats, beards and pocket protectors abounded. He spotted Gina and smiled. She smiled slightly, then looked away.

The door at the front of the room opened and the buzz of conversation receded to a low mumble. The Hispanic man who strode in was not tall, had an unexceptional face, and sported a buzz cut, yet his presence was commanding. His short-sleeved khaki uniform shirt had two stars on left and right shoulders, adding to his air of gravitas. A lean woman, also in khaki, her face impassive, came in behind him, followed by a shorter uniformed woman with greying hair. Director Harris entered last, somber and out of place in an aloha shirt. The last three sat to one side of the flatscreen while the man with the stars on his shoulders stood in front, hands clasped behind him.

"Good morning," he said in a clipped tone. "For those of you I have not met, I am Rear Admiral Diaz. I am in charge of this mission." He gestured at the seated stoic woman. "This is Lieutenant Commander Amundsen." She nodded slightly. "Captain Murphy of the *USS Shanklin*." The Captain nodded as well. "And I'm sure most of you know Mr. Harris, Director of the Gershon Oceanographic Institute." Harris steepled his fingers and leaned his chin on them. Diaz continued. "I will now turn this briefing over to Lieutenant Commander Amundsen."

The slim woman rose from her chair and stood to one side of the flatscreen. "This is a classified mission," she said in a penetrating contralto. "You have all been required to sign nondisclosure agreements and I'm sure you have noticed that none of your outside communication devices work. No cell phones, no internet. This is standard security protocol."

"You can't do that!" someone shouted from the crowd. "We're not military!"

Amundsen raised her voice. "This is a Navy operation and as such you are subject to Navy security. You'll understand why in a few minutes." She waved her hand over her head and the room dimmed. A map came up on the video screen of an elongated atoll with an irregular lagoon in the middle. It was surrounded by a coral reef, white against the darker blue of the deep ocean.

Amundsen gestured at the flatscreen. "Palmyra Atoll. Just over four and a half square miles. A worn-down extinct volcano a thousand miles south-southwest of the Hawaiian Islands. About as remote as you can get. Nineteen days ago, at approximately eleven hundred hours Greenwich Mean Time, the Fish and Wildlife Service lost contact with their research station on Palmyra Atoll. They were in radio contact when the loss occurred. The last words from

Palmyra were about a meteor in the sky, then the line went dead. Fish and Wildlife contacted the Weather Service to see if they had picked up any anomalous events. They had seen nothing, nor had NASA. The USGS registered no seismic activity."

"What does this have to do with us?" came an impatient voice from the audience.

Lieutenant Commander Amundsen tilted her head to the side. "Please hold your questions until after I'm done." She eyeballed the room for a couple of beats, then continued. "Fish and Wildlife called the Navy and we sent out a recon team from Hawaii. The plan was to land and contact the research team and report in. A drone would land first."

She paused in her staccato delivery and cleared her throat. John noticed that Admiral Diaz was sitting rigidly, as if trying to remain composed.

"Twelve miles from the atoll the plane disappeared," she continued. "Vanished. The pilot was in radio contact with Pearl Harbor when the transmission cut off in mid-sentence. The drone had already been launched, though. When the radio operator could not raise the pilot, he had the presence of mind to start recording the drone's feed." She looked to the back of the room and circled her hand over her head.

The map changed to a view of flying over the ocean. A dot of green showed on the horizon. Amundsen continued, "The search and rescue planes sent out to look for any wreckage also vanished. The drone footage is the only record we have."

"What kind of drone?" John recognized Barry's voice.

"Strategic Design SV-150A," she said tersely. "Experimental model, microjet engine, radar resistant and self-guiding. In stealth mode it glides in for a landing."

The green speck was getting bigger, resolving into a spatter of interconnected islands. A red light in the upper right corner of the image switched off. "The drone is now in stealth mode," Amundsen said. The view began to descend. The atoll grew bigger. "We'll be coming in over the lagoon toward the landing strip. Watch screen left."

The drone dropped ever lower. A bright blue lagoon stretched out to a long landing strip at the right of the screen. To the left was a cluster of small buildings. Or the remains of them. A quick glimpse of smoking ruins flashed by as the drone homed in on the runway. A nervous murmur ran through the room.

"Quiet," she snapped. "Keep watching."

The drone landed jerkily and came to a stop well shy of the end of the runway. Several yards away a figure stepped out onto the tarmac, there was a flash of light and the screen went blank.

Amundsen's voice spoke in the dim quiet. "We had that last part enhanced."

The video came on again, only grainier and much zoomed in. There was movement in the trees to the right of the pavement, the image stuttering in slow motion. A figure scuttled from the trees onto the landing strip.

It was a giant crab. Carrying a ray gun.

The image froze.

The room went crazy.

When the slo-mo giant crab stepped out of the trees John was as floored as everybody else. A chill ran down his spine and the hair on his arms and neck stood up. This was first contact! Every sci-fi addict, action movie director, and conspiracy junkie had been fantasizing about this since forever. And here it was in jiggling video freeze-frame right before his eyes! This lasted for a heartbeat or two until a sharp pain told John that Oliver's grip had tightened to the verge of crushing his finger. John gasped at the pain and looked over at the octopus. In that insane second of shock and sensory overload, John had a flash of zen. He saw himself looking from one intelligent alien to another, from the menacing crustacean wielding a ray gun (a ray gun!) to his strange and gentle alien friend. Oliver was bright, pulsating red, with white horns covering his skin, the ridge above his eyes glowing white and almost quivering. His eyes actually bulged out of their sockets. John had never seen Oliver this excited.

John rapped frantically on the aquarium's glass, trying to free his finger. Oliver released the digit, never taking his eyes off the screen. John pulled his hand out of the water and massaged his finger to get the circulation going. A single tentacle descended from the rapt octopus and made its way over to the keyboard. After some hesitation, one tap.

"Crab," the synthetic voice said.

"No kidding," John replied. "Big crab."

Lieutenant Commander Amundsen let the hubbub go on for a while, a bemused smile resting on her lips. People were shouting at each other, jabbering into the air, pointing at the jittering image on the flatscreen. A few sat quietly with beetled brows. Eventually, Amundsen called for quiet. She had to call loudly and several times. After the crowd quieted, Amundsen looked at the seated Admiral. He nodded and she continued. "Just so you know, not only am I the intelligence officer with this operation, I also represent the First Contact Unit of the United States Navy."

Another voice from the crowd: "Wait a sec…the Navy actually has a unit specifically designed to deal with alien contact? You're kidding."

Lieutenant Amundsen frowned. "This is not a laughing matter, sir. The Navy is prepared for any contingency. And the First Contact Unit has certain protocols. The aliens are a complete mystery so far. The aliens must…"

A tall, bearded scientist stood and raised his hand. "Excuse me!" he said in a loud voice. Not used to being interrupted, the lieutenant paused. The scientist continued. "We should have a name for them instead of just calling them 'the aliens.' It would make the problem of approach more organic."

Amundsen sighed with frustration. "Civilians," she muttered. "Alright, discuss it among yourselves and see what you can agree on." She looked at her watch. "I'll give you ten minutes."

The room rang rampant with suggestions for several minutes. "Crabs" was a bit obvious and a few pubic-louse-and-blue-ointment jokes were offered. Several wild takes on scientific nomenclature were suggested, as well as one guy wanting to name the giant crabs after his mother-in-law. It got tiresome and rowdy until John Rauchenberg stood up and said his piece.

"Listen, we're all science fiction fans here, right?" John had to yell to be heard over the hubbub. A murmur of agreement rippled through the room. "Remember in *Forbidden Planet* how the only hint of what the Krell looked like was the shape of the doors? Well, the doors look perfect for our alien crabs."

"The movie's doors are bigger though," said Larry.

"Yeah, bigger. But we should honor that classic film and name the crabs the Krell. That's what I say. It's only five letters and it's easy to remember."

Admiral Diaz jumped in. "Well it's certainly easier to remember than 'The Evil Doris Bickerman.'" Laughter filled the room.

Ten minutes had elapsed and the lieutenant put the entries up for a vote. She read the results. "Mr. Rauchenberg's suggestion of 'the Krell' wins by a wide margin." John stood up and took a bow. "I won't go through the entire tally, but 'The Evil Doris Bickerman' was in last place with only one vote. And by the way, 'Crustacea xenoinimicus' will be the official scientific nomenclature used in the papers that I am sure all of you are itching to write once you get back."

That being settled, Lieutenant Commander Amundsen opened the floor to questions.

Where did the Krell come from? No idea. How big were they? About a meter tall and a bit more than that wide, the size of a kitchen table. They appeared to be oxygen breathers. They also appeared to be from a world with similar gravity to Earth, judging by how easily and quickly they moved. What about the ray gun? What kind of weapon was that? An even grainier zoom-in on the weapon the Krell held showed it to have a smooth barrel and a wide stock. Beyond it being an energy weapon, there was no concrete information. Was the Krell wearing or carrying anything else? There appeared to be things clipped to the shell, but they couldn't be sure because the image was of such poor quality.

"But why are they here?" asked one of the computer engineers.

"That is the big question," Amundsen replied. She turned to John and Gina. "For that we have our experts on alien intelligence."

Gina looked puzzled. "I don't know anything about what crabs think. My dolphins are mammals with brains like us." She gestured at John. "You want an alien intelligence, talk to this guy."

"What do you have to say to that, Mr. Rauchenberg?"

"Oliver is kind of an alien, I guess. But I have no idea how a giant space crab thinks and I'm sure he doesn't either."

"So what do you want from us?" Gina asked.

"We're not asking you to read the Krells' minds," Amundsen said. "What we need from you two is reconnaissance."

"Can't you just send in some drones or something?" Gina asked.

"As you've seen, the Krell can spot approaching machines. We need organic penetrators. Spies who can make intelligent decisions."

"Then send in some scuba divers or frogmen or whatever the Navy calls them," Gina said.

Amundsen ignored her and turned to John. "I hear your octopus can be easily trained."

"Oh, he likes to do just about..."

"Can it carry a camera?"

"Oliver's a he, not an it," John frowned. He turned to the aquarium. "Do you want to carry a camera, Oliver?"

Oliver jabbed at his keyboard. "Does Oliver get a crab?"

Admiral Diaz went to where John was sitting and looked into Oliver's traveling tank. "That's some fish you have there, son," he said

"Actually, sir, he's a cephalopod," John said. "If you want you can put your hand in the water and he'll smell you." Puzzled, Admiral

Diaz frowned. John stumbled on. "It's how he gets to know you. Through his skin. He uses his sucker cups to sort of 'smell' stuff." He made air quotes for the word 'smell.' "But only if you want. He won't bite or anything."

The admiral cautiously dipped two fingers in Oliver's traveling tank. Oliver extended a tentacle and gently wrapped the admiral's fingers. "Oliver," said John, "this is Admiral Diaz. He's our friend."

Oliver's color brightened, flashes of red drifting across his skin, and he tapped at his underwater keyboard. "Pleased to meet you," came the synthetic voice. The military man and the octopus held their contact for several seconds. "Ad-me-rahl Diaz is very strong." The admiral smiled.

John saw Oliver raising his siphon toward the surface. He rapped on the aquarium's glass. "If you squirt the admiral I'll have you for lunch! No crab!" Oliver paused. Admiral Diaz looked perplexed. Oliver's siphon swiveled over to John and squirted him full in the face. The synthetic voice issued a wicked "bwah-ha-ha!" and laughter ran through the room. Even Admiral Diaz laughed, pulling his fingers from the water. Bands of bright blue and purple flickered across Oliver's skin, his visual way of laughing.

John did his best to appear nonplussed. He used his sleeve to wipe his face. "Thank you, Oliver."

"You're welcome." The octopus manipulated the timbre to make the synthetic voice sound like a condescending game show host.

John turned to Admiral Diaz. "Sorry, sir."

The admiral smiled, drying his fingers with his handkerchief. "I believe a sense of humor is a sign of intelligence. We're hoping that you two will help us figure out what these damn Krell things are up to. We need you and Ms. Martinelli to send your animals to the atoll to take a look around."

"And I don't know about John here," Gina said, "but my pod is not a military resource."

Amundsen's voice was chisel-sharp. "Actually, it is. Above and beyond the contract you signed when the Gershon Institute hired you, you realize, do you not, that our planet has just been invaded by aliens from outer space wielding advanced weaponry. I had hoped to get your voluntary cooperation rather than ordering you to do so. Voluntary cooperation is always more productive than…"

Without looking at the Lieutenant Commander, Admiral Diaz held up a hand to stop her. His eyes were on Gina. "Tell us your concerns."

Gina took a deep breath. "My pod and John's octopus are living, sentient creatures who have never been in the open ocean. The world they know is the size of a large swimming pool. They could easily get lost out there, or be attacked by sharks, or any number of bad things. It just doesn't seem right—or smart—to put them in danger." She glanced briefly at John.

Amundsen jumped in. "Your contract states unequivocally that…"

Diaz held up his hand to silence her again. He gave Gina a rueful smile, his tone of command softening. "You're right, this operation is dangerous. But we need the reconnaissance so we can figure out what to do next. The eight of you—and that includes our two submarine operators—are riding point because you have the skill sets to ride point. Believe me, if I could do this job myself, I would do so without hesitation. I would send Navy personnel if I could. However, no one but you can do it. Do you understand?"

Gina dropped her gaze to her lap.

"Do we have your full and voluntary cooperation?" Diaz asked.

She looked up, her lips taut. "Okay." A slight pause. "Sir."

"I'll take that as a yes," Diaz said, settling back in his chair. He gestured for Lieutenant Commander Amundsen to continue.

"So far," she said, "we have only this crappy video and a suspicion of where their spacecraft might be. Ms. Martinelli, we need your dolphins to scout the west end of the atoll where we suspect the Krell spacecraft is, with cameras. Their task will be to locate and get video footage. Can they do that?"

Gina shrugged. "Yeah, they can do it."

"Good," Amundsen said, turning her attention to John. "Mr. Rauchenberg, I have a more challenging task for your octopus."

"Oliver loves adventure!" the octopus's artificial voice said.

"We need it...sorry, Oliver to get into the reef area around the atoll," she continued. "Particularly the area where we think the Krell are setting up a base. If he can infiltrate all the way into the lagoon in the middle of the atoll, even better. Your octopus can blend in with the natural surroundings, yes? Look like a piece of coral and so forth?"

"Oh, yes!" replied John enthusiastically. "Dr. Schreiner spliced *Thaumoctopus mimicus* DNA into Oliver's genome, plus several other subspecies. Oliver's got mad skills."

Admiral Diaz waved his hand toward Oliver's travelling aquarium. "Demonstrate, please."

"Sure thing," John replied. He turned to the octopus. "Oliver, show us the seaweed."

Oliver transformed before their eyes into a mound of seaweed, his tentacles becoming strands of plant matter waving in the water. A murmur of appreciation went through the watching crowd. "The rock," John said. The waving arms tucked in around the octopus's body, as he became a lump of rock covered with sea moss. More appreciative murmurs. John smiled. "Rubik's Cube." Oliver took on an almost cube-like shape, colored squares covering the sides. The crowd laughed. He began shuffling the colored squares as if he were an actual Rubik's Cube. A scattering of applause rippled through the room.

John smiled at the admiral. "Oliver's kind of a show-off."

"I can tell."

"Oliver is Rubik octopus," the synthetic voice said. He settled down to a contented speckled reddish brown.

"So what do you need him to do?" John asked.

"We need him to carry a video camera into the reef area," Amundsen replied, "and get footage of what the Krell are up to."

"Shouldn't we try to talk to them first?" said Gina.

"That's my department," Amundsen replied with quiet authority. "We will not attempt to contact the Krell until we have a better understanding of them." She looked at her watch. "It's almost thirteen hundred. I'm sure all of you need some lunch or have work you need to attend to. We will meet back here in three hours to finalize the particulars of the mission. Dismissed."

John looked over at Gina and smiled. She looked worried and sad, but gave him a wistful smile, then got up and left. John nodded his respects to the officers, and wheeled Oliver's aquarium away.

When John got back to his lab, Oliver was still excited. The big octopus clambered into his tank and drove his crank-powered car round and round the sandy bottom. He was still bright red and the white horns had disappeared only to be replaced with coruscating bands of neon blue that ran across his mantle and down his arms. After several minutes of this he abandoned the car and crawled into his den. The light of the television came on. John hypothesized that Oliver was dealing in his own way with the recent revelations and decided to leave him alone.

John walked to Gina's lab and found the door open. She was in a foul mood, scowling down into the dolphin tank. Her dark hair was tied back in a tight bun and the front of her lab coat was soaked. The entire cargo bay had been cleared to allow an enormous saltwater tank some seven meters wide by twelve meters long and two meters deep. It looked huge in the cramped room, but was painfully small for the dolphins.

John knocked politely. When Gina looked up, her scowl did not fade.

"Hi," he ventured. "How ya doin'?"

"What do you want, John?" Her tone was curt as she brushed an errant strand of hair from her forehead.

"Well," he replied, "since we're going to be working together, I thought I would come by and…visit." He looked around at the machinery, computers, and stacks of boxes filling her cramped work area. "Wow. This looks almost as chaotic as my lab."

"I don't have time for small talk, John. Don't you have an octopus to take care of?"

"He's holed up in his cave, probably watching season six of *Game of Thrones*. That's what he does when he's trying to sort something out."

"I'm kinda busy, John. Really."

John gave a little shrug and a shy smile. "Sorry to bother you," he said and turned to go. "I'll check in later."

"Hold it," Gina said. "I'm sorry I snapped at you. My guys are being a pain in the rear."

John stepped back into the lab. "Are they giving you grief?"

She sighed and leaned against the edge of the tank. "You have no idea." A dolphin stuck its head out of the water and chittered at her, then turned and slapped its tail on the water, splashing the back of her lab coat. She did not flinch. A green light flashed on a stack of electronic components and a computer voice translated the dolphin's squealing chatter. "Ugly bad fish. Stupid." She reached over and switched the speaker off.

"Maybe I do," John replied. He stepped up to the edge of the holding tank, resisting the urge to sidle up next to her. "Oliver has been a petulant snot ever since we came on board."

She gave him a dark sideways glance and said nothing.

"I keep telling him he looks like a booger with eyes, but he doesn't get it." Gina made no response. John looked at the sleek forms darting about under the water and tickled the surface of the pool with his finger. "You could introduce me to your pod."

"Sure. Why not." Gina tapped a button on her console twice and three dolphin heads poked up out of the water. "John, I'd like you to meet Nancy, Sheila and Gary," she said into a microphone. "Guys, this is my friend John." She touched another button and John could hear a rapid burst of underwater squeals.

"What do I do?"

"Touch their noses. Gently."

John softy touched the snout of each of the dolphins. They ducked back under the water and swam in circles. He could hear them squealing and chittering.

"What are they saying?"

"You don't want to know."

"Maybe I do."

Gina flipped the speakers back on. Computer voices tumbled from the speakers, talking over each other. "He's ugly! We should all orgy! Gina wants him to…" She flipped the speakers off, a blush reddening her cheeks.

John tried to change the subject. "So what's the problem here?"

She leaned on the edge of the tank, staring blankly into the water. "The tank's too small. I could only bring three dolphins, and they're pissed that they don't have their other pod mates with them. They're not getting enough exercise in this dinky tank, and they're bored out of their minds. So, like the children they are, they act up in creative and aggravating ways."

John smiled. "Bored? Maybe they'd like to play a game!" He plucked a soccer ball from atop a stack of boxes and tossed it into the pool.

"I don't think you want to do that," Gina cautioned.

John looked over at her, still smiling. "Why not? How could…"

At that moment the largest of the dolphins, Gary, rose up out of the pool carrying the soccer ball on his nose. He flipped the ball up and smacked it with his snout, sending it into the side of John's head with a ferocity that caused him to stagger back, losing his glasses. The other two dolphins stuck their heads out of the water and cackled.

"Not nice!" Gina scolded the laughing marine mammals. John waved his hand at her to stop, then slid his glasses back on and scooped the ball off the floor. He tossed it from hand to hand while the dolphins watched, then threw it at the two smaller ones. One fielded it over to the larger dolphin who did the lifting it out of the water and smacking it with his snout trick again. But this time John was ready. He butted the soccer ball with his chest, directing it to splash down at one end of the pool. One of the smaller females hit it from underneath, lifting it out of the water, then batted it toward John. He caught it, faked tossing it to them a couple of times, then spun the ball and balanced it on his forefinger. All three dolphins watched with rapt attention. One slapped the water with a flipper.

"They want you to throw it," Gina told John.

"I bet they do," he replied. He dropped the ball and hit it with an upward swing of his arm in a volleyball serve. The ball hit the ceiling and splashed down in the middle of the pool. The dolphins chittered and cackled and squealed, tossing it from one to the other. John yelled "Hey!" and formed his arms into a sideways circle. One of the female dolphins flicked the ball in the air and leapt up out of the water, expertly smacking the ball with the side of her snout. The soccer ball shot through the center of John's arm circle. John whooped and raised his fists in the air. All three dolphins rose up out of the water and chattered madly.

Gina looked at John quizzically. "Where did you learn to do that?"

"Played volleyball in college," he smiled. "'Scuse me. I got a game going."

John and the three aquatic mammals batted the soccer ball back and forth for another twenty minutes. Gina joined in, retrieving the ball and sometimes surprising the dolphins by smacking it into the pool. Gary tried bouncing it off the ceiling and achieved good accuracy after several tries. John at times held the ball and turned his back on the dolphins, pretending to ignore them while they whistled and clamored until he threw it back. The dolphins would then turn the tables on him while he waved and shouted. Mostly it was hitting the ball back and forth, occasionally pulling off some extended volleys. At the end of the session the humans were smiling and laughing and the dolphins were slapping the water with amusement. She had John give each of the dolphins a fish treat.

"That was fun!" John exclaimed.

"Thanks for playing with them," Gina smiled. "You're part of the pod now." John glowed as if her smile was a match and he was tinder. "They're going to probably indulge in a little sex play," she continued. "We have a couple of hours until the next meeting, so maybe we should get some lunch."

"I know an excellent ocean-going restaurant nearby," he smiled back. "Then maybe we can go look at the submarine."

The cafeteria provided Gina and John with a not-bad-but-not-exemplary mid-day meal that they ate while discussing the play habits of augmented ocean creatures. After a rather tasteless fish filet, John poked around at his salad.

"So what do you think of this whole Krell thing?" he asked Gina.

"I think we should definitely contact them right away." Gina said. "Yes, they shot the drone, but that doesn't necessarily mean they're hostile."

"Shooting at stuff is pretty much the definition of hostile," John said. "Don't you think we should check them out before rushing in?"

"Of course we should. But they're alien in every sense of the word. We should initiate contact, give them a chance."

"They killed the entire research team..."

"Seemingly," she countered.

"...burnt the buildings to the ground and fired on our drone."

"The burnt buildings could have been an accident," Gina said. "Heat of atmospheric entry and all that. And there could be survivors. As for the drone, they probably thought they were being attacked."

"We can't go all woo-woo on this. The evidence so far points to them being not very friendly."

Tired of the impasse, Gina shook her head and took a bite of her salad.

A man stopped at their table and John recognized him as the slight, well-dressed guy he had seen at the back of the room during the briefing. The man smiled warmly. "May I join you?" he asked.

"Uh, sure," Gina replied. "And you are...?"

"I'm Kyle Montgomery," he replied. He stuck out his hand and Gina shook it.

"Gina Martinelli. Pleased to meet you."

Montgomery extended his hand to John. "And you must be the infamous John Rauchenberg, master of octopi."

John shook the proffered hand. "Have a seat." The slight man slid into a chair and set a small salad on the table. "How do you fit into this crab hunt?" John asked.

"I work for Strategic Design," Kyle said with a shy smile. "They have a lot of equipment attached to this expedition and I'm here to babysit it. Kind of an observer. Fix any problems that might come up."

"I love Strategic Design!" Gina exclaimed. "They made most of my video equipment and an amazing underwater keyboard. I think John has one for his octopus, too."

"Always nice to hear from a satisfied customer."

"What kind of problems do you anticipate?" John asked.

"If we knew what to anticipate, they wouldn't be problems. SD makes durable stuff." He took a bite of his salad, dabbing his lips with his napkin. "I've spent years wanting to get the hell out of the office, so you can imagine how quickly I jumped at the chance for a South Pacific cruise." He turned to Gina. "I read your paper on *Crosscultural and Interspecies Content Interpretation*. Or at least most of it. From what little I understood, you're onto some groundbreaking stuff."

She was obviously pleased and smiled back. "Thank you."

"I'd like to come by and meet your pod, if that's alright."

"My door is always open," she replied.

"And I'd like to meet Oliver," Kyle said to John. "He seems fascinating."

"Yeah, he's one amazing mollusk. Feel free to drop by anytime."

"So what do you think of the Krell?" Gina asked Kyle. "Dangerous or benign?"

"Right now there's no way of knowing, but I think they're intelligent enough to be peaceful" he replied. "We could learn a lot from the Krell if we can figure out how to communicate with them."

"Gina here is a genius with alien languages," John said. "If anybody can figure out how to talk to them, it's her."

Kyle smiled. "And what's first contact without at least a little bit of contact?"

"I know Dolphin, John, not Krell."

"You can learn," John said. "Hopefully it will be more *Arrival* than *War Of The Worlds*."

Gina plucked a cherry tomato from John's salad. "Might even be *ET* for all we know."

"Only not as cute," Kyle added. Gina laughed lightly. "I would be very interested in anything you learn about the Krell language," he said seriously. "I'm a bit of a linguistics buff myself."

"No problem," Gina replied.

Montgomery rose from his seat and picked up his empty plate. "Well, nice meeting you two." He nodded to Gina and said, "I'll be by soon to meet your pod." He turned to John. "And I look forward to meeting Oliver. So what are you guys up to next?"

"John said he'd show me the submarine," Gina replied.

"Ahhh, the *Beagle*. She is a beauty. SD built the electronics and drive interface." He smiled again at the two marine scientists and walked away.

"Seems like a nice guy," Gina commented.

"Looks can be deceiving," John said flatly.

She let this slide off her. "Do you need to look in on Ollie?" she asked.

"He doesn't get as bored as your guys do. He's got his car to play with and besides," John glanced at his watch, "he's probably still watching *Game of Thrones*."

"Doesn't Ollie get lonely? Wouldn't he like a lady octopus to cuddle up to?"

John looked down at his hands in discomfort. "Octopuses don't, uh…mate…like we do."

Gina kept her expression neutral, waiting for him to continue.

"After octopuses mate, which they do at the end of their lives, the male dies within a month or so. The females lay their eggs and starve to death caring for them." John looked up from his hands into her calm eyes. "So Oliver had the sex drive edited out of his DNA."

"Aww. That's too bad. He can't fall in love, I guess."

"Love and sex aren't necessarily tied together. I mean, mammals are a different story. Humans, y'know, and dolphins too, I guess. We're all, uh, tied up in, uh…"

"I know what you mean," Gina said. "But isn't there some lady octopus he could get together with? Pass on the DNA? Is he even fertile?"

"We're pretty sure he's fertile. And the Smithsonian has an augmented female named Octavia over on the East Coast. But the muckety-mucks don't want to chance it. Maybe in a few years. Or decades. Remember, the females die after breeding too."

"That's so sad." Her mouth formed a little moue of melancholy.

"Yeah," he agreed. "Sad." He slapped both hands on his thighs and put on his game face. "Let's go check out the submarine."

Kyle Montgomery quietly opened the door to John's lab and stepped inside. Going to the cabinet where the cameras were kept, he removed two cameras. He verified their model number: SDCL4514-7, Strategic Design's top-of-the-line. Using a bent paper clip, he poked it into a small concealed port on the bottom of both each instrument, then returned them to their cabinet. That done, he turned and looked at the octopus's tank. Oliver was perched on what appeared to be a crude rolling platform, watching the company man with emotionless, alien eyes.

"Hello, Oliver," Montgomery ventured. "I'm your new friend."

The octopus tapped on an underwater keyboard, and a synthetic voice came from a hidden speaker. "Oliver does not smell you."

"Call me Kyle."

"Put Kigh-yull's arm in tank."

Montgomery balked. Strategic Design had contracted to build the computer network at the Gershon Institute, and with covert corporate access like that, it was easy for him to go in via a back channel and access all the information he needed. So he was aware of the octopus's almost psychic abilities and was loath to let Oliver touch him lest the cephalopod see through his veneer. "Kyle cannot put his arm into the water. Is there anything else?"

"Does Kigh-yull give Oliver a crab?"

Montgomery saw a bubbling aquarium full of crabs against the far wall. "Of course I'll give you a crab." There was a padlock on the crab tank. Montgomery looked at the serial number on the bottom of the lock. It was a Series 917 from LockMaster, another subsidiary of Strategic Design. Kyle Montgomery took what looked like a Swiss army knife from his pocket and opened a hidden compartment containing a lock pick set. He unlocked the aquarium and used a pair of tongs hanging nearby to snag a crab and drop the struggling crustacean into the octopus's tank. Oliver rose up and squirted a jet of water toward him. Montgomery was able to dodge most of it, but a goodly amount soaked his shirt.

"I love you too, Oliver," Montgomery exclaimed. "Does this mean we're friends?"

"Oliver does not smell Kigh-yull," came the synthetic voice.

The octopus extracted the crab from where it had hidden under a rock and settled on it to feed. Swiping at the water on his shirt, Montgomery returned the tongs to their hook and locked the crab aquarium, leaving the padlock precisely in its previous position.

Oliver expelled the emptied crab shell from under his nest of arms and jetted up on to the rolling platform.

Montgomery turned and faced the octopus tank. "John does not love you."

"John is Oliver's friend." The octopus regarded Montgomery with his unreadable gaze.

"No, he's not," Montgomery continued. "He is using you. You are just a lab rat to him."

"Buggabugga."

The company man was taken aback. "What?" Dark flecks began to form on Oliver's neutral beige skin. "You are just an experiment to John. Understand? A lab rat. Do you know what that is?"

Tentacles tapped the keyboard. "No."

"A lab rat is something you can throw away," Montgomery said. "I'll come back later and explain it more. OK?"

"Oliver wants more crab."

"And I will give you crabs. Many crabs. We'll talk later."

Oliver's beige briefly flashed a light blue. "Oliver understands."

"You're just an experiment. A lab rat. Remember that."

Kyle Montgomery, loyal employee of Strategic Design, slipped into the corridor, easing the door shut behind him.

The Gershon Oceanographic Institute's submarine, the *Beagle*, was at the stern of *Darwin's Dream*. Larry and Barry, the sub techs—or as they liked to call themselves "subtext"—were tinkering with something under one of the submarine's stubby wings.

The vessel was cigar-shaped, some fifty feet long and ten feet in diameter, with a glass bubble for a nose and truncated wings on the side. A low superstructure with an entry hatch sat on top amid-ships. A cluster of propulsion units clung to the stern and the skin of the submarine was dotted with blisters for sensors and cameras. The submarine was bright yellow on the underside and the top was being painted blue by several Navy personnel. Or several shades of blue, it seemed. The paint appeared to shimmer and move in the bright tropical sun. John had heard of the Navy's new photomimetic paint, but had never seen it in use. It was supposed to make the submarine blend in with the color of the water when seen from above.

Larry and Barry looked up when they heard footsteps. They smiled broadly at the two visitors. "Who's your friend?" Larry asked.

"Larry, Barry, this is Gina. Gina, this is Larry and Barry," John said. "Gina works in dolphin intelligence."

Larry nodded. "Pleased to meet you."

"Would you like a tour of our Yellow Submarine?" said Barry, waggling his eyebrows.

"As long as we don't get lost in a sea of green," she grinned. "I have to be back in time for dinner."

Larry and Barry were almost apoplectic with eagerness to show off their enormous toy. Inside there were switches and consoles and a universe of video screens. There were gauges and joysticks and electrical panels and even a tiny galley. Eventually John and Gina went into sensory overload and begged to go back outside.

Once they were on the deck again, Larry and Barry's enthusiasm still simmered. Larry knelt down to look under the huge yellow cigar. "Check out the remote arm!"

"Larry!" John exclaimed. "Enough. My brain hurts."

"OK." Larry was undaunted. "Maybe we can all go out on a cruise together sometime."

"I'm sure we will," John said.

The four quietly soaked in the smell of salt air and the view of open ocean, watching the nearby Navy ship cut through the water beside them. Larry suddenly jerked his head to the side as if hearing something, then looked out to sea. "Perhaps we should seek the wisdom of mighty Neptune," he intoned.

Barry knelt and put his palms together in mock supplication. This was obviously a bit that the two had done many times before. Barry spoke with submissive adoration. "What do you see, oh Wise One?"

Larry puffed out his chest and set his jaw, his gaze stern and distant. "Water," he said sonorously. "Lots and lots of water."

They held their visionary-and-acolyte poses for a couple of seconds, then dissolved into laughter. It got the two marine biologists laughing as well, as they all shared in the absurdity. This lasted until Director Harris emerged from a doorway and strode over to the group.

"Martinelli, Rauchenberg, I assigned you two an acclimation exercise over an hour ago," Harris declared. He looked at John. "You need to have your fish meet Miss Martinelli's fish."

Gina was frowning. "You realize, do you not, that neither species are fish."

Harris glowered at her. "I was being poetic. I don't want your dolphins treating one of our major assets as lunch when they're on this mission. Mr. Rauchenberg will be at your lab in a half-hour and you two will introduce your animals. I'll want video and notes. Got it?" Neither Gina nor John made any reply. "Silence means yes," Harris said. "There's a mandatory meeting in the mess hall in an hour and a half. Don't forget."

# CHAPTER FIVE

Twenty-seven minutes later, John rolled Oliver's travelling tank into Gina's dolphin lab. "Ready here!" he said. "Dolphins ready?"

"You concentrate on your octopus and I'll concentrate on my dolphins," she said. Her tone indicated she was all business. "Now…what's the objective of this exercise and how do we implement it?"

"I think Dennis the Menace's point—and it's a good point—is that our guys are going to work together, so we need a new paradigm. A better one than the 'prey-and-predator' one they have in the wild, so they should have a cautious meet and greet."

Gina crossed her arms and gazed into the dolphin tank. "I've explained the parameters of the situation to my pod and thoroughly gone over the kind of behavior I expect. They like to please, so I'm sure they'll go along with it. What did you tell Ollie?"

John bit his lower lip and looked at her sideways. "Um…I told him we were going to meet some friends and it would be OK."

"That's it?"

"I told him to remember what my Aunt Zelda used to say: 'Make nice and say hello.'"

Gina gave him a doubtful look. "Aunt Zelda, eh? OK, let's give this a go."

John transferred Oliver into a bucket of salt water, secured a wire mesh lid onto it, and put the bucket on its side at one end of the dolphins' tank. As a double precaution, Gina placed a clear plastic box over the bucket. She spoke into her microphone and the water sang with high-pitched dolphin language. Meanwhile, John kept his eye on Oliver. The octopus's skin was a pulsating brick red and little white horns stood up all over his mantle. He was intensely curious.

One by one the dolphins swam up to the clear plastic box and eyeballed Oliver. Gary, the big male first, then the two females. They made short chirping sounds at him, then swam vigorously from one end of the tank to the other. Oliver remained motionless, pressed up against the mesh screen.

"They're excited," Gina commented.

"You're sure they're not just hungry?"

"I fed them a big lunch before you got here. Don't worry."

"You ready to take the box away?"

Gina reached into the tank and lifted the clear box out of the water. She flicked on the microphone and said "Oliver is a friend." The underwater speakers sang a translation in Dolphin. She spoke each dolphin's name as, one at a time, they nosed up to the bucket's mesh screen and made short squeaks and chitters at the octopus. Oliver had retreated to the back of the bucket, his skin still pulsing brick red. One tentacle was pressed up against the wire mesh, smelling the dolphins as they peered in at him. Gina and John watched with silent intensity, each on edge in case anything might go wrong. But nothing went wrong. Gary, Nancy and Sheila each went up to the octopus a few times. After that they returned to dashing around the tank. John dragged Oliver in his bucket out of the dolphins' realm and returned him to his travelling tank. He smiled at Gina and some of the tension drained away.

"That went well," John said.

"Better than I thought it would," Gina replied.

He looked at his watch. "We've got twenty minutes until the meeting starts. Do you want to get a cup of the mess hall's terrible coffee?"

"I really have to get ready. Glad this went well," she said. "I'll see you at the meeting." Hearing the dismissal in her voice, John picked up his bucket and left.

The chairs in the mess hall were set up in a semi-circle. John had hoped to sit next to Gina, but by the time he arrived most of the seats had already been taken. At the front of the room Rear Admiral Diaz, dressed in his working uniform, leaned back in a chair, while Lieutenant Commander Amundsen, also in crisp khaki, addressed the group. "We are here to go over the particulars of this operation and hash out any problems," she said. She paused as if anticipating annoying interruptions, then continued. "The experimental submarine, the *Beagle*, piloted by Mr. Stokowski and Mr. Lambert..." she gestured at Larry and Barry, who smiled and waved. "...will carry Mr. Rauchenberg and Ms. Martinelli to Palmyra Atoll. Ms. Martinelli will deploy her pod of dolphins equipped with recon cameras to document the alien spacecraft. The reef itself will be surveilled by Mr. Rauchenberg's octopus."

Rear Admiral Diaz smiled and looked at John. "How's Ollie doing?"

"Just fine, sir," John said.

The admiral tipped his head, then waved at Amundsen to continue.

"Once the reconnaissance team has returned, we will process the data and send our conclusions to Washington."

"I thought we were keeping radio silence," said one of the technicians.

"We will shoot a compressed picowave burst via laser up to a comsat, and hope that it's too brief for the Krell to notice. Any other concerns?"

No one expressed any other concerns.

Amundsen continued her spiel. "The Krell were able to neutralize our aircraft from approximately twelve miles away. We don't know their weaponry or its full capacity, but we do know that they can detect machines and home in on them. Not all machines, though. This is borne out by the fact that our drone was able to glide all the way to a landing at Palmyra's airstrip.

Only when the Krell were able to visibly identify it as a machine did they destroy it."

Norma Ellison raised her hand. "Excuse me, ma'am, but wasn't the drone sending out a video signal? Why didn't the Krell home in on that?"

"It makes sense that an advanced species would be able to detect electromagnetic signals, but again, we just don't know," Amundsen replied. "Maybe they detect only certain frequencies. Everything is speculation at this point. Our mission is to collect data. Nothing more."

"That's it?" exclaimed a tall man at the back of the group, obviously agitated. "Then what the hell is the destroyer for? You would think—"

Rear Admiral Diaz broke in, using his command voice. "You would think that you would respect Lieutenant Commander Amundsen enough to let her finish." The irate man sat back down.

Amundsen looked at the admiral. "Thank you, sir." She turned to the gathered personnel. "Our first concern is a safe approach. For that we have the Institute's submarine's silent running technology to thank."

"Yeah! The SQUID drive!" Barry said excitedly. "Even the fish get fooled!"

Diaz crinkled his brow. "Squid drive? An underwater jet?"

Larry put a hand on Barry's shoulder to calm him. "Not quite. SQUID stands for Surprisingly Quiet Undulating Impelment Device. Barry here came up with the name, of course. It copies the locomotion pattern of fish by moving piezoelastic membranes in a semi-stochastic sequence. We have been able to infiltrate and swim within various fish groups."

John raised his hand and spoke up. "Lieutenant Amundsen, your first concern is a safe approach. What's your second concern?"

"Our second concern," she said, "is to deploy your animals without them being detected. Our third and overriding concern is to get the reconnaissance footage back here for analysis."

One scientist raised his hand. "Will we be able to watch the video feeds?"

Amundsen shook her head. "Negative. We go in full stealth. No video feed, no GPS, record only. We will provide all appropriate parties with the data afterward. But we go in silent. Whatever the animals bring back is what we get."

John glanced over at Gina. She was frowning and did not look his way.

Lieutenant Commander Amundsen brought the map of Palmyra Atoll up on the flatscreen. The *Beagle* would approach the atoll in a random pattern to better emulate marine life. It would cruise at an approximate depth of thirty meters so the submarine and Gina's dolphins could keep sight of each other. A Navy representative would be on board to watch over the mission. The dolphins and the octopus would be deployed a kilometer offshore.

At the west end of the elongated atoll the coral reef sloped down into a bowl twenty to twenty-seven meters deep. It was thought that the alien spacecraft was at the bottom of the declivity. The area was deep enough to avoid orbital detection and close enough to the channel leading to the inner lagoon for cargo to be easily trans-ferred. Two hours were allotted to complete the surveillance.

Gina raised her hand. "And after the two hours?"

"After two hours," Amundsen said, "the animals are to be abandoned."

John leapt to his feet. He had never leapt to his feet before, but there is a first time for everything. "Hold it! You want me to aban-don Oliver? What the hell?" At the other end of the semi-circle Gina was shouting too. "I'll never abandon my pod! Your commander just said they are precious souls! What kind of monstrous?..."

Amundsen held her hand up. "Stop!" she ordered. She did not shout, but her iron voice filled the room. John and Gina stopped, still fuming. "We can expand the time frame and give you some leeway to make a situational determination, but we cannot allow you to put the lives of everyone at risk, not to mention jeopardizing the mission. Do I make myself clear?"

Both John and Gina opened their mouths to object, but Diaz cut in. "We're gambling here that the Krell won't detect you. But we don't know the extent of their capabilities. The longer you're out there, the greater the probability of them reacting. Lieutenant Commander Amundsen and I are willing to give you some leeway. But only some."

They could tell from his tone that the decision was final.

When John got to the lab, Oliver was lazily driving his miniature car around the tank, his color rippling through hues of red, orange and brown. John had a hard time coaxing him to focus on instruction.

It was an arduous slog getting Oliver to understand his upcoming mission. First, John had to get him to understand what a mission was. Fortunately, they had all eight seasons of *Game of Thrones* as reference for strategy and purpose. Octopuses are naturally solitary creatures, but years of interaction with humans gave Oliver a flair for cooperation. So John found himself in an extended conversation with his highly intelligent cephalopod friend about the social and political intricacies of the various houses and characters in *Game of Thrones*, plus a few oblique forays into *Spongebob Squarepants*. It took awhile. Oliver's understanding of metaphor was just different enough from John's human take on it to be slightly maddening. Eventually they settled on the Krell being the White Walkers and Oliver being a combination of Jon Snow, Arya Stark, and Mr. Squidward heroically protecting Bikini Bottom.

Learning the miniature video camera was much more up Oliver's alley. They would be working out in open water without the voice synthesizer, so before the instruction started they agreed on new hand signals for "camera," "good," and "bad." The sign for "camera" was two fingers against the forehead; the signs for "good" and "bad" John borrowed from Plains Indian sign language: hand swooping up for "good" and down for "bad." Plus there was the tried-and-true kisses gesture of touching the back of one's open hand to one's mouth, but that was something they would probably not be using in the field.

John hooked up a video screen so Oliver could see what the camera was seeing. Learning to aim and frame took a little while, but the cephalopod's dexterity came to the fore and he turned out to be very good. They did several exercises and played some games to keep Oliver interested. Even when John took the video screen away, Oliver continued to do exemplary camera work.

The two were playing an interspecies game of video-the-moving-object when Gina knocked lightly at the door and came into John's lab. She did not look happy.

Oliver turned a rippling blue upon seeing Gina. He stretched a couple of tentacles over to his keyboard. "Gee-nah!" his synthetic voice exclaimed. "Oliver is Jon Snow!" He brandished the miniature video camera.

"Hi, Gina," John smiled. "How's it going?"

She offered a wan smile. "Oh, pretty good."

The smile faded from John's lips. "You don't sound all that good."

"I just need some octopus time, I guess." She stepped to the tank and stuck both arms into the water. John sensed that this was not the time for silly banter or words of comfort. He stuck his arms into the water as well. Oliver placed the camera on a rock and swam over to the humans, wrapping tentacles around their arms. The three communed quietly.

Oliver tapped his keyboard. "Gee-nah is sad." Oliver keyed gentleness into the synthetic voice.

"Is that true?" John asked softly.

"I guess," she sighed. "Not exactly."

"What's the problem?" John asked, looking at her and hoping it was not the wrong thing to say. Gray blotches swam across Oliver's skin as he experienced her turmoil.

She shook her head, her eyes fixed on the water.

The octopus tapped again at his keyboard. "Gee-nah is afraid."

"Really?" John tried to keep his tone light.

Her gaze shifted from the water to John, dark eyes flaring. "I'm scared for my guys."

"Don't worry, they'll be OK."

Her eyes caught fire and she pulled at the restraining tentacles. "They'll be OK? Really?" She turned to the octopus in the tank. "Kisses are over, Oliver. Let me go." Oliver did so, also releasing John's arms, and swam over to sit on his car.

Gina jerked a towel from a nearby table and dried her arms. "Have you thought this through at all?" she said. "We're sending our best friends out into the open ocean. It's bigger than anyplace they've ever been by infinite orders of magnitude. And it's dangerous. What if they meet a shark?"

"I thought dolphins could kill sharks."

"*Wild* dolphins, John. My guys are couch potatoes compared to wild dolphins. They've never even seen a shark. They can't take care of themselves." Gina was getting worked up. "We're sending our friends up against space aliens with ray guns, you idiot! Armed with what? Cameras?! If you're not afraid, then you're stupid."

John took a towel and calmly dried his arms. "We agreed to do reconnaissance. Nothing more."

"You yourself said the Krell aren't friendly."

"I did, yes. And I still believe it. But we're just sneaking in for a quick look," John said. "And our guys are mighty smart animals..."

"Don't call them animals!" she burst out. Then her shoulders drooped and she looked at the floor. "You're right. They are animals. We're all animals. It's just that this is just so goddamned dangerous. My pod trusts me to keep them safe, and I'm not sure I can."

Gina's brow knotted and she looked like she was about to cry. John reached out and put his hand on her shoulder, trying to think of the right thing to say. She jerked herself away.

"Excuse me, John. I have work to do," she said coldly, and stormed out of the room.

John didn't know what to do. Oliver picked up on the vibe, turned a mottled brown, and jetted into his den. John suspected that he had said the wrong thing, but for the life of him could not pinpoint what it was. He mentally threw his arms in the air and vowed not to think about it. As if that was possible.

A few troubled hours later John finally worked up the courage to go to Gina's lab, but the door was locked and there was no answer to his knock. He moped around his lab for a little bit, then joined Larry and Barry in the mess hall, only half-listening to their banter. Over his macaroni and cheese, he tried to figure out what he could have done to be more supportive of Gina. Hadn't he simply been trying to raise her spirits? Had he done something wrong? Compared to the intricacies of cephalopod intelligence, John found women far more complex, nuanced, and mysterious.

# CHAPTER SIX

Gina was in her lab putting the final touches on the translation into Dolphin of the mission instructions for the next day, when Kyle Montgomery rapped lightly on the open door.

"Hi, Gina. May I come in?"

She turned in her chair to face him, but did not smile. "Hello, Kyle. Nice to see you."

He stepped into her lab. The dolphins saw him and set to squealing and cackling. Gina waggled a finger at them and tossed a knotted rope into the tank, then stabbed at a button on her console. A faint, muted burst of dolphin song came from the water.

"I told them to go play. What can I do for you?"

"Sorry to bother you. I came to turn on the sound recording function on your cameras."

"Shouldn't the Navy take care of that?" Gina asked.

"Actually, the Institute leases the cameras from Strategic Design. I want to check the settings. I already checked John's camera."

She stared at him for a long second. "Fine," she said. She opened a file cabinet drawer and set six underwater cameras in front of Montgomery. "How good is the fidelity?"

"Excellent," he replied. "I hope the Krell have a language."

"I'm sure they do. Any intelligent race would."

"I meant a spoken one. Language is the key to contact."

"Language is the key to civilization," she replied.

Montgomery nodded. "Do you mind if I look in on you occasionally as you figure out their language? That sort of thing fascinates me."

"Feel free," Gina said. "I like to bounce ideas off other minds."

Kyle arched an eyebrow. "Not John's?"

"Well, yeah, him too. But I like multiple viewpoints."

Kyle Montgomery turned one of the cameras over, examining its underside. He looked up at Gina.

"Do you have a paper clip?"

Rear Admiral Diaz was at his desk in the office he had commandeered from the Gershon Institute's staff, when there was a polite knock at his door. It came from a somewhat muscular Black man in Navy khakis. He stood casually at-ease.

"Ah, Gunnery Sergeant Davidson," the admiral said, smiling. "Come in, Gunny."

"Please, sir, just call me Dave." He closed the door in response to the admiral's gesture and eased himself into a chair.

Diaz shut the laptop he had been working on and regarded the sergeant silently for a few seconds. "You work in personnel, yes? And you're a Marine."

"It's just a humble desk job, sir," Davidson said. "I'm good at paperwork." He paused. "And yes, I'm in the Marine Corps, but I work for the Navy now and then. Right now I'm in personnel."

"Admiral Westminster recommended you," Diaz said. "Told me you were the best at what you do. Said you could get things done."

Davidson shrugged slightly. "That was very nice of the admiral, but I'm just the guy who goes over requisitions and assignments."

Rear Admiral Diaz stared at the sergeant for a few seconds. "Riiiight." The ghost of a smile crossed his lips. "I have a little job for you, Gunny."

Davidson nodded. The admiral continued. "I want you to be my eyes and ears on the submarine tomorrow. These are civilians, and civilians can make mistakes. I want you to make sure their actions are in line with Navy protocol."

"Just a ride-along, sir?"

"Yes. Just a ride-along," Diaz replied. "Unless the situation warrants more than that."

Kyle Montgomery did not bother to knock at John's open door. He just stepped inside and said, "Hey, John. How's it going?"

John turned away from the report he was writing. "Hello, Kyle. What brings you to my humble laboratory?"

Montgomery stood well back from Oliver's glass fronted tank. The octopus eyed him with unreadable eyes, all the while passing a half-finished Rubik's Cube from arm to arm to arm. The company man flashed John a warm smile.

"I just came by to wish you and your lab rat good luck tomorrow."

John frowned. "Oliver's not a 'lab rat.' He's not even a mammal."

"I'm sorry," Montgomery countered. "I meant it metaphorically. Your octopus is the focus of your study. That's all I meant."

John stood and went to the tank. Oliver jetted over to the glass. "Come on over and get acquainted," he said. "Oliver is one of the most fascinating individuals you'll ever meet. Stick your arms in the water so he can get to know you. You can apologize to him yourself for calling him a lab rat."

Kyle held up his hands, palms outward. "Not today, thanks."

"It's just a little water. Oliver won't bite you."

Montgomery shook his head and clasped his hands behind his back. "I have one helluva case of eczema. Doc says I should avoid saltwater. Notice you never see me swimming."

"OK then," John said doubtfully. "Let me introduce you. Kyle Montgomery, this is Oliver the Amazing Octopus. Oliver, this is Kyle."

The octopus tapped at his keyboard. "Oliver does not smell Kigh-yull."

"He really wants to meet you," John said to Montgomery. "Oliver can 'smell' you with his skin and sucker cups."

Montgomery replied with a tinge of nervousness. "Some other time."

"Is Oliver lab rat?" the octopus's synthesized voice said.

"No," John said to Oliver. "Oliver is an octopus." He frowned at Kyle.

"What is lab rat?" Oliver insisted.

"It's just an animal scientists use for experiments," Kyle said to Oliver. The octopus turned fire engine red.

John put his hand on Montgomery's shoulder and guided him to the door. "You really got him going there, Kyle."

"Not what I meant to do. Just joking around," Montgomery replied, guilt pulling at his features. "Sorry. I just wanted to wish you good luck on your mission tomorrow."

"I like jokes to be funny, and so does Oliver. Thanks for the well wishes. Now if you'll excuse me, I've got an octopus to calm down." The marine biologist stepped back into his lab and closed the door behind him.

In the corridor, a grin settled on Kyle Montgomery's lips.

Gina forced herself to eat a salad and some bread. The recon mission was tomorrow morning at eight, and her stomach was in knots. Plus, Anne and Simone, techs from the chem lab, had invited themselves to her table and were ribbing her about John.

"Your boyfriend looks kinda nice, for a nerd," Anne enthused loudly. "You get a gander at his tentacles yet?" This brought on giggles and snickers from the two women.

"He's not my boyfriend," Gina responded. She took a healthy bite of salad.

"You guys looked awful cute hangin' out on the aft deck," Anne taunted.

"Small ship, small world," Simone said smugly.

Norma Ellison set her tray on the table and slipped into the seat beside Gina. She waved her hand dismissively at Anne and Simone while Gina worked on her salad. "You two run along now. I have actual non-boy stuff to discuss with her."

"Tell you what," Simone said to Gina. "When you're done with your boyfriend you can send him over to me."

Gina swallowed her mouthful of greens and said, "He's not my boyfriend." Norma waved goodbye to the two lab techs.

Simone stuck out her lower lip in a mock pout. "Selfish." Anne and Simone left with their trays, complaining to one another how hard it was to find a man with a brain above his beltline.

Norma turned to Gina. "How you doin', girlfriend? Haven't seen you since the big reveal." She made crab claw motions with her hands.

Gina ducked her head and nibbled at her bread. "Sorry. I've been really busy."

"I've been thinking about how the Krell language might sound. You'll be recording, of course."

Gina nodded. "Of course."

"I bet Krell sounds either like a bunch of bubbles or like fingernails on a blackboard. They either push water through a membrane to make sound—like our larynx—or they rub something together."

"What if their communication is chemical?" Gina countered. "Like ants. Or some sort of quasi-telepathic electrical signals."

Norma sipped pensively at her drink. "Hadn't thought of that."

"Whatever it is, it will be a challenge to translate," Gina said. "If we can even record it." A comfortable silence sat between the two women. Norma broke it.

"So," she said. "What are you going to do about John Rottweiler?"

"That's Rauchenberg. John Rauchenberg. And I'm not going to 'do' anything about him. We just happen to be working together. That's it."

"Uh huh," Norma replied with a poker face. "Well I hope you two have a good time smooshed together in that submarine. And I hope you get some good data. Anything that you might call language, let me know, OK? This is getting exciting."

"I'm nervous about the whole thing."

"You'll do fine," Norma said. "Just relax into it." She paused and gave Gina a cool look. "You know, they were right about one thing."

"'They' who?"

"Those two yappy hens who were ribbing you."

"What were they right about?"

"John Rauchenberg is kinda cute, in a nerdy sort of way."

# CHAPTER SEVEN

The morning came far too early. John had not slept well; worry and doubt had plagued him with insomnia. Gina was right: he was sending Oliver into real and deadly danger. John had managed to grab some fitful sleep in the wee hours of the morning, but was haunted by a dream of Oliver turned into a giant rat that he was dissecting. When John got up he felt like he'd been dragged behind a tractor. He went over the mission again with Oliver while slurping down a bowl of tasteless cereal and inhaling three cups of the dense and corrosive fluid the Navy called coffee.

John put Oliver in a ten-gallon bucket of salt water and clamped the octopus-proof grate over the top. He grabbed his scuba gear and the cumbersome bucket and managed to lug it all up to the rear deck not much past seven-thirty. Larry and Barry were doing an inspection of the *Beagle*. They wore costume captain's hats and were talking to each other in bad British accents. John was simultaneously happy and embarrassed to have such weirdos as friends.

He clanked his way down the gangplank that led to a floating pontoon dock moored alongside *Darwin's Dream*. Gina was donning her scuba gear. He was thunderstruck yet again by her beauty. She always wore outfits that spoke of serious science, but her one-piece swimsuit frankly stated her fulsome figure. Her raven hair was braided and draping down her back past her shoulders. John decided against offering to help her get into her diving gear, thinking that it might be construed as too forward. Besides, he might start trembling. He set Oliver's bucket down and watched Gina swim out to commune with her dolphins as he donned his own scuba gear. Sergeant Davidson, the Navy ride-along, sat in a deck chair someone had nailed to the plywood, watching Gina cavort with the dolphins. His sleeves and pants were crisply creased, and he carried a sidearm. The sergeant turned a cool eye to John.

"You ready for this?"

John smiled. "Ready like Freddy."

"How about your octopus?"

"Oliver knows what he has to do. And his camera work is pretty damn good."

"Good." Sergeant Davidson turned his gaze back to Gina and her dolphins. "I want this mission to go smoothly."

They had been over the operation a hundred times. The *Beagle* would be put in the water and, after a systems check, pull fifty meters away to await John and Gina. The end of the pontoon dock had mooring points the *Beagle* could tie up to, but for safety reasons the higher-ups had decided to not bring the submarine too close to *Darwin's Dream* for this maiden voyage. John and Gina would swim out to the submarine, and John would secure Oliver in a special housing bolted to the port wing while Gina would introduce her pod to the submarine. They would then enter the vessel through its waterlock—the aquatic equivalent of an airlock. The *Beagle* would submerge to a depth of approximately thirty meters and wend a meandering path to Palmyra Atoll. The octopus and dolphins would be deployed and return to the submarine with gathered reconnaissance. Then they would all merrily meander back to *Darwin's Dream*. Easy peasy.

Rear Admiral Diaz and Lieutenant Commander Amundsen arrived at precisely fifteen minutes before the hour, both in crisply ironed uniforms. Sergeant Davidson saluted, and Larry and Barry took off their fake captain's hats, leaving John and Gina feeling awkward in their scuba gear. Diaz and Amundsen shook hands with everyone and wished them luck. The Rear Admiral gave a little pep talk about how proud everyone was of them and wished them God speed. Larry, Barry and Sergeant Davidson climbed into the *Beagle* and a crane deposited the vessel into the ocean. The submarine floated awkwardly for a minute or two, then, as if it had come alive, steadied itself and silently moved out fifty meters, leaving no wake. Its blue photomimetic paint blended seamlessly with the surrounding ocean. Gina was the first to fall backward into the water. John picked up the heavy octopus-laden bucket, whispered, "Here we go, buddy" into it, and followed her.

He was always amazed at the difference of the underwater world; the way that light was filtered by the water, the deadening of sound, the floating, buoyant wonder of weightlessness. There was a cathedral feel to it, especially since there was no bottom to be seen, just vastness. He adjusted his mask and swam toward Gina. Her dolphins came over to greet him and he held his hand out, running his fingers over their skin as they swam by. He tickled one of the females on her tummy and she squealed and did a barrel roll. Gary, the large male, was the first to check out the octopus in the bucket, sticking his snout up against the grate. John could feel the dolphin's chitters and clicks through the bucket's handle, but couldn't see Oliver's reaction. Gary moved off, swimming over to Gina as the two females took turns chattering at the octopus. John was fascinated. The dolphin tank meeting back on *Darwin's Dream* seemed to have worked.

In the clear tropical water only the yellow underside of the submarine could be readily seen. John swam around to the stubby port side wing. A box with a screen mesh door was clamped to the wing. John poured the octopus into it. He held out a finger and Oliver wrapped a tentacle tip around it. They communed for a couple of seconds, then Oliver settled at the back of his box and John closed the mesh door.

John swam around to the starboard side and squeezed into the waterlock. Once through, he peeled himself out of his diving gear, stowing it next to Gina's. She was up at the front observation bubble, drying her hair.

John grabbed a towel and joined her. The front of the sub was one enormous glass hemisphere. Two seats projected into the bubble and Larry and Barry occupied them, but there was adequate standing room behind the chairs. Gina was leaning over Barry's shoulder and giving hand signals to the dolphins just outside the glass. They were obviously very excited, swimming in circles, blowing bubbles and making dolphin faces at the humans within. Larry and Barry, captain's hats back on, mumbled their way through a checklist. Sergeant Davidson sat at one of the data stations that lined both sides of the middle aisle, his face impassive.

John stepped up beside Gina and leaned over Larry's shoulder to get a better view. "They are beautiful," he whispered *sotto voce*.

"Aren't they though," she replied, not looking away from the water dance of the dolphins.

The two submarine techs finished their checklist. Larry turned to Gina and spoke in a bad, stodgy British accent. "Are you ready, Mizz Martinelli?"

She made a two-handed gesture at the dolphins. All three dove together out of sight, then zoomed up past the glass bubble and leapt high in the air. They landed as one in a hail of bubbles, then gathered in front of the glass, mouths open and laughing their high-pitched delight. Gina clapped, and all the others joined her. The dolphins nodded and squealed. She made a "let's go" gesture at them and the dolphins backed off, waiting for the submarine.

With that the *Beagle* began to glide forward through the water and dive at a gentle angle. The sliver of daylight at the top of the observation bubble dimmed to rippling blue and silver.

"Seventeen meters," Barry said. "Seems to be pulling to port a bit."

"Probably the octopus box," Larry countered. "I can feel it in the stick. Can you compensate?"

"No problem," Barry muttered, his fingers dancing across his console. John could feel the subtle correction of the submarine righting itself. They continued to descend. Larry switched the cabin lights on.

Problems averted and the mission underway, Larry and Barry turned to each other. They had obviously been practicing for this moment for a long time. They both gleefully started singing the Beatles' "Yellow Submarine." They knew all the words, did all the sound effects, and gave an animated performance. John, Gina, and even Sergeant Davidson joined in for the chorus and the cabin resounded with "We all live in a yellow submarine! Yellow submarine! Yellow submarine!" When the song eventually wound its way to an end, everybody laughed and clapped.

"Depth thirty-two meters," Barry said, back to being all business. The *Beagle* stopped its descent. "Cruising speed six point seven knots."

"Roger that," replied Larry and a calm settled on the group. Even in the clear waters of the South Pacific, not much light penetrated this far down. The outside lamps were left off and the cabin lights dimmed. Conversation ensued.

For the approximately two hours it took to arrive at their appointed spot, they discussed the intricacies of invading another planet. They all agreed that the Krell had probably been surveilling the Earth for quite some time from the moon. All the satellites in Earth orbit had been thoroughly mapped and tracked, and an alien object would have been noticed. How the Krell detected incoming machinery was briefly discussed, with volumetric displacement, bending radar, and aerial observation platforms giving way to the notion of listening for the sounds made by machines. Then they discussed theories of interstellar travel and ray gun technology for a bit. One of the more chewy subjects was how a water-based life-form with only partial land-based functioning could ever develop advanced technology, given the need for fire to smelt the metals that were the underpinning of a technological civilization. They agreed that they were basing their assumptions on terrestrial crustacean biology and that they needed to wait and see what the crab-like Krell were really like.

But the biggest question, the one that completely stumped the five human minds, was why the Krell had such a small footprint. Why stage whatever they were doing out on this insignificant little dollop of coral in the middle of nowhere? Why no communication, no "take me to your leader," no set of demands from a superior, starfaring race, no sign of scientific curiosity—if they were indeed a scientific expedition? And why the wait? Were they building something? The Krell had been inhabiting Palmyra Atoll for going on a month. What was their plan? Eventually the conversation ground to a halt, leaving each alone with their dark thoughts.

Gina turned a hull mounted camera toward the surface to see how her three dolphins were faring. They were easily keeping up with the *Beagle's* meandering gait and had made contact with a local pod of striped dolphins, *Stenella coeruleoalba*. They were playing and chirping at one another, feeding on the occasional fish, and doing the social things dolphins do. Gina was filtering the feed of the outside microphones to capture the chitters and squeals of the mammals cruising the surface. She fed the conglomeration into her computer's translation algorithm. "Visiting," she said to her companions, then turned back to her computer.

John used another exterior camera to watch Oliver's box. Not much to see there. The octopus had finagled the tip of a tentacle through the mesh-covered door of his box. The thin appendage fluttered in the current, tasting the water. John worried about Oliver's upcoming rendezvous with the unknown. He felt that they were on the verge of something truly momentous, but could not put his finger on exactly what that might entail. More than just the danger of venturing into the lair of hostile space aliens. Something else. John felt a pang of kinship with the cephalopod riding just a few feet away. He sighed and turned the camera feed off.

Sergeant Davidson put a friendly hand on his shoulder. "That's some octopus you have there, John. A regular Einstein."

"Thanks." He smiled a wan smile.

"You're worried."

John allowed himself sarcasm. "Oh, no. Why should I be worried?"

"This is big," Davidson said. "We're all a little on edge." John shrugged, at a loss for a reply. Davidson patted John on the back and gave him a solemn nod. "This is a noble endeavor. It's gonna be

OK." John nodded and mumbled another thank you, then turned to his computer and pretended to work.

Larry had been watching Sergeant Davidson's interaction with John. "You're a Navy Seal, aren't you." It was not a question.

The sergeant seemed taken aback. "Me? I'm just a desk jockey. I work in personnel."

"Yeah, right. Personnel." Larry said sarcastically. "My uncle Cecil was a Navy Seal. The way you wear your gun, the way you stand. Dead giveaway."

"I'm in personnel." His tone was cajoling. "Really. Been there for six years. The admiral tapped me for this duty because I was available."

Larry was unrelenting. "Navy Seal. Am I right?"

Davidson's demeanor did not crack. "And if I am?"

"Don't make me no never mind," Larry replied. "I just like to know who I'm working with."

"You got me wrong, Mr. Stokowski. I'm just a Marine Gunnery Sergeant."

"Then welcome aboard, Gunny," Larry smiled. "Nice to have a Navy Seal on board."

Barry looked up from his computer screen. "When you're a Jet you're a Jet all the way."

Larry nodded. "From your first cigarette to your last dying day."

Sergeant Davidson made a sound of disgust and went back to looking out the front observation bubble. He tapped his finger on the side of his seat for a few seconds, then said, "I'll let you guys in on a little secret." The rest all looked at him, curious. "That jet that dropped the drone, the one that got zapped..." Davidson paused for effect. "Admiral Diaz's son was the pilot."

The only gasp came from Gina. The others just stared at the sergeant. "Explains why he's so adamant about this mission," Davidson continued.

Barry frowned. "So they send the grieving father off with an outdated destroyer to escort a bunch of science geeks into hostile alien territory. What's up with that?"

"The top brass think the video was a fake," Davidson replied. "Sure, the jet was lost and then the planes they sent to look for it, not to mention the drone blowing up, but the bit with the giant crab…the Pentagon didn't believe it, thought it was the Russians or the Chinese. But they had to do something: it was a rear admiral's son. So to shut him up they sent him out with a toothless old boat just to let him know what they thought of his 'hoax.'" The sergeant made air quotes with the last word.

"How do you know all this?" Gina asked skeptically.

"I work in personnel," he replied. "I hear stuff."

"Well, there you go," said Larry. "Answers many questions. So here we are heading toward giant crabs with ray guns, and the brass thinks it's a joke."

"You can just feel the love," Barry muttered under his breath.

The air was tinged with gloom, and no one said anything for the rest of the journey. Eventually they arrived at Palmyra Atoll. Larry and Barry had relied entirely on speed, direction, currents and what Larry called "the feel of the stick" to guide them. They ended up within a hundred meters of their target point, a little more than a kilometer offshore. The *Beagle* slowly rose to twelve meters while John and Gina donned their diving gear, wordlessly helping each other as divers will. Gina wore a sound generator the size of a soup can strapped to her shoulder and a keyboard on her left arm. She seemed grim and determined. John chose not to look her in the eye.

Sergeant Davidson wished them luck and held the waterlock's door for them. The cramped chamber was doubly cramped with the two marine biologists jammed into it. Pressed tightly face-to-face, Gina looked John in the eye. "Don't get any ideas," she frowned as water began to swirl in around their feet.

"Never in a million years," he grinned at her. They put their mouthpieces in, stopping conversation. The waterlock filled and the door opened into dimness. The two swam around to the port wing and detached Oliver's transport box.

Gary, Nancy, and Sheila were waiting for them in the cool blue light near the surface. It seemed so relaxed and normal—just a typical day hovering over dark oceanic depths, preparing to send their augmented animal friends off to spy on space aliens. Then it started to turn strange.

Gina's pod greeted her enthusiastically, chittering and whistling and rubbing up against her. Then they came over to greet John. Gary, the big male, came first, and John did what he thought was the correct protocol, putting out his hand to stroke the dolphin. Gary accepted the gesture, then turned his attention to the box holding Oliver, putting his snout up to one of the grate holes and making dolphin noises. To John's surprise, the octopus extended the tip of a tentacle through the mesh and laid it on the dolphin's snout. They held this for a few seconds, then Gary swam away and surfaced to get a breath of air. John was puzzled by the interaction. The two females, Nancy and Sheila, approached separately, and the scenario was repeated. John's puzzlement morphed into astonishment. This was groundbreaking. He looked over at Gina. He could not see her expression behind the mask, but sensed her shock.

The three dolphins swam back to Gina and she attached two cameras to each of their left fins, one looking forward and one to the side. She tapped at the keyboard on her forearm and the soup can on her shoulder emanated a series of whistles and clicks, followed by a complex series of chatterings. When the instructions were through, the dolphins swam in circles around her, squealing with excitement.

John opened the door of the octopus box and Oliver flowed out like liquid smoke. He briefly twined a tentacle through John's fingers, then floated away to hang suspended in the water, arms spread and slowly writhing. John gave him the small video camera and the octopus cradled it in a curled tentacle. Everything was proceeding as planned. John gave the octopus the "OK, go" hand signal, but instead of heading toward the atoll, Oliver jetted over to Gina and landed on her shoulder.

John went into panic mode. Not for Oliver, but for her. This was an in-the-wild situation, a totally new experience for Oliver, and Gina was not octopus-trained. John mentally slapped himself. *Octopus-trained, my uncle's mustache!* he shouted in his head. *Who was training whom?* Oliver was like a cat—although minus the fur and bones—in that all interactions were on his terms.

Gina froze, not knowing what to do. Oliver briefly touched a tentacle to her cheek, then reached two tentacles across to her forearm keyboard. Gina fought him, trying to pull her arm away, but Oliver used his great strength to hold her arm in place. John frantically swam to her. An octopus of his size had the strength of a grizzly bear; if he got excited he could do some real damage to Gina. He grabbed Oliver's tentacles and tried to pry them loose. The octopus used one of his free arms to block John.

Then Oliver started typing on Gina's keyboard.

Oliver's tentacles flashed across the keys, eliciting squeals, clicks and squawks from the canister on Gina's shoulder. She stopped struggling and held as still as she could while Oliver typed madly. The water was filled with the high-pitched sounds of dolphin language. This was getting stranger by the moment.

Soon the dolphins started responding and Oliver's input became more complex, the squeals and squawks sounding more and more like language. This went on for several minutes. John had never seen this combination of dexterity and focus from Oliver before. If Greek sounds like Greek to you, try Dolphin. It was otherworldly. He saw Gina relax and took it as a cue to do the same. The two scientists watched Oliver's tentacle tips manipulate the keyboard on Gina's arm, filling the water with high pitched noise. This was behavior John had never seen before and would never have guessed possible; it gave him chills. And the dolphins were responding to the noisy onslaught with equally escalating complexity. The interplay grew and grew, the ocean alive with sonic harmonies.

Then the dolphins uttered a single squawk in unison and the cacophony abruptly stopped. They shot to the surface for a breath of air and quickly returned to Gina and John.

Oliver released his grip on John and Gina and jetted several feet away to hang in the water like a half-opened flower. John put his hand on Gina's shoulder and tilted his head in question. She looked at him and nodded. John saw no fear in her eyes. He did see pink sucker cup marks on her arm, though. This was not going the way he had thought it would.

The three dolphins circled John and Gina in perfect unison, then the two females headed toward Palmyra Atoll. Gary, the big male, swooped up toward Oliver, and John's heart stopped in his throat. But the dolphin did not attack. Instead, Gary slowed to a glide under the waiting octopus and Oliver grabbed onto his dorsal fin, plastering himself to the dolphin's back. He looked like a giant asterisk against the dolphin's mottled grey. Oliver's chromatophores kicked in and the octopus took on the dolphin's color, blending perfectly. Then Gary took off to join up with the two females. Moments later the two marine biologists watched them hit the surface and speed toward the atoll. Oliver still clinging to the dolphin.

John was beyond shocked. Dumbfounded, gobsmacked or pole-axed didn't even come close. He was so stunned, he actually let go of Oliver's transport box, thanking his lucky stars that he had remembered to tether it to his wrist or he would have lost it to the inky depths. Floating there in the massive blue, with silver sky above and dwindling darkness below, Gina and John looked at one another and simultaneously did the *"what the heck?"* shrug, lifting their open palms. They watched the dolphins race away until they could no longer see them, then turned to go back to the submarine.

The *Beagle* had all but disappeared. The blue camouflage paint and the fact that it was at a darker depth made it almost invisible. John detected a faint shimmer from the special paint and pointed at it. They had drifted a ways in the current. John kept his eyes trained on the *Beagle* and was careful about equalizing the pressure in his ears as they slowly descended. Gina concentrated on the simple task, too. Anything to take their minds off the strange developments they had just witnessed.

Gina Martinelli was the first out of the waterlock. She ripped her mouthpiece out and tore her mask off. "That was the weirdest thing I've ever seen!" she exclaimed.

John was right behind her, pulling at his mouthpiece and mask. "They were talking to each other!"

The two launched into a jumbled description of the incident, talking over each other while shedding their diving gear. Sergeant Davidson made them go back over some parts, extracting details.

"So you say the octopus and the dolphins were having an actual conversation."

John and Gina both nodded.

"Does your dolphin speech device have a record function?"

"Of course," she replied. "It records everything. Both sides. I use it for reference."

"Can you figure out what was being said?"

"Probably." Her brow furrowed and she chewed her lower lip, her eyes far away. "I can search for known words, but the structures sounded off. Maybe an algorithm for spatial resonance overlays..." Her gaze came back into focus and she turned to John. "I don't even know what language Ollie thinks in."

"Oliver thinks in octopus," John frowned. "He knows some English, but..." His voice trailed off.

"I'll get right on it," Gina said and went to her computer.

Sergeant Davidson nudged John's shoulder. "Maybe you can help her out."

John looked at Gina, intense at her keyboard. "I think she prefers to work alone," he replied.

# PART THREE
# THE KRELL

# CHAPTER EIGHT

Oliver the octopus clung comfortably to Gary as the three dolphins cruised toward Palmyra Atoll. They would arc up out of the water in their drive toward the island, then surge forward again beneath the surface. Oliver enjoyed the taste of the water and the shock of the air. It was an adventure. He liked adventures. The water was too warm for his taste, but he was genetically altered to tolerate both tropical and Northern Pacific temperatures. Nonetheless, he looked forward to returning to the cooler environment of his tank back at the ship. Maybe John would give him a crab or two. This led Oliver to think about the giant crab he had seen on the video and considered that soon he might be basking in the aqueous alien smell of them. He was excited in his octopusian way, holding cool thoughts and making cool plans in his widespread synaptic system. His arms were ready, his color controlled and neutral, relaxed but on the trigger, like an athlete. The dolphins raced through the water, leaping into the brilliant sunlight, chattering and singing to one another. Oliver heard it through his skin and let the sounds wash over him with the warm water, hearing not language but music. The distance to the atoll rapidly diminished.

The sea floor rose from indigo depths to a visible bottom and all of a sudden they were at the reefs that comprised the outer edges of the atoll. The majority of Palmyra Atoll was the reef skirting the island. The three dolphins turned right toward the western end where they were to do their assigned camera tasks. Their pace slowed, but they remained out over the edge of the reef where it sloped down to the abyssal depths. Oliver could see the palm trees and low hills that comprised the land portion of the atoll. The trees passed from view, and they were at the wide, shallow expanse at the west end of the atoll.

Oliver tapped a tentacle by Gary's blowhole. The dolphin slowed almost to a halt and the octopus released himself from the cetacean's back. Oliver flashed a happy blue and a passionate red at the dolphin. In response, Gary did a barrel roll and sang a squealing song. The dolphin then darted away to join his podmates. Oliver hung suspended in the water, his skin a neutral beige, and assessed his situation.

He sensed that the water quickly became shallower a few meters away. He felt the push and pull of the waves and smelled the nearby coral. There were life forms all through it. The vague flail of fish, many sizes, mostly small. And the smell of crab, a type Oliver had not smelled before, was distinct in the water. Remembering John's warning of danger, Oliver became a floating chunk of seaweed and swam toward shallower water.

Coral heads billowed up from the white sand and the fish population increased. The octopus nestled into a hollow in the coral, his color and skin texture taking on the exact appearance of the polyp structure. He fished the little camera from the depths of his tentacles and slowly panned the reefscape as he had been instructed. He jetted over another head of coral and crawled around to the far side.

And there it was, facing out to sea.

Oliver knew what a machine was, and this was definitely a machine. He had been told to be on the lookout for machines, but ordered not to touch them. The octopus oozed down the face of the coral to get a closer look, all the while training the camera on the alien object. The machine was a narrow triangle about a meter and a half long, with several bumps and spikes on the wide end. It was made of a dark metal and sat on articulated legs. The narrow end faced out to sea while the wide end with the bumps and spikes faced the reef. An orange light slowly blinked on the wide end. Oliver extended the tentacle holding the camera, hoping to get a closer shot. Suddenly one of the bumps began to flash red and a high-pitched warble came from the machine. Oliver pulled the camera back into the folds of his tentacles and went completely motionless. He waited to see what would happen next.

He was just about to leave his position when he sensed something sizeable approaching. From around another knot of coral, one of the Krell emerged. The alien crustacean was huge to Oliver's eye, the size of his traveling aquarium. The smell of strange crab became overwhelming. Oliver had a hard time staying still, the sight of the big crab creature was so shocking. Had the octopus had salivary glands, he would have been drooling; had he had bones, they would have been trembling. He made sure the camera was aimed at the alien.

The Krell was reddish brown on top and a dusty white on the bottom, like Earth crabs. Most of the other aspects of the alien were also analogous to Earthly crabs: large and small claws, several legs, and eyestalks that constantly swiveled side to side. The Krell carried a ray gun in its large claw. It moved strangely, walking not only sideways like Terran crabs, but forward as well, like the cat that sometimes wandered through John's lab. The Krell had an almost mammalian mouth with lips hidden behind fidgeting mandibles. Most odd, though, was the third eye located above the mouth, its jagged pupil standing out against the russet carapace.

The enormous crab creature sidled up to the machine. Two of the mouth mandibles reached out, revealing themselves to be small arms with multi-jointed hands. The hands turned off the blinking light, then folded back beside the third eye. Had Oliver been a marine biologist he would have been floored. As it was he merely observed, reining in his hunger and holding the camera steady. The Krell stood by the machine for awhile, less than a meter away from the octopus, scanning the water and the reef. Several times the eye stalks looked directly at Oliver but did not see him. The smell of crab was overwhelming in the warm water. It took enormous self-control not to let his skin turn to the colors of desire and hunger.

The upper carapace of the alien crustacean was a single hard shell with bumps and ridges, and the outer edge had several spiky protrusions. A raised ridge behind the eye stalks was pierced with metal objects, some inlaid with faceted stones. One had a slowly pulsing bluish light, another a moving disc inside a square, another was a metal ring. inscribed with alien runes. A strap ran crosswise over the top of the shell, and then under. The strap supported a variety of small tools and a pouch.

The crab creature aimed the weapon held in its large claw out toward the open sea, the tip of the claw resting on an illuminated blue button. After a minute or two, the big claw folded back, holding the ray gun at a rest position. The smaller claw snapped out and skewered a passing fish, feeding the struggling creature into the alien's gesticulating mandibles where it was torn apart and fed to the awaiting mouth. Oliver's hunger kicked into overdrive, but he remained motionless—his ancient survival trait.

Having finished its snack, the huge crab moved away into the reef. Oliver swiveled an eye to note the direction it took. He waited before moving, eventually sliding down to the sandy bottom and taking on its color. There was so much new here. Oliver was delighted with his adventure, yet tempered by a deep animal sense of caution. He lifted himself from the bottom and became a piece of drifting seaweed again. A slight current wafted in the direction of his primary objective: the entrance to the channel into the lagoon. Oliver used the jet action of his siphon to propel himself a little faster. There were crab tracks—big crab tracks—on the sand below him. He was John Snow and Arya Stark walking the borders of Bikini Bottom. He was Mr. Squidward and Spongebob infiltrating the realm of the White Walkers.

The smartest octopus on the planet drifted and jetted with the current, observing everything, his blue blood tingling with excitement.

The mood inside the *Beagle* was tense and awkward. Three of the men assiduously pretended to ignore the intense woman hunkered over her computer. Larry and Barry played a game of checkers on the submarine's computer, angling the screen so they could see Gina's reflection. Sergeant Davidson pretended to do a crossword puzzle, watching her out of the corner of his eye. He had entered a mere two words in the entire time of staring at the puzzle. Only John actually looked at Gina, sitting behind her and to the side. He found her intensity alluring, the strong set of her jaw, her midnight hair pulled back.

"John," she said without looking up, "take a look at this."

He got up from his seat and looked over her shoulder. Her screen was covered with waveforms, squiggles and words—dolphin sounds and their translation. "What do you have?" he asked.

She tapped the computer screen with a fingernail. "It appears that Ollie ran through just about every sound my synthesizer could make. Like he was trying it out. But look here." She tapped at a point farther down the screen. "These three are the dolphins' names. See: that's Gary, that's Nancy, and that's Sheila. But then they add a fourth one. Closest translation is 'has no bones.' Your octopus repeats it back and adds the dolphin suffix for 'friend!' How could he possibly know that?"

"Oliver's a fast learner. You named them back at the ship and called them friend."

"OK, so he was somehow able to pick up a couple of words. But then it gets weird." She brought up another screen. By this time Sergeant Davidson was looking over her other shoulder and the two submarine nerds had put their checkers game on hold.

"This is where Ollie stopped his noodling around on the synthesizer and went into a whole different mode," Gina continued, her brow furrowing. "All of a sudden it has structure. A simple structure, but definitely coherent."

"Are there any actual words?" John asked.

"Some. But it's like pidgin Dolphin. Like a 'me shiny island swimmy' kind of thing." She shook her head. "How the hell does he do that? Anyway, it gets weirder." She scrolled down and pointed out a series of waveforms. "They corrected him! The dolphins corrected the octopus and he corrected his, his…speech, I guess you'd call it." She sat back in her chair, wide-eyed. "I'm at a loss."

Sergeant Davidson leaned in. "What were they talking about?"

"It's mostly pidgin Dolphin and regular Dolphin is hard enough. They talked about swimming and carrying. The word for reef came up a lot. Some other stuff that I'm still working on."

Davidson pressed on. "The dolphins all said the same thing just before they swam away, right? What was it?"

"Yes. They all said yes. But it's a pod call, the way you would say yes to other pod mates."

John moused down the screen and stopped at a complex waveform and its equally complex breakdown. "This is the biggest word so far."

"That one has me stumped," Gina said. "The inner trigram means 'animal' or 'other' or sometimes 'danger.' It's bracketed by all sorts of modifiers. This one here…" she tapped the screen, "usually means 'big shark' but it can also mean 'hate.' For some reason they added a sublingual for 'ocean.' And here's 'reef' again. And, strangely enough, 'sky.' It's like a new word."

"Who came up with it?" John asked.

She squinted at the screen. "Looks like Ollie came up with the first form. Then the others modified it and they all agreed on the final form." She turned to John. "He can't just make up words in Dolphin!"

"Apparently he can." The three gazed at the computer screen in silence until John spoke softly. "I'll bet it means 'alien.'"

The ocean Gary swam through was warm and alive and the air was sweet when he leapt into the sparkling burn of the sun. What fun! The water was clear and endless and the reef was beautiful and mysterious. He had grown up in an aquarium and had never seen anything this vast. It was glorious to flash through the warm sea with his two female consorts. They sang and joked and played just offshore from the atoll. The mission laid out for them by She Who Would Not Have Sex (they called her Gina to her face just to humor her, but used the off-color nickname among themselves) was complex and challenging and sounded like a grand adventure. They were glad to do it, glad to be out in the sea and swimming free.

Cruising west along the edge of the atoll they saw only one giant crab hunkering below the waves on the edge of the shallow reef. The three dolphins dove and made their way past at a darker depth. The water was cooler and Gary found that refreshing. Then up to the surface again for a taste of the glorious tropical air.

The shoals of fish and forest of coral sang like a chorus of angels in the music of cetacean sonar. He Who Has No Bones tapped at Gary's blowhole and the dolphin slowed down to let him detach. Then a fond farewell to his new friend, and back to the racing swim. The cameras strapped to their left fins looked both ahead and to the side, and the three dolphins took turns mugging into each other's side-facing cameras. This was a fun adventure.

The reef slowly deepened and became less spectacular, and the dolphins veered south. They took turns diving toward the bottom, now ten meters, now twelve, pretending to forage for fish. They cavorted at the surface, partly to look normal and partly because they enjoyed it, then dove for the bottom again. The sea floor held nothing of interest; no tracks, no machines. But their sonar and the flow of the currents told them that up ahead the bottom dropped away suddenly. The large depression that was their target was twenty-five to thirty meters deep, not a difficult stretch for a dolphin. Sonar could tell them everything, but She Who Would Not Have Sex wanted video, so video she would get. Gary called Sheila and Nancy to the surface and they gave each other the ready sign. The dolphins swooped down into the coral bowl.

They cruised over the edge of the hollow in unison. Below them the seafloor fell away to dimmer depths and a jungle of coral bloomed in their sonar. A couple of hundred yards away, a light shone among the coral. Sonar showed a hard-edged, regular shape. Exciting! Gary and his two female companions headed up for a breath of air.

They had been drilled on procedures and counter-procedures; this would be an elaborate dance, show-boating at its best. The dolphins loved it.

Gary took the inner part of the run at twenty meters, Nancy higher and farther away for the wide shot, and Sheila nearer the surface, looking down. They headed for the strange object that sang so harshly in their sonar.

The alien spacecraft was huge and rounded, some fifty meters across and nearly ten meters high. Light came from the opposite side of the ship, the one facing the atoll. Sheila hovered above while Gary and Nancy executed a wide, graceful arc toward the lighted side. Bluish illumination poured from a wide doorway. Gary slowed to take it all in. A constant stream of Krell, some walking, others driving aquatic tractors with trailers, milled around the portal. The area was alive with the alien crab creatures, most lugging oddly-shaped packages from the spacecraft and loading them onto trailers. Two Krell stood on either side of the portal, ray guns in their claws. An underwater road had been cut through the coral and paved with crushed reef material. A parade of giant crabs stretched along the road rising toward the lagoon.

Gary swooped low to get a better view. One of the Krell guarding the door perked up and aimed its weapon at him. The dolphin knew a threat when he saw one and flashed upward and away, twisting and dodging in a broken pattern. A bolt of coruscating red light shot through the water, missing him. Gary felt the electricity and heat of the bolt and veered away. He sang the retreat signal and headed up, Nancy by his side. They joined Sheila at the surface and exchanged messages of fear and wonderment.

The smell of crab was heavy in the warm water. As Oliver got closer to the channel into the lagoon, he began to see random globs of grayish jelly clinging to the coral. They looked like excrement. Oliver avoided the ugly goo. *Do not touch alien stuff*, he reminded himself. His caution slowed his progress, but the slower, avoid-the-grey-jelly pace let the octopus observe more.

That was how he caught the crab. It was just a little one, but Oliver saw it scrabbling across the bottom and was on it like sand on the seashore. He was famished from his efforts so far and dug into the little crustacean with gusto. The taste was gamier and more robust than the tame aquarium crabs he got from John. Oliver gobbled it down, hiding the empty shell under a piece of coral to cover his tracks.

Refreshed, he continued south, drifting and darting across the shallow reef. Once, he had to camouflage himself as a moss-covered rock when a large underwater machine came crashing through the reef several yards away. The machine ate up the coral and spit it into a vat, making the water vibrate like crazy. Oliver got good footage of the machine as it crunched by. Another time he came upon a Krell backed up against a head of coral. It had lifted its rear end and was spraying grayish jelly onto the coral. Oliver was reminded of how he expelled his own waste through his siphon. The octopus made sure to get a steady shot. Other than those two, Oliver did not encounter any more Krell until he got to the channel leading to the lagoon.

Floating up over a head of coral, Oliver beheld a strange sight. To the right a road had been cut through the coral and a line of giant crabs and underwater tractors pulling trailers stretched away, dropping down into dimmer depths. Oliver thought he saw a flash of red light in the distance. It did not repeat. To his left the procession passed under an arch of dull metal. A blue light flashed on the front of the arch every time a Krell or a Krell-driven machine went through. Beyond lay a regularly shaped trough that disappeared into a brighter distance. This was undoubtedly the channel the humans had dug to access the lagoon, Oliver reasoned. The octopus swam closer, aiming the camera at the oncoming crab creatures.

Hanging in the water, Oliver was startled to see a Krell guard with a ray gun coming in his direction. The octopus jetted over to the nearest outcropping and settled onto it, altering his coloration to blend in. To his horror he found that he had landed on an expanse of the grayish jelly. But the armed Krell was approaching and Oliver had to wait for the alien to pass. His fear turned to wonder as his sucker cups assessed the ook. It felt comfortably squishy and there were dark granules scattered through it. He sensed its chemistry and concluded that this stuff could well be edible. The armed Krell passed by and Oliver allowed himself a careful nibble of the jelly. It was delicious! He took another bite, then another. Then his sense of caution kicked in and he ceased feeding, but enjoyed the lingering taste.

Oliver noticed that two Krell were gradually approaching from the deeper direction of the road and were randomly sticking their little mandibular arms into the blobs of gray jelly. Time to leave. The octopus cast off from the coral head and jetted north, away from the busy channel road. It was a long way back to the edge of the atoll, but Oliver made good time against the light current. He had seen all that he could see and was anxious to get back to John and the cool balm of his regular tank. He fantasized, as he jetted along, about the big, fat crab John was going to give him.

It was because he was daydreaming that Oliver ran into the Krell warrior. Literally ran into it. The giant crab crossed between two rows of coral and Oliver jetted right into the side of its big claw. Before the octopus could react, the giant crab had grabbed a tentacle with the smaller claw. Oliver wrapped three arms tightly around the big claw. Then the crab's smaller claw cut into his flesh and Oliver felt excruciating pain.

Larry and Barry were back at their game of checkers, Gina and John consulted over a computer screen, and Sergeant Davidson was deep in a crossword puzzle trance. Something hard hit the front of the glass bubble and everybody just about jumped out of their skins. One of the dolphins swam back and forth outside the bubble. It rapped at the glass again, the sound loud in the metal tube. Gina darted to the front of the sub.

"It's Sheila!" she exclaimed. "They're back!"

Gina put her hand on her heart, then gestured out to the dolphin. It was a love gesture and the dolphin responded in kind, doing a barrel roll and giving off a series of smooth clicks. Gina made an upward gesture and the female dolphin took off for the surface.

The marine biologist strode to her scuba gear and began donning it. John stepped to join her, but Sergeant Davidson put out a restraining hand. "I'll go."

"But I have to get Oliver..."

"I said I'll go," the officer glowered at John. "I have instructions to secure the data. Have a seat." Sergeant Davidson pushed John back into a chair and went to his own diving gear.

Gina was not happy. "John is the qualified one here, Mr. Davidson and—"

Davidson smiled. "Call me Dave."

The ice on Gina grew a couple of inches thicker. "Ok, 'Dave' ... Mr. Rauchenberg here has a very independently-minded octopus coming in and he is really the one to deal with—"

Davidson interrupted her again. "I have my orders, Ms. Martinelli. Now suit up."

They donned their scuba gear in silence, she fuming and he clinical. Davidson insisted they cycle through the waterlock together and John found himself feeling a flash of jealousy. Then they were out and Davidson retrieved Oliver's transport box. Gina gave John a small wave and he waved back.

The two divers headed for the surface.

John was fuming. He vented mightily to Larry and Barry, who had nothing encouraging to say. "That's really messed up," was Barry's contribution. Larry wasn't much better. "Looks like 'Call Me Dave' has the upper hand here."

John wasn't buying it. "That's my octopus out there!" He began to don his diving gear.

Just then they heard the outer door to the waterlock open and shut. Puzzled looks passed among the three men; it was too soon for Gina and Davidson to be back. The sound of the water being pumped out of the lock was loud in the quiet submarine. The pump abruptly stopped and they looked expectantly at the waterlock door.

The door opened and Gina came storming out. "Damn it!" she exclaimed loudly. She turned to John. "You're not gonna like this!"

John's heart trembled in his chest. "Is it Oliver?"

Sergeant Davidson emerged from the waterlock, holding four dolphin cameras. "Only the two females came back. No sign of the male or your octopus."

John put his hand to his mouth. "What happened?"

Davidson opened his mouth to speak, but Gina interjected. "The girls say Gary is waiting for Ollie." She touched the underwater speaker on her shoulder. "I asked if anybody was hurt and they said no."

"And just how accurate is that translator of yours?" Davidson demanded.

"Pretty damn accurate, 'Dave.' And 'no' is extremely easy to translate."

"What about Oliver?!" John's voice was nervously loud. "We have to go get him!"

Gina put her hand on his arm and looked him in the eye. "I trust Gary. We wait."

"Now hold on a minute," said Sergeant Davidson. "You're not giving the orders around here, Ms. Martinelli."

"Neither are you."

"This is a Navy operation and I represent command."

"I don't take commands from you," scowled Barry, hunkering into his chair.

"It's been two hours. We have our data and our window has collapsed. We go back."

"We stay!" Gina growled.

John was right behind her. "We're waiting for Oliver," he said through gritted teeth.

Sergeant Davidson wasn't having it. "I'm in charge here! And I say we return to the ship now!"

In the charged moment of standoff, Larry cleared his throat. All eyes turned to him. "I'm the captain of this vessel. We wait."

"Bloody well right!" Barry chimed in with his bad Cockney.

They waited.

If you could have bottled the silent tension that filled the submarine, the vitriol would have stripped the paint from a '57 Cadillac with enough left over to poison the water supply of a medium-sized city. The five retreated into computer screens and games, lost in frustration.

All of a sudden Sheila and Nancy were tapping at the observation bubble, repeating a series of clicks and squeals. Gina got her sound can out and aimed it at the front glass. She looked at the translation on her computer. "Gary's on his way!" She gave the dolphins a thank you sign and they left for the surface.

There was a rush to the scuba gear. Davidson stopped John. "You're not coming."

John was intense. "Yes, I am. He's my octopus." The two men stared laser bolts at each other. "What are you going to do?" John taunted. "Shoot me?"

The sergeant smiled mirthlessly. "You got mojo, I'll give you that. OK, you can come along, but just remember who's in charge. You and I go out together first."

John nodded, not saying anything, and continued to slip into his scuba gear. All manner of sarcasm bubbled through his brain, but the gatekeeper to his tongue wisely turned it away.

"What do they mean 'on his way'?" John asked Gina.

She slipped on her tanks and tightened the straps. "There's this adverb thing they do when they talk about swimming. If you think all those Eskimo names for snow are impressive, dolphins have ten or twenty times the number of nuances for 'swimming.' So they used the modification that means 'slow,' with another overlay indicating caution."

"Is Oliver hurt? Or Gary?"

"There's a very specific signature for 'injury' and it wasn't there." She adjusted a strap on John's diving gear. "So no, I don't think so."

"We'll know soon enough," Sergeant Davidson said. "Let's go."

John retrieved his flippers and made a show of holding the door to the waterlock for Davidson. The two men shoehorned themselves into the cramped space and cycled through into the blue, cathedral ocean. Gina followed. The ascent was efficient and uneventful.

Sheila and Nancy waited at the surface. Gina joined the two men and the three stared intently south toward Palmyra Atoll, hoping to catch a glimpse of the approaching dolphin. Sheila and Nancy started clicking and chittering excitedly, swimming in circles. The humans all squinted into the watery distance. The dolphins, of course, had already spotted their approaching pod mate with their sonar and heard his distant song through the water. Eventually, a moving dot that was Gary resolved itself out of the silvery blue. John noticed that he seemed to be slower than usual and felt concern for Gina, knowing she'd worry. As the approaching dolphin became an actual form, he noticed that Gary had a large lump on his back that was a little too big to be Oliver. A tingling apprehension grabbed at his guts. Gary was swimming asymmetrically; the irregular thing on his back was heavy, throwing his balance off.

The large dolphin went directly to Gina, squealing and squawling. She stroked him while the two females nuzzled against his side.

The lump on his back was Oliver, dolphin gray and shot through with black. He was covering something, tentacles desperately wrapped around the dolphin's body. John swam up to Oliver and noticed a gash on one of his tentacles. The wound was not bleeding and appeared superficial. Sergeant Davidson approached as well, but John waved him back. John touched two fingers of his other hand to his face mask: the sign for "camera." Oliver's skin turned a warm reddish-brown and a tentacle holding the small camera uncurled from under him. John took the device and stowed it on his belt.

He gestured for Davidson to approach. When the Navy officer was beside him, John tugged gently at a tentacle, then tapped his own shoulder. Oliver slowly flowed from the dolphin's back onto John's shoulder, moving with the cloud-like grace of heavy cream poured into iced coffee. He gradually revealed the lump on the dolphin's back, holding it with three tentacles and passing it to Davidson's eager hands.

It was a massive crab claw, its cream and dusky red carapace broken and missing in places. And it was holding a ray gun.

# CHAPTER NINE

A glow of victory permeated the *Beagle* all the way back. They were relieved that their animal cohorts were safe, and were completely blown away that they had an actual Krell claw and ray gun. There was a lot of laughing and joking on the return voyage.

Their arrival at *Darwin's Dream* was all business. Once they were moored to the pontoon platform deck at the rear of the ship, John and Gina exited through the waterlock. Sergeant Davidson, toting a duffel bag with the cameras, alien claw, and ray gun, left through the top hatch and up the gangway from the pontoon platform onto the rear deck of the ship where he was whisked away by the brass.

While Gina went off to commune with her pod, John retrieved Oliver in his transport box. Up on the pontoon platform was John's mesh-top bucket full of seawater that Larry—or maybe Barry—had thoughtfully left for him. He dumped Oliver in and closed the mesh cover. Gina was with her dolphins and he waved to her. She waved back and he gave her a gesture to come in. She patted each dolphin on the snout and swam toward him. He liked being with her, liked her intensity and her intelligence, even enjoyed her ribbing him. Like their dolphins and octopuses, they were different species, both very smart yet seemingly able to get along. He helped her up and she sat on a deck chair, removing her flippers.

"Aren't you going to put them back in their tank?"

She smiled at him. "That takes four people and three trips, and the dolphins hate it. I had a talk with them and they promised they would stay close to the ship."

"Wow. I wish I could do that with Oliver."

She rested her hand on the bucket's mesh. The tip of a tentacle poked through and caressed her finger. "Doesn't Ollie want to swim free?"

"He's more of a resting-on-something kind of guy. What Oliver really wants is to get back into his tank and eat a crab."

At the mention of crab, the octopus stuck three more tentacle tips up through the mesh and waved them excitedly. Gina laughed and John laughed with her at the dancing tentacles. "Might as well head on up. You know they're going to grill us."

"Debrief," she said, making air quotes. They laughed again.

John and Gina were allowed to go to their quarters to freshen up. John gave Oliver two crabs, praising him highly for a job well done. Then a quick shower and some clean clothes. The debriefing was not all that bad. Lieutenant Commander Amundsen recorded their recollections and observations, then let them go, reminding them that there was a mandatory meeting in the morning at oh eight hundred.

When John returned to his lab, Oliver was sitting on a rock, idly flipping through the color possibilities of a Rubik's Cube. John asked to see his wound. Oliver set the Rubik's Cube down and swam over to the front of the tank, extending his tentacle. John gingerly touched the gash, causing Oliver to wince slightly. Cephalopods have an amazing healing ability and the cut appeared to be healing nicely. When the inspection was over, Oliver returned to sitting on the rock, his chromatophores shifting through shades of brown and muted reds. "Play chess?" Oliver typed into his keyboard.

"Not now. I'm tired."

Oliver sulked, his skin turning a bland beige. "John does not play chess."

John tried to lift the mood. "That was some adventure,." he said.

"Oliver likes adventure."

John wished for the thousandth time that Oliver had some physical way of showing emotion other than color. "How did you manage to speak to the dolphins?"

"Gee-nah keyboard," Oliver replied.

"I know that, you silly octopus. How did you know what to say? How did you figure out how to actually speak Dolphin?"

"Oliver sees."

"Sees what?"

"Everything."

This stopped John in his tracks. Even after all these years, he was still on the outskirts of understanding how Oliver thought. It was something John had been pursuing for years, gathering only snippets along the way. John's senses sharpened, the air becoming crisp and fraught with possibility.

"How do you see everything?"

"Big water speaks to Oliver."

"The ocean," John said. "How does the ocean help you speak to the dolphins?"

Oliver's color turned brick red and purple, indicating knowledge and surety. John had seldom seen this color combination "Big water speaks," the octopus continued. "Oliver sees. Oliver remembers."

John was trying to interpret the octopus's cryptic answers. "The ocean helps you see the dolphin's language? Like with your eyes."

"Smell, see, listen. Lan-gwij is not … octopus."

"But you talk to me."

Blue circles flashed across Oliver's skin. "John does not smell. John is not octopus."

John was still trying to make sense of Oliver's oblique replies. "So you're reminding me that you, octopuses in general, don't think in language." Oliver sat impassively, watching the marine biologist. "Then how *do* you think?" John asked.

Oliver rose from the rock he had been resting on. A tentacle tapped at the voice keyboard. "Rubik cube." With that he jetted into his lair. Moments later the light of the television came on.

John was flummoxed by the conversation with Oliver. *There's more here than meets the eye*, he said to himself. *Way more.* A wave of fatigue swept over him and he decided to puzzle it out later.

John dropped a piece of fish into Oliver's tank. He then kicked off his shoes and stretched out on his cot, succumbing to the warm tide of sleep. He dreamed of Oliver reciting Shakespeare in Dolphin.

Kyle Montgomery made it a point to be on the rear deck of *Darwin's Dream* when the *Beagle* returned from its reconnaissance mission. Sergeant Davidson, the Marine spook Rear Admiral Diaz had sent with the mission, emerged from the Institute's submarine and strode up the gangplank onto the ship. He stopped to shake hands and exchange brief pleasantries with Diaz and the imperious intelligence officer. It was during this brief stop that Montgomery used the scanner in his pocket to download the accumulated data from the seven cameras Davidson carried in his duffel bag. It took less than five seconds for the miniature device to vibrate lightly against Montgomery's palm, indicating that the download was complete. Kyle nodded and smiled at Davidson as he walked by, but the officer pointedly ignored him.

In the privacy of his cabin, Kyle transferred the camera data to his laptop. The computer looked like last year's model, nice but nothing spectacular. Inside, however, it was a powerhouse sizzling with Strategic Design's latest AI upgrades. Making sure the door to his cabin was locked, the company man turned the lights low and began to review the data. As he watched the video and let the AI's higher-order language programming look for patterns, Kyle Montgomery casually filed his fingernails. They were perfect.

John Rauchenberg was dragged from the arms of Morpheus by an insistent knocking at his door. He glanced at his bedside clock. Evening already, just past dinner time. Answering the door he found a sailor with a flash drive containing the video reconnaissance. All the scientists were getting copies and they were to share their observations at the morning meeting. The sailor put a plastic case marked "classified' in John's groggy hands and hurried to his next delivery.

John splashed some water on his face, checked on Oliver (still in his den watching *Teletubbies*), then slotted the drive. The first minute was Rear Admiral Diaz asking everyone to analyze the data and bring their findings to the morning meeting, then reminding the viewers that the information was classified and blah blah blah. The menu screen came on and John selected Oliver's video. The camera was recording from the moment it left the *Beagle*, so the first fifteen minutes were of the underside of an octopus clinging to a dolphin. Fast forward through the black to Oliver detaching from Gary. Some floating in the ocean and swimming to a reef. Then the octopus found the Krell weapon and things got real interesting. When the alien arrived to check on it, the scientist in John came to the fore and he noticed details about the giant crab creature. His recall of the intricacies of crustacean features was not deep, but the particulars of the alien's physiology were apparent. The third eye and the arms that came out from the mandibles were especially interesting. He smiled at the thought of Hank Lodge, the Institute's lead crustacean specialist, going ape over this.

Oliver had been instructed to get good, steady footage of every-thing, and he did so admirably. John watched intently, searching the coral and sand for any sign of Krell presence. Many big tracks but no giant crabs. Oliver caught and ate a small crab. The coral became dirty, covered with some kind of grey goop. The Krell coral crusher lumbered by and Oliver stumbled on an alien crab taking a crap on a coral head. The intermittent goop on the coral became more common and there was light up ahead. John was blown away by the parade of Krell and their machinery. Oliver landed on a goop-covered blob of coral, his camera work amazingly steady. A couple of alien crabs were approaching, poking at the coral and Oliver jetted away, trailing the camera behind him.

On the video the octopus headed back toward the open sea. The trip back was just coral passing by, giving John's brain ample time to chew on the amazing images he had seen. Watching Oliver wrestle with the armed Krell warrior, ripping off his eye stalks, injecting the giant crab with poison, then breaking off the large claw holding the ray gun raised John's excitement to a fever pitch. The excitement sharpened his thinking. He remembered that the coral had been showing less of the gray goop as Oliver headed away from the Krell highway.

Something clicked in his head. He stopped the video and sat in thought for several seconds, then ran the video back to where Oliver was sitting on the goopy coral. John step-framed through the video until he had a relatively clear shot of the grey jelly. He zoomed in as far as he could; the stuff was translucent snot with large, oddly shaped chunks of black embedded in it. John stared at the screen, lost in a deep fugue.

A chill ran down his spine.

He rewound the video even farther, to before the coral crushing machine. Oliver had caught a crab. He found the cephalopod's pounce onto the crab and went frame by frame until he found a good shot of Oliver's incipient meal. The frame was a little blurry, but the evidence was right there, especially the third eye. Horrified, he fast-forwarded again to the close up of the goop on the coral. Yes, it was obvious.

They were eggs.

Gina's attention was only partially on the graphic breakdown of the Krell sounds on her computer screen. It was late, she was tired both mentally and physically, and her mind kept returning to John Rauchenberg. His hand on her shoulder, firm and warm, as they looked at language. The way he had looked at her in the waterlock, eyes sparkling with gentle amusement as the water lifted past their knees. Her concentration on the Krell sounds was scattered and she found herself going over the same information more than once.

Norma Ellison was sitting beside her, taking notes. Without looking up she said, "Quit thinking about the octopus boy."

"Sorry," Gina said.

Norma tapped the screen with her pencil. "Go back a little." Gina rewound the video until Norma said to stop. "Now hit play."

A grainy video played on the computer screen. "We've been looking at the wrong thing," Ellison said. "Can you boost the sound?" Gina brought the sound up. This was Gary's camera, swooping low over the Krell supply line. The muted rumble of underwater machinery and the sluice of water running over the microphone made other noises difficult to discern. "Listen to those two guys passing each other." Gina tickled the frequency filters and isolated a distinct scraping whistle coming from two alien crabs. "Now do it when those other two pass." It was the same sound. "I think we're onto something," Norma smiled. She and Gina high-fived one another.

Gina knitted her brow as she compared the spectral display of the two similar sounds. "We were looking at each Krell separately, trying to match sound and action. We were missing the conversation."

Norma stood and patted Gina on the shoulder. "Now you figure out the rest of it, girl. I'm gonna get some shuteye." She left, closing the door behind her. Gina went back to the computer and began comparing snippets of video with the strange Krell language, looking for repeating patterns. She became the data, and time disappeared.

A light tapping at the door made Gina jump. She peeked out the door's small window and saw Kyle Montgomery's calm eyes looking at her. She opened the door.

"Kyle," she said. "What brings you here?"

He stepped into her lab holding two cups of coffee and handed one to her. "Not the Navy stuff," he smiled. "This is my personal stash. Dark Roast Kona Primo."

Gina gratefully accepted the cup, the aroma heady and dense. She took a sip and let it wash over her tongue, tasting the bitter-sweetness of the brew.

"You even put creamer in it," she marveled.

"Half-and-half, actually. Thought you might like it." He sat on a packing crate and sipped his coffee. "I saw your light on and thought I'd see if you'd made any language breakthroughs."

Gina drank more of the delicious coffee, feeling a wave of alertness wash through her. "Well, the audio was difficult to isolate and the frequencies were all over the place. Fortunately, everything seems to lie within the sound range of Dolphin."

"Did you find anything?"

"Hard to tell what's just noise and what's language. But I've been looking for repeating patterns and one thing did stand out."

Kyle Montgomery leaned forward, interested.

She moused up the computer screen and highlighted three short sound bursts, then tapped a key to play them. There came a muffled scrape and whistle from the speakers, repeated three times.

"This is the sound repeated most often. The Krell say it whenever they encounter other Krell. Lieutenant Ellison spotted it. Some sort of a recognition signal, we theorize, like a 'hello.'"

Kyle nodded and pursed his lips. "We can use this to our advantage."

John's brain was throbbing. He sat in a funk for a good five minutes, staring at the freeze frame of the Krell eggs until the screen saver cycled into its dance of random color. He dragged himself out of his chair and headed topside. Back by the now-empty cradle for the *Beagle* submarine was the spot where he would go to ruminate; it was relatively private and there was a nice ocean view. The tropical air was warm and humid, but his mind was boiling with calamity and he found no comfort in the night. He leaned on the rail and stared up at the stars, not seeing them. Footsteps came across the deck and he recognized Gina's walk. She settled on the rail next to him. He looked away from the sky and gave her the best smile he could muster.

"You look like you found something," he said.

There was excitement in her smile. "I found a word!" John gave her a puzzled look. "I isolated a Krell word!" she enthused.

"I hope it's not 'kill all the humans.'"

"I can tell you've had a bad night," she replied, her face turning serious. "No, it looks like a greeting. A greeting! We could use this."

"Bolstering your theory in favor of contact."

"This is an amazing time, John. Language is everything. We are on the verge of meeting a starfaring race and we now know how to say 'hello.'"

"Are you sure?" he countered. "You ever woof at a dog?"

"What do you mean?"

"What I mean is that you might think you're saying 'hello,' but what does the dog think? You might be saying 'my foot is a hamburger.'"

She turned from him and looked out at the dark sea. "I got a bubble going here. Try not to pop it, OK?"

"Sorry," he mumbled. "But don't forget they're aliens and they have alien motivations."

"I know that," she replied. "But I believe that all intelligent beings share common traits. One of them is curiosity."

"We have to be careful about using a human yardstick to measure an alien mind," John countered.

Gina looked at him with her calm gaze. "Ever the philosopher." A pause. "How is your research going? Did you find anything?"

"Kinda." He looked at his feet. "I'm still checking my data."

"That bad, eh?" She gave him a warm smile. "You should get some sleep, John. We can reveal our findings to each other at the morning meeting."

John tried to keep the sadness and worry away from his eyes. "Sounds good," he replied.

"Sweet dreams," Gina said. She patted his hand and left.

But John's dreams that night were not sweet.

Gina stood at the front of the crowded mess hall, a graphic representation of a sound burst on the flatscreen beside her. Rear Admiral Diaz, Captain Murphy and Lieutenant Commander Amundsen sat to the side. John quietly entered the back of the room and stood in the shadows. Gina was wrapping up.

"To summarize, I think this might be the key to Krell social interaction," Gina said. "They always say it when they meet each other." She paused, reveling in the moment. "This could be our door into first contact. I suggest we send in a probe. It would have to be unmanned, of course. We would broadcast this 'hello' word and see their reaction."

Admiral Diaz spoke quietly to Amundsen. "That would give us away. They would know we were here."

"Don't kid yourself, Hector," she said. "I'm sure they already know we're here." She turned to Gina. "Excellent presentation, Ms. Martinelli. We'll open it up to discussion and—"

John strode toward the front of the room. "I have something important," he said in a loud voice.

Lieutenant Commander Amundsen frowned at him. "You're late, Mr. Rauchenberg. You'll have to put your name on the roster. Dr. Lodge is next up to talk about Krell physiology."

"What I've got to say is more important than physiology." He looked at the crustacean specialist. "Sorry, Hank. I know that these are giant crabs and you're dying to talk about them, but this is game-changing." Henry Lodge nodded his acceptance.

Amundsen was furious, shown only by the rigidity of her back. "You are out of order, Mr. Rauchenberg. I'm sure that Ms. Martinelli—"

"Let him talk," Gina interrupted. "I trust John." She nodded at him, then went to her seat. John took her place beside the large flatscreen.

Amundsen leaned back into her chair. "This better be damned good." She glanced over at Diaz.

"Lieutenant Commander Amundsen is right," Diaz said. "You are out of order and I should have you thrown out of this meeting. But you have Ms. Martinelli's blessing. And apparently Dr. Lodge is willing to delay his presentation. You have five minutes, Mr. Rauchenberg."

"I'm sure Hank will find this riveting," John said. "What's the name of the person handling video playback?"

"That would be Ensign Peterson," Amundsen replied flatly.

John directed Ensign Peterson to run the video to the part where Oliver had caught the little crab and freeze it when the alien crustacean was full frame. Hank Lodge actually gasped. John pointed out that this was a small Krell, barely six inches across. Lodge at first postulated that this could be a different order of the alien species, a worker used for fine work or a courier caste. John held up a hand.

"Hold that thought," John admonished. He had the ensign fast-forward and freeze-frame on an extreme close-up of the gray jelly covering the coral. "Take a look at this, Hank. What do you see?"

The crustacean specialist could only stammer.

John addressed the room, raising his voice. "Those are eggs. Krell eggs. Thousands, probably tens of thousands, of Krell eggs. And at least one has hatched already. Oliver ate the evidence, but there are sure to be more." He turned to Rear Admiral Diaz, who was still staring at the screen. "That's why they landed only one ship. They plan to breed their soldiers here."

Diaz cleared his throat. "It makes sense."

"It makes a lot of sense," Amundsen said. "It looks like they plan to hatch an army. Brilliant strategy."

"Those eggs could start hatching any day now," John said. "And Lord knows how fast they grow or how smart they are." He turned to Hank Lodge. "Any ideas about that, Hank?"

Hank Lodge shrugged. "They certainly appear to be eggs. I don't know what their gestation period is, but it does look like they might be getting ready to hatch."

Amundsen leaned forward in her chair. "The primary directive of the First Contact Unit may be to make contact, but this doesn't look good."

"We have a chance to make contact with a starfaring race," Gina insisted, "and we can't blow it."

"I think they're a danger and we should do something about it," John countered.

A voice from the crowd shouted, "Nuke 'em!" Another voice shouted "We can't take a chance!" Other voices were raised in opposition. A few chanted "First contact! First contact!"

Amundsen stood and held her hands up. "Quiet!" she said firmly over the hubbub. And then again, "Quiet!" After a few moments the crowd quieted. "Nobody's nuking anybody today," the lieutenant commander said.

Murmurs swept through the assemblage and several voices shouted out. "How about tomorrow?" and "Nuke 'em now!"

"Stop it!" The iron in her voice rang through the room. "Absent any alien attack, the directives of the First Contact Group mandate that actual contact must be initiated. I intend to follow that directive. We will be cautious, yes, but we *will* try making contact with the Krell."

Pretty much everyone was on their feet, all giving their opinions. John waved his arms for attention and shouted above the other voices. "We've got one of their ray guns. Maybe we can use that technology against them."

The Rear Admiral's features hardened and he shook his head. Amundsen's frown shot daggers. "That's classified Navy intelligence," she hissed at John.

There was a moment of stunned silence, then cacophony. The cat was out of the bag and the scientists and technicians were in an uproar. People demanded to see the alien weapon immediately.

Rear Admiral Diaz was a study in controlled fury, as was Lieutenant Commander Amundsen. Captain Murphy remained seated, wearing a look of confusion. Admiral Diaz glared at John and hissed, "You and I are going to have a talk about this later."

Eventually the crowd quieted down. Amundsen looked out over the room with her steeliest stare. She let the silence settle. "Yes, what Mr. Rauchenberg said is true: we do have one of the Krell weapons."

"Oliver got it!" yelled Barry from the back of the room. John smiled to himself. *Good ol' Barry.*

"True," Amundsen continued, "Oliver the octopus was able to obtain the weapon."

"And the entire claw that held it!" yelled Gina. She smiled at John.

"Yes, Ms. Martinelli," the admiral replied. "We also have a specimen of Krell body tissue."

"Screw 'classified'!" yelled one of the more excitable scientists. "We need to see 'em!"

Amundsen nodded. "Alright, you can see the specimens. I'll have them here in fifteen minutes." The sea of scientists and technicians babbled loudly. "This is why we brought you people, I suppose," she said. "To give us your expertise."

Admiral Diaz turned to the crowd and spoke loudly. "Lieutenant Commander Amundsen will lead a discussion of how we can use Ms. Martinelli's discovery to initiate first contact. If it is even feasible." He turned to John and glowered. "Rauchenberg. In my office."

The admiral gave John a blisteringly thorough dressing-down. John remained mute, knowing that nothing he could say would change anything. Near the end of his tirade, Diaz intimated that if, in the future, John tried a stunt like that again he would have him thrown in the brig. John apologized profusely, then excused himself and returned to his lab.

Instead of communing with his cephalopod friend, John readied Oliver's portable aquarium. He figured that since the octopus was the one who retrieved the ray gun, he should be in on the examination of it. Oliver was a bit perplexed at the "no kisses" rush, but willingly got into the aquarium. He loved outings.

When they arrived back in the cafeteria the debate was still going on. John, with Oliver in his aquarium, lingered at the back of the room. Larry and Barry were at the front of the crowd arguing with Amundsen. "We're going to be up to our asses in crabs real soon," Larry declared. "Giant intelligent crabs with ray guns." A slight pause. "Ma'am." Larry, for all his gangly, easygoing spirit, could be amazingly intense at times.

"And who knows what hellish machines they're building in the lagoon!" Barry did not have Larry's intensity, but he had volume. "We gotta do something!" A murmur of agreement swept through the assemblage, along with a few more "nuke 'em" mumblings.

"Enough!" Amundsen's voice filled the room. The crowd quieted. "First of all, we don't have any nuclear missiles. Captain Murphy can confirm that."

The captain of the *Shanklin* pursed her lips. "Lieutenant Commander Amundsen is right. We're bare bones. Left port in a hurry and with minimal armament. We have rifles and a few rounds for our deck cannons, but nothing of any consequence."

"You could call it in," one of the scientists argued. "We're out of the blast zone radius. Call Washington. Boom. Problem solved."

Amundsen was firm. "Out of the question. We may be out of the primary shock wave zone, but we are not out of the secondary shock wave zone. Plus we would be exposed to heavy doses of radiation. And we all know how ugly that can be." She paused and swept the room with a steely glare. "Again—our primary directive is first contact. Ms. Martinelli has given us a possible avenue of communication with the Krell. Captain Murphy has a few Zodiacs and I'm sure we could rig something. The eggs are probably not going to hatch tomorrow. Too bad we don't have a scaled down *Beagle* submersible, but we will do what—"

A voice came from the back of the crowd. "I think I can help." Kyle stepped forward.

"Mr. Montgomery." Amundsen did not smile. "Don't tell me Strategic Design sent along a miniature submarine."

"Actually, they did," he smiled. "It's over on the *Shanklin*."

"Next to the filet mignon, I'm sure. Are you willing to donate it to the cause, or do I need to commandeer it? And how big a submersible are we talking about."

"It's about three meters long," he replied. "I can have it prepped for you by tomorrow morning."

"Can it carry my voice synthesizer?" Gina asked.

"No problem," he said to her.

"You'll need a SQUID drive on your little submarine if you want to get anywhere near the Krell," Barry said with a certain smugness.

"Actually," Kyle countered, "Strategic Design has been working on something along those lines for a while now. Maybe you can give us some pointers. Or we can give you some."

Barry could not hide his ire and had just opened his mouth to object when a rolling table carrying the Krell claw, still clasping its ray gun, was wheeled in and the disagreement was forgotten. John and Oliver were accorded a front-row spot. Avidly interested, the octopus rose up out of the water to get a better look, his skin bright red with little white horns popping out all over him. Some time was spent examining the weapon's fit into the claw. The firing mechanism was well forward on the oddly-shaped stock, placed so that the movable part of the pincer could push the recessed button. The weapon was carefully removed from the claw and placed on the table. An eager set of biologists, led by Hank Lodge, took the claw to another table for closer inspection. Everybody else was fascinated with the Krell weapon, especially Oliver.

The ray gun was surprisingly light for its size, weighing in at three point eight kilos. It was just over a meter long. The stock was wide and weirdly shaped to fit the Krell's large claw. Most of the weight was in the stock and it was postulated that the energy source was located there. The ray gun had not yet been test fired.

The power source was the big mystery. Certainly a battery of some sort, but it would have to be mighty powerful in order to have enough energy for a weapon of this size and ferocity. Perhaps nuclear, someone posited, although no radiation had been detected. Maybe, said someone, it's a cube of condensed light folded into a molecular reflection matrix. Several voices rose in dispute and the conversation became loud and esoteric. Oliver sank down into his tank and John wheeled him back to the lab.

# CHAPTER TEN

The next morning Lieutenant JG Norma Ellison sat at a table in a corner of the empty mess hall with Lieutenant Commander Amundsen and five Navy Seals. Gina Martinelli strolled in, a cup of coffee in her hand.

"Sorry I'm late," she said lightly. "Got hung up in a muffin. What'd I miss?" She sat next to Norma.

Amundsen scowled at her, but Norma gave her a smile. "Lieutenant Commander Amundsen is outlining the mission." She turned to her superior officer. "Sorry, ma'am."

Amundsen nodded at her and turned to the Seals. "One and a half klicks out you will cut your trolling motor and row the rest of the way. Petty Officer Michaelson will control the submersible and Lieutenant Ellison will enter the water and ride along with it to the atoll where she will deploy—"

"Hold it!" Gina said. "I thought this was an unmanned mission."

"That was your suggestion, as I recall," Amundsen replied. "Protocol demands otherwise. We will be taking every possible precaution by setting up a synthetic voice device to say 'hello' in the Krell language—and thank you very much for that breakthrough, Ms. Martinelli—then we will fall back and observe."

"Can't you send in the drone sub by itself?"

"Protocol requires a human presence."

Gina flared. "What right do you have to tell another human—"

Norma put her hand on Gina's arm to stop her. "I volunteered," she said.

Gina looked at her incredulously. "Really?"

"Yes, really," Norma replied. "You've never been in the military. This is what I do: I serve. I know ASL and Native American sign, I can speak five languages, and I'm scuba certified. I can do this."

Amundsen rested her hard gaze on Gina. "I asked her and she volunteered. Do you have a problem with that?"

"Well, I guess if..." She trailed off.

"It's first contact, Gina!" Ellison beamed. "Who could turn down that chance?" Her brow furrowed. "I thought you were in favor of contact."

"I am ... but this could be really dangerous."

"Now you're starting to sound like your boyfriend John," said Norma, forcing a smile. "He's actually kinda handsome, y'know. Give him a hug for me." Her smile was beginning to turn nervous.

Gina sensed the fraught moment and turned her sigh into a bright smile. "Will do. Congratulations, Norma. You've been given a tremendous honor." She flashed her friend the American Sign Language sign for "luck." Ellison signed "thank you" back.

The day had not gone well for John. He had hit his head on a hatchway, spilled hot coffee on his arm on the way back to his lab, and had had a weird encounter with Oliver. It all started with an uncomfortable scene with Gina in the hallway. She and Kyle Montgomery were deep in conversation and smiling at something when John passed them.

"Gina!" John had exclaimed. "Congratulations! Looks like you got your first contact!"

She stopped and gave him a glowing smile. "I get to watch it on the bridge with the admiral."

"Can I come, too?"

"Sorry. Invitation only," Kyle said, and they were off, striding down the hallway and chatting about aqueous sound distortion. Miffed at being brushed off, John bonked his head on a hatchway on his way to the lab and spilled coffee on his arm.

Then Oliver refused to come up to the glass for "kisses," opting instead to ride around the tank on his crank car, ignoring John. Ignoring was not part of Oliver's normal suite of responses. John pulled a chair up to the glass wall separating their worlds. "What's wrong?"

The octopus made another circuit of the tank, then went to his keyboard. "Why is Oliver lab rat?"

John was puzzled. This again? "Oliver is not a lab rat," John asserted calmly. "Who said you were a lab rat?"

"Kigh-yull."

John nodded ruefully. "I remember him saying that. Oliver is not a lab rat. Kyle is wrong. I love you."

The octopus did not return the emotion. "Oliver does not smell Kigh-yull."

"Then how do you know he is telling you the truth?"

Oliver turned almost black, then lightened to a dull white. Random spots of brick red came and went on his skin. "Oliver wants chess."

"OK," John replied, retrieving the chessboard and pieces from a shelf under his computer. "Lord knows you've been bugging me enough about it."

"Oliver is not a bug."

"Figure of speech," John said. He took a black pawn and a white pawn, mixed them up behind his back, then held out two closed fists. Without hesitation Oliver gestured at John's left hand. It was the white pawn.

"You always pick the white one, Oliver. How do you do that?"

Oliver briefly turned into a Rubik's Cube, colored squares moving over his skin. "Buggabugga."

"Yeah, I know. Buggabugga. You'll have to explain it to me some time. If you can."

They set up the game on a shelf attached to the tank. Oliver employed two tentacles simultaneously, one positioning the front row of pawns, the other the back row of major pieces, a process

John always found fascinating. Play began and the game progressed with the usual opening gambits, putting major pieces in strength positions, then attack-and-parry interplay with pieces being lost on both sides. They were neck-and-neck for awhile until John backed Oliver's king into a corner.

"Looks like you're not so smart after all, my eight-armed fiend."

Oliver managed to shoot a splash of water square into John's face. "Oliver gives chess to John."

John mopped his face with his sleeve. "What?"

"Oliver gives chess to John. Chess is John's crab."

'Hold it," John said, his brow knitting. "Are you saying you're letting me win?"

"Yes."

"Oh really," John replied sarcastically. "You've done this before?"

Oliver's color was a relaxed shade of beige. "Yes."

John was at a loss for words. It occurred to him that, just as when the octopus had communicated with the dolphins, Oliver contained unexpected depths of intelligence. "Why are you doing that?"

"Oliver loves John."

"I appreciate that, Oliver, but that's not the way chess works. You are supposed to do the very best you can, not just let the other person win." Oliver made no reply. "Do you understand?"

"Yes." Oliver moved a knight to put both John's king and queen in danger. "Check."

From there it was only four moves for Oliver to checkmate John. Chagrinned, John put the pieces back in the box while Oliver gloated by turning green with purple circles. He swirled the purple circles around on his mantle and triggered his usual evil laugh on the voice synthesizer.

John leaned his forehead against the cool glass. "I love you, Oliver," he said softly. "Never forget that."

Oliver's chromatophores flashed brief bands of blue. "Oliver loves John." He slipped into his den.

Perturbed by the way the chess game had gone, John brought up 3-D solitaire on his computer. It was the closest thing he had to meditation. Thoughts danced unbidden in his head. Was he jealous of Kyle Montgomery? *Heck yeah!* Was this rational? *Not really, but at some level...perhaps.* Black two on red three. Did he have any claim on Gina Martinelli? *Absolutely not. No human being has a claim on another human being.* But he liked her a lot and wanted to have a firmer relationship. And this Kyle dude set off all his intuition alarms. Why couldn't she see that? Red six on a black seven. *Let it be,* John told himself. *Just like the song.*

The next morning, in a windowless room on *Darwin's Dream* just aft of the bridge, several sets of eyes were glued to a large flatscreen. It was divided into four camera feeds: one from Lieutenant Ellison's helmet camera, two on the miniature submersible—hastily dubbed *Robby* after the robot in *Forbidden Planet*—and one on the tail mast of the Zodiac. Both ships were getting a full feed of the proceedings, partly to keep the crews of the *Shanklin* and *Darwin's Dream* from rioting, partly to have as many eyes as possible on the encounter, and partly because Lieutenant JG Norma Ellison, communications specialist and linguist, wanted everyone to see her make first contact with a starfaring race.

The Zodiac cut its electric motor a kilometer and a half from the atoll and four of the crew paddled it to a half klick from the shore. The Zodiac came to a stop in the slowly rocking water. Petty Officer Michaelson guided *Robby* to a halt directly under the boat. Ellison made a show on the Zodiac's video feed of double-checking the voice synthesizer controls on her left arm and flashed a thumbs-up to the camera. Aboard the *Shanklin*, Gina gave a thumbs-up and sent a little smile to the video screen.

Lieutenant Ellison fell backwards into the water off the edge of the Zodiac and latched onto a grab bar on *Robby's* underside. The submersible got underway again, leaving the inflatable boat behind.

The five seals watched her progress on a small video screen. After about ten minutes of bubbling nothingness on the three underwater cameras, the reef came into view. Strategic Design's version of the SQUID drive proved its worth when the *Robby* slid past a Krell perimeter gun less than fifty meters away. The mood was tense in the briefing room as the submersible moved into shallow water.

John had not slept well. He sat in front of his computer, drinking the dark brown linoleum cleaner the Navy called coffee and watching the progress of the first contact team. Oliver watched from the glass front of his tank. John was excited for Gina's breakthrough. A glimmer of hope shone somewhere near his heart. John did his best to ignore it, favoring his doubts.

On his computer screen Lieutenant Ellison fell backwards into the sea and moments later was clinging to the *Robby*. The game was afoot. The reef eventually came into view. The submersible seemed to take forever to reach shallow water.

"I am at the edge of the reef now. Thick coral ten meters ahead." Her voice sounded canned and flat on her face mask's microphone. "No sign of any Krell." Norma Ellison let go of her handhold and settled to the bottom. John leaned forward in his chair, eyes transfixed on the screen, shoulders clenched.

"Be careful," he whispered.

The gathering in the briefing room watched silently, faces tense in the blue light of the flatscreen. They watched as Norma's helmet camera scanned the reef. The room was full of the sound of her breathing. "Activating communication module now," she said, her voice made flat by her mask's microphone. The screech and whistle of the Krell greeting came from a speaker on the submersible.

Then, barely visible at the edge of the screen, something moved.

"Michaelson, pan right!" Amundsen barked.

A camera on the submersible panned right to an outcrop of coral. "You've got company, Lieutenant," Amundsen said with forced calm. "Two o'clock."

"I see it," Ellison said.

The alien crab moved slowly toward Ellison, stopping some five meters away. The Krell made a short, high pitched sound.

"What's it saying?" Rear Admiral Diaz demanded.

Gina frowned at her computer screen in her lap. "I don't know. It's not 'hello.'"

The cameras on the small submarine hovering nearby showed the Krell watching the lieutenant. Ellison stood still, both hands upraised. "Drop back," Amundsen said into her microphone. "Let the voice box do its thing." Ellison took a step backwards.

"Here comes another one," Kyle Montgomery said. He was excited, his foot bouncing against the chair leg.

Two more Krell scuttled into view, then a fourth, this one larger. They stood regarding Norma. The voice box on the submersible emitted a Krell 'hello.' The larger Krell replied.

Gina was jubilant. "He said hello back!"

"Good work, Lieutenant," Amundsen said. "Now drop back."

"I can still engage." Norma replied.

"Fall back, lieutenant."

"I'm going to have to respectfully refuse, ma'am."

"Fall back, dammit! That's an order!"

Ellison's helmet camera looked at the gigantic crab in front of her. "Can't give up now."

She turned to the Krell and slowly moved toward them, her hands held up, palms out. The speaker on the submersible again issued the alien 'hello.' The alien crustacean replied.

Lieutenant JG Norma Ellison's heart was racing. She worked to control her breathing. This was the moment. The speaker on the submersible screeched the strange alien word. The largest Krell replied. She formed the American Sign Language sign for "I love you" pinkie and index fingers up, thumb to the side—with both hands.

"I'm trying some sign language," she said. "In case gesture is part their communication." In truth, the ASL sign was more for her than the Krell; something to calm and focus her. She continued slowly advancing. "Four meters now. Closing."

The largest Krell handed its ray gun to another alien and advanced toward Lieutenant Ellison. The voice synthesizer sent another "hello." The massive alien crustacean again replied.

Norma took a deep breath, trying to calm herself. "*Fear is the mind killer*," she said to herself.

The Krell stopped a few feet away from Ellison and she found herself looking into the eye at the tip of one of the alien's eyestalks. She avoided looking at the fidgeting mandibles. She and the Krell faced each other for several seconds. The giant crab reached out its large claw and gently gripped the lieutenant's left arm, the one with the synthesizer control keyboard, just above her elbow. She found the grip not what she had expected; it was very light yet decidedly firm. Ellison decided to play this as a peaceful greeting. She slowly nodded her head. The synthesizer pinged another "hello."

"We have contact," Ellison said, excitement tinging her voice. "The Krell's grip is gentle and seems—"

The Krell's claw snapped shut, severing the lieutenant's arm.

A gasp went through the briefing room, followed by exclamations and expletives. The Krell's large claw moved up what remained of Ellison's arm to her bicep and gripped her more tightly. The two cameras on *Robby* watched as her severed forearm was grabbed by the Krell's smaller claw. The room rang with Ellison's scream and her helmet camera jerked as she thrashed in pain. Then a deep intake of air as she worked to steady herself. The helmet camera stopped its jerking and focused on the lead alien. The stump of her arm spewed red blood into the water.

"Get her out of there!" Gina exclaimed.

"Quiet!" Amundsen ordered.

"I'm going into shock," Norma said through clenched teeth. "This could be a greeting ritual." Quick as a whip, the large claw released the stump of her arm and grabbed her by the neck. Her helmet camera looked into the unblinking eye of the alien crab while the submersible showed her twitching in pain. The Krell held her for several long seconds as her twitches weakened. Norma Ellison's last words were, "Please, no..." The giant claw snapped shut and her decapitated head sank lazily to the sandy bottom.

Gina cried out, putting her hands to her face. Others shouted or sobbed. The camera on the Zodiac showed the Navy Seals, watching on their own screens, frozen in shock. The two cameras on the submersible showed the large Krell holding Ellison's now limp corpse, clouds of blood billowing from her neck and arm. Her head gently settled on the sand, its camera facing upward. Everyone watched in horror as three cameras showed the giant crab using its small manipulator arms to tear the lieutenant's body open, spilling her guts into the sea. The small arms tore bits of flesh from Ellison's torso and fed them into the palpitating mandibles. The voice synthesizer onboard *Robby* said "hello." This time there was no response.

Lieutenant Commander Amundsen had the presence of mind to shout into her microphone, "Get that sub the hell out of there!"

The camera view from the submersible began to back up. The three other Krell warriors raised their ray guns and fired on the retreating sub. Radio contact went silent and the cameras sank with the blasted submersible. The nose camera was buried in the sand, but the one on the tail, as well as Norma's helmet camera, continued to show the big Krell eviscerating Lieutenant Ellison and shoving portions of her flesh into its writhing mandibles.

Meanwhile, the three smaller alien crabs made adjustments to their ray guns and fired at an upward angle. The Zodiac was in the process of coming about, its outboard motor at full power, when bright rays of red sliced through the craft and cut its crew to ribbons. The camera, mounted on a short mast at the aft, recorded the swift carnage before the video device was destroyed by the alien barrage. Back at the reef the lead Krell retrieved its ray gun, approached the camera on *Robby's* tail fin and pressed the barrel against the lens. The display disappeared in a flash of red. This left only the camera on Ellison's decapitated head looking steadily up at the looming Krell. It tossed the lieutenant's body to the side where it was grabbed by another Krell and dragged off camera. The Krell's lesser claw then lowered Ellison's arm in front of the mandibles and third eye, where the small manipulator arms began to go over the synthesizer's control keyboard. The claw holding the ray gun swiveled down to the camera on Norma Ellison's head and the last video feed ended with a flash of red.

A shocked silence settled on the briefing room. Gina was openly crying and stumbled out of the room, brushing aside any comforting words or touches.

"Well," Sergeant Davidson said from the back of the room, "So much for first contact."

Kyle Montgomery leapt to his feet, frantic. "We've got to try again!" He turned to Diaz and Amundsen. "We were almost there!"

Amundsen leaned her face on her hands. "Go away, Mr. Montgomery."

Diaz was equally stern. "We are not going to try again."

"Why not?" Montgomery insisted. "I can have another mini-sub flown in! We can get another crew and..."

Captain Murphy gave in to her anger. "My crew is not expendable merchandise! We are not going in again. I'm sure Lieutenant Commander Amundsen will agree."

"They're not interested in communicating." Amundsen's eyes began to fill with tears. "First contact is...severely compromised."

"No!" Montgomery shouted. "We have to go back! I'll go myself! It's imperative—"

"Sergeant Davidson," Rear Admiral Diaz said sharply. "Escort Mr. Montgomery to his quarters and confine him there."

"Gladly," Davidson replied. He took the still agitated company man by the arm and forcibly walked him to the door.

"You won't like the way this turns out!" Montgomery snarled at the admiral. Davidson pushed him out of the room and pulled the door shut behind them.

"I don't like the way any of this is turning out," Diaz said quietly.

John watched the death of Lieutenant Ellison with horror. It was everything he had feared and worse. The Krell's ability to locate and destroy the Zodiac as the point of origin of the submersible was frightening at an entirely different level, but was outweighed by the gruesome death of Norma Ellison. Oliver was stunned as well. He turned solid black, the color of deep upset. John got out of his chair and put his arm in the octopus's tank, hoping that their bond would calm his pain and fury. Oliver wrapped the tip of one tentacle around John's wrist. That part that touched John briefly turned a dusky blue, then faded down through gray to black again. He stretched a tentacle out to his keyboard. "Gee-nah is sad," Oliver's synthesized voice said. Oliver then released John's wrist and retreated to his den.

John realized that Gina must be even more devastated than he by the violent failure of the mission. She had held such heartfelt hope for a sane and intelligent encounter. And she had become good friends with Ellison. John knew where he would find her.

Gina was down on the pontoon dock moored to the aft of *Darwin's Dream.* She sat with her lower legs in the water and was bent over almost double. John at first thought she was crying until he saw the dolphin noses poking up out of the water. She was gently stroking their snouts and they were making soft cooing squeaks, sensing her grief. John made some noise as he came down the gangplank. She turned to see him and attempted to smile. John stepped out of his flip-flops and sat beside her, dangling his feet in the warm tropical sea. A dolphin nudged at his insole and he lightly stroked the snout that poked up out of the water. Gina threw a floating toy out into the water and the dolphins dragged it away and played a splashy dolphin game with it. The two marine biologists sat quietly. It was John who spoke first.

"Pretty heavy."

Gina nodded. "Yeah," she replied hoarsely.

More silence. John looked up at the sky. "I bet they'll nuke 'em now."

Gina leaned back on her hands, lifting her face to the sun. Her eyes were puffy and John saw the tracks of tears on her cheeks. "Naw. Washington will drag its feet like they always do and Palmyra Atoll will be overrun with giant crabs and their ray guns and war machines. And there will be a war and the big corporations will make a lot of money. For a little while. Until the human race is wiped off the planet. I can hardly wait."

The moment lingered, unwarmed by the sun.

"Or we could win," John said. "Some kind of pre-emptive strike that cripples the enemy. Or maybe even wipes them out. A nuke or a virus or...I got it! A secret alien army! You know, little grey guys with big eyes and their own ray guns."

She rolled her head toward him and opened one eye. "This is not a time for levity."

He looked down. "Maybe it's the best time," he replied.

"You are such a dreamer, John." She sighed and sat up. "But it's out of our control. Face it. There's nothing we can do."

"I'm so sorry it didn't work out," John said.

Gina put her hand on his. "So am I, John. So am I." A tear rolled down her cheek and clung to her chin. She took her hand off John's to swipe at a tear. "So is Norma. Mika. God rest her soul. She said to give you a hug." Gina leaned into John and wrapped her arms around him, draping her head over his shoulder. She squeezed him tightly for several seconds, then dropped her arms and scooted away a little, wiping another tear. "That was from Norma."

They sat quietly awhile, their feet in the warm ocean, the dolphins splashing nearby.

"You have to keep going, Gina," John said at last. "You actually translated the Krell language."

"One word," she snorted. "I translated one word. And I got it wrong. And it killed Norma."

John turned to her. "No. Not your fault. You probably got it right and the Krell just don't want to talk to us. But you got a foothold. You should translate more."

Gina frowned down at the water. "What for? If we nuke the Krell we'll never know what their plans were and if any more are coming. If not, we become crab food."

"Everything's a maybe," he assured her. "So why give up? We could—just could—make a difference. Not to quote Aunt Zelda again, but most clouds do have at least a hint of a silver lining."

Gina was not about to be convinced. "And according to Spock there are always possibilities. Yeah, I know," she said sourly.

"Here's a little bit of a silver lining," John offered. "We saw a miracle."

Gina turned to him. "What do you mean?"

"We saw amazing interspecies communication. Our totally different critters actually talked to each other."

Gina nodded. "Yeah. That was pretty amazing. Almost makes up for the end of the human race."

John's smile faded and he looked out to sea. "That's not a certainty. Something's going to happen."

"It always does." Her voice was flat and dusty.

John stood up and put his flip-flops back on. "I think I need some octopus time." He turned and climbed the gangplank to the rear deck, sighing inwardly.

Rear Admiral Diaz and Captain Murphy stood on the observation deck outside *Darwin's Dream*'s bridge. Each was lost in thought, still in shock over the horribly failed first contact. The tropical sun was hot on their skin.

"Not good," Captain Murphy said. "Not good at all. We should have sent the Seals all the way in with her."

"It would have turned out the same," Diaz countered. "The Krell have us outgunned eight ways from Sunday."

"But to send her in alone like that?" Murphy shook her head. "Unconscionable."

"Take it up with Amundsen. She claims it was part of the protocol."

Murphy shook her head again. "Damn shame."

Diaz straightened up from leaning on the rail and looked at Murphy. "I gotta ask you, Janet...what the hell's with your brother-in-law?"

Captain Murphy stiffened somewhat in response. "Kyle? What about him?"

"He just seems...off."

"What do you mean?"

"He's sneaky as a cat. Always seems to be in the right place at the right time with his corporate opinion. Plus he got in my face. He reeks of Strategic Design."

Murphy hung a wry smile on her lips. "Well, he does work for them."

"True," the admiral responded. "But doing what? I don't buy his 'I'm just an observer along for the ride' story. I mean, he brought along a remote submersible. Who does that?" Diaz paused. "Did it ever occur to you that he might be using you?"

"He's family." Murphy's tone was defensive.

"Did he tell you anything about this mission?"

"Of course not. Only a handful of people knew." Murphy beetled her brow. "No, he just told me he had gotten wind of a bunch of scientists headed for the South Pacific who needed a Navy escort.

And we had to leave pretty much immediately. Made it sound like a vacation."

"You ever wonder why he chose your ship?"

"He's my sister's husband. We keep it in the family. He told me he needed a Navy ship to accompany a scientific expedition. I figured it was one of Strategic Design's projects. How could I say no? I don't get to take the old girl out much anymore."

Diaz's eyes narrowed. "With a skeleton crew and no armaments. No questions asked. Just off on an ocean cruise with your brother-in-law."

"He told me it was a simple run."

"I'm sure he did. Didn't any of this raise red flags for you?"

"I don't like where you're going with this, Hector. I didn't have time to request anything. Kyle got me an assignment, a mission. Said we had to leave in two days." Murphy paused, thinking back. "But he was pretty secretive about it. I put it down to him not wanting to tangle the strings he was pulling. I was just glad to be going out to sea again."

"And look what it's turned into," Diaz sighed.

"Yeah. Look what it's turned into."

"I'm going to release Mr. Montgomery from his quarters tomorrow," he said. "But I don't want to see him at the memorial."

"You were pretty hard on him."

"He earned it." Rear Admiral Diaz's tone was stern. "Keep him away from me tomorrow. Memorials are tough enough as it is. Also, I've got enough evidence for the big brass to convince them to OK some sort of strike, and I don't want to hear any of his objections."

Captain Murphy's face showed doubt. "Do you really think they'll go for it?"

"They have to," Diaz replied, looking out to sea. "All those eggs are about to hatch."

Frssk F'tig, sub-commander of the Overview Caste of the True Race, finished eating tidbits of the pink biped. He breathed deeply of the warm tropical water. The water tasted strange: too much tang and not enough of what he would call *clstet*. But then the waters of every world embedded in his genetic memory had tasted strange at first. The next generation would find the taste of the sea normal, as they would this robust, oxygen-heavy atmosphere. The True Race would surely flourish here.

Frssk F'tig poked at the sliced up ruin of the machine the pink bipeds had sent with their emissary. His ancestral DNA memory informed him that many races had sent emissaries to contact the True Race. They were always destroyed or chased away, and seldom was a second attempt made. The True Race was not interested in conversation, or even surrender; they were interested only in conquest. This particular emissary was not that much different from the hundreds of emissaries on other planets the True Race had conquered. The pink biped had come in peace, as almost all other races had, was cautious in its approach, also a norm, and had met the usual fate of destruction. Plus its flesh had tasted tolerable. A good food source for the True Race conquering horde that would soon hatch. Nothing unusual there.

What was unusual—vexing even—was the word spoken by the machine that had accompanied the emissary. It was a simple recognition signal, and not a very good one at that. It was missing some of the beat frequencies and sounded like something a simpleton would say. The vocal synthesis apparatus and drive mechanisms of the submersible were being figured out, but that did not answer the overarching question that niggled at Frssk F'tig: how had the pink bipeds learned the recognition word of the True Race?

He poked at the shattered and burnt remains of the emissary's machine, hoping to find a clue. All Frssk F'tig found was a shard of metal with a drawing on it of a bulbous robotic machine that vaguely resembled the shape and proportions of a pink biped. This revealed nothing, and there was nothing in his ancestral memories to explain the mystery of how the pathetic and weak occupants of the planet had learned such an important word of the True Race's language. None of the pink bipeds had managed to penetrate the atoll stronghold. They were clumsy and soft and hard to miss. Nor had any of their crude mechanical devices been detected. That left only the possibility of an extremely focused and powerful listening device or some other means of infiltration that the True Race had not yet thought of.

Frssk F'tig tossed aside the piece of metal with the crude drawing on it and continued to shuffle through the wreckage of the emissary's machine. The True Race would figure the puzzle out in due time. They had conquered thousands of planets and had seen everything. Right now they had to focus on readying the stronghold for the hatching and training. Food and weapons were being prepared for the massive army to come. Everything was progressing well. The time of glorious battle was drawing near.

# CHAPTER ELEVEN

Rear Admiral Diaz's cabin was small and cramped, meant for only one person. He sat on the edge of the bed while Lieutenant Commander Amundsen sat in the only chair.

"It's mandated in the protocol," she said. "Two attempts at contact. Orders from the top brass. The very top."

Diaz shook his head. "You saw what they did to Lieutenant Ellison."

"I was sitting next to you, Hector," Amundsen replied softly.

"Norma Ellison is a hero. We cannot abandon that. A strong response is called for," Rear Admiral Diaz said, his voice hard. "We cannot be seen as weak. They'll run all over us."

"I'm sorry, but the protocol for first contact..."

"I know," Diaz growled. "Two tries." A grave silence sat between them. "But we have to come at them from a position of strength," Diaz said at last.

Amundsen cocked her head to the side. "What do you have in mind, Admiral?"

"A compromise," Diaz said. "A show of force that still leaves open the possibility of contact. Call in some fire power. A submarine, preferably *Los Angeles* class. They have Tomahawk missiles."

Amundsen was taken aback. "You want to nuke the Krell? That doesn't..."

Diaz held up a hand to stop her. "Let me finish. Every living thing understands force. Instead of a nuke we drop a couple of thousand pounders on them. Detonate them in the air at five hundred feet. Big shock wave, but not lethal. A shot across the bow. Let the Krell know we mean business."

"And if it doesn't work?" Amundsen frowned.

Diaz's face was hard as stone. "The Navy has JMEWS bunker busters, and they pack one hell of a wallop. Detonate one of them underwater in the lagoon and another one over their spaceship. The shock wave will cause major damage. Bring them to their knees."

"I'm not sure a starfaring race can be bombed into negotiating."

"It's a chance we'll have to take, Gladys."

Amundsen stood. "I'll get a video package together right away, sir." She turned at the door. "Do you really think they'll send a *Los Angeles* class sub?"

"Let's hope so."

Oliver would not come out of his den. John had long ago given up trying to psychoanalyze the blue-blooded cephalopod's intelligence, so he turned to the standard enticements: toys, crab, and kisses. It was the kisses that finally lured Oliver out. He flowed over to the glass and rested on the sandy bottom, his skin a dull shade of brown. Thin bands of blue rippled across his skin and his tentacles undulated with the "kisses" dance. John plunged his arms into the water and Oliver threw a tentacle around each of them. Black patches of doubt wandered across Oliver's skin.

"You are sad," Oliver's synthetic voice stated.

"Yes."

"Why?" Oliver asked.

"The lady and the big crabs today," John replied. "Very sad."

"Sad. Oliver knows."

Gina slumped into the room, exuding angst. "I need some octopus time," she announced, barely glancing at John. She plunged her arms into Oliver's tank and Oliver wrapped tentacles around them. "Hello, Ollie," she said softly.

The two humans stood quietly, arms immersed in the cold water, the velveteen touch of Oliver's tentacles against their skin. Gina was the first to speak.

"We're doomed, you know."

"Let's hope not," John replied.

"Hope won't do much to save us." Her voice was heavy with resignation. "Diaz won't nuke 'em. He could call in a strike."

"We'd die from the radiation."

"I don't care," she said.

"Don't give up hope."

"Hope," Gina scoffed. "The handmaiden of despair." She scowled down into the tank for several seconds. "Damn. I think I left the dolphin communicator down on the dock. I should go get it."

"Nobody's going to steal your communicator."

The air in the room felt heavy.

"I wish we had that alien army you fantasized about," Gina said at last. "I wish we had a thousand dolphins."

"And I wish we had a thousand Olivers," John replied. "But we don't."

"Then we have nothing." Resignation pulled her voice down. "So we're doomed."

John turned to her. "There are always possibilities," John said. "Spock..."

"Star Trek Two. I know. There are always possibilities. But not this time. This time we're all..." Gina's eyebrows suddenly shot up. "Omigod!" she exclaimed. "Look at Ollie!"

The octopus holding onto them had turned a sickly grey with black horns of worry moving across his body amid spasms of yellow. Fear gripped John's stomach. "Oliver! Are you OK?"

Oliver, still swarming with colors, unwound his tentacles from their arms and swam over to the keyboard. He hovered for a moment before tapping out a reply. "Doom," the synthetic voice intoned. He scurried into his den.

Gina then did something John was not expecting. She walked over and hugged him, putting her head against his chest. She was shaking with fear and frustration. "I'm scared," she said meekly.

Not knowing quite what to do, John patted her gently on the back. "Me too."

She sniffled and pulled away, not looking at him. "I gotta go lie down," she said and left, wiping at her nose.

Larry and Barry were deep in their own funk. John picked at forgettable food while the two submarine techs groused about the impending deluge of heavily armed space crabs. The lack of any aggressive action by the government was the overriding concern, followed by speculation about what a world ruled by crabs would be like. Dark humor surfaced.

"We could see the horrible introduction of new and unsavory dishes," Barry offered in a dreary deadpan. "Think of it: people puff pastries, bisque of baby, minced teenager. Crab Louie salad becomes their human Louie salad."

"I guess the only question is: classic Louie dressing or creamy ranch?" John added in a somber tone.

This elicited only the mildest of sad smiles from his dinner companions. The humor was just not funny. John tried putting forth his secret alien army attack force idea, hoping that Larry and Barry would enjoy it and run with it, but levity had no seat at the table. Larry said that they could perhaps use the *Beagle* to ram the alien spaceship, but declared that it would be a suicide mission. Barry observed that doing nothing would have the same effect as suicide, just take longer.

John moped down to Oliver's tank and put his arms in the water, hoping that the octopus would come out of his den and maybe exchange an empathetic touch. After several minutes he had not emerged from his rocky lair and John's arms were getting numb. He dried off and dropped a piece of fish into the cephalopod's tank, then grabbed a pillow and light blanket and headed topside.

The afternoon had lost its heat and given way to a tropical evening. A light breeze carried the saltwater scent of the ocean, the air was warm, and the stars arching over the dark sea burned with a mad brilliance. John was blind to all this. He retreated to the aft deck to nurse his troubles.

He stood at the railing for a long time, lost in thoughts of giant crabs swarming through the seas and across the land. He had read a lot of science fiction. Superior technology always wins. A niggling voice in the back of his head said, *tell it to the North Vietnamese.* He ignored the idea as an anomaly and concentrated instead on the effect the European colonizers had on all of the indigenous peoples they had encountered. A fatigue born of hopelessness pulled at him.

John found a wadded-up pile of burlap and tarps and nestled into the pile, pulling the blanket over him. Gazing up at the stars, he wondered which one was the home of the Krell. He wondered about their technology and how they had come to tame fire. He wondered what the Krell would do with the human race, indeed with the entire biosphere. His thoughts turned to Gina: how their relationship (could he even use that word?) had evolved, how sadness had dampened her fire, how graceful she was swimming with her dolphin pod, how he wanted to dance with her keen mind and wild beauty. He fell asleep trying to remember the smell of her hair.

Kyle Montgomery was deep into his computer's AI language program, hot on the trail of anomalies contained in Gina Martinelli's translation of the Krell "hello" word. She had said that the aliens' language fell within the vocal range of dolphin communication, an assumption born of seeing things through a limited lens. The Strategic Design AI program embedded in his laptop had no such limitations. The program was currently searching for sounds above the dolphin range. The outlook was promising and Kyle had confidence it would find something he could use.

There came a sharp knock on the door and the sound of the lock turning. Montgomery tapped a key on his computer and the screen changed to a game of solitaire in progress. He feigned concentration. Sergeant Davidson opened the door and leaned against the doorframe, arms crossed on his chest, and Kyle turned to him.

"Sergeant Davidson," Montgomery smiled. "To what do I owe this honor?"

Davidson made no move to enter the cabin. "Rear Admiral Diaz has decided to cancel your confinement to quarters."

"How kind of him," the company man replied with faux gratitude.

"It was pretty stupid to shout demands at a high-ranking United States Navy officer."

"Am I free to go, then?"

"Not quite yet. The order goes into effect at oh seven hundred hours tomorrow. With one condition."

Montgomery casually moved a red eight onto a black nine. "And that is...?"

"The admiral is making an announcement tomorrow and doesn't want to see hide nor hair of you. Probably for several days. He's pretty peeved. Try the black four on the red five."

"I know how to play," Kyle responded, making the move. "Where is he making this historic announcement?"

"From the main deck of the *Shanklin*."

Montgomery smiled up at the lieutenant. "A memorial service, I presume. If the admiral pleases, I'll just stay on *Darwin's Dream*. I'd like to visit with some friends."

"I didn't think you had any friends."

Kyle Montgomery put on a mock pout. "I have lots of friends."

"Sure you do," Davidson said with unveiled sarcasm. Then, after a pause, "What's your story, man? Why are you really here?"

"I'm here representing Strategic Design," Montgomery replied innocently. "That's all."

Sergeant Davidson let the silence hang in the air. "Right," he said at last. "See you at oh seven hundred." As he turned to go he looked over his shoulder. "You missed an ace in your discard pile."

Montgomery looked abashed. "Thank you, sergeant."

Davidson was not subtle about closing the door. The lock slid to with a click and Kyle Montgomery brought the AI language program back up.

John Rauchenberg awoke to cool morning air and someone gently shaking his shoulder. It was Sergeant Davidson. He handed John a cup of steaming coffee and spoke softly. "Mandatory meeting on the foredeck in thirty-five minutes. You might want to grab some breakfast."

John sat up and mumbled his thanks as Davidson strode away. Holding the cardboard cup with both hands, he took a sip of the dark liquid. The vicious caffeine instantly made the world clearer, if not more coherent. He made his way to the mess hall and had bacon, scrambled eggs, and an English muffin, washed down with a second cup of ferocious coffee. Mandatory meeting on the foredeck? There must be some kind of important announcement. Probably that we're pulling out, John speculated. He still had ten minutes so he treated himself to another English muffin and a third cup of coffee.

Kyle Montgomery watched from a shadowed stairwell as Sergeant Davidson shook John Rauchenberg awake and gave him a cup of coffee. He then surreptitiously followed Rauchenberg to the cafeteria and observed him groggily get breakfast and sit at a table. Perfect. He found his way to John's lab and slipped inside, making sure the door was fully closed.

Oliver was perched on a piece of coral, his skin a neutral beige, running through variations on his Rubik's Cube. He did not stop his rotation of the puzzle cube's sides as he tapped at his voice synthesizer keyboard.

"Kigh-yull."

Kyle smiled his corporate smile. "Hey, Ollie. Howzit goin'?"

Oliver set the Rubik's Cube down. "Oliver does not smell Kigh-yull."

Montgomery's smile faded. "That again. Not gonna happen." He quickly slapped a friendly look back on his face. "Does Oliver want a crab?"

The octopus blushed with excitement and a few white horns raised on his skin as he flowed over to the glass wall separating water from air. He made a complex gesture with his tentacles that Montgomery found confusing, then repeated the gesture.

"I'm sorry, I don't understand."

Tentacles tapped at the keyboard. "Oliver wants crab always."

Montgomery unlocked the crab tank and used tongs to extract the largest crab he could find. He locked the tank and held the wriggling crustacean where Oliver could see it.

"I'm going to give you this juicy crab, but then I want to show you something. So no going into your den, OK?"

Oliver turned a mottled brown, black patches crawling up and down his tentacles, then displayed a few blotches of sky blue before settling back down to a neutral beige. A single tap at his keyboard. "Yes," the synthetic voice said.

Kyle dropped the struggling crab into Oliver's tank and watched with rapt attention as the octopus captured and devoured it. Montgomery always liked a good kill. His meal finished, Oliver flowed over to the glass and looked at the company man with strange, inscrutable eyes.

Montgomery took his laptop computer from inside his shirt, opened it and tapped a few keys. "Remember how I told you that you are a lab rat?"

The octopus tapped a single key. "Yes."

"Good. Because when they're done with lab rats they always kill them." He turned the laptop around to face the saltwater tank. "Take a look at this."

The scene on the computer was of a dissection table. The camera looked down on a dead Giant Pacific Octopus pinned to a table. A gloved hand holding a scalpel reached in and slit the octopus's mantle open. Oliver, his skin darkening and rivulets of sickly green running down his arms, rose to the upper part of the glass. Kyle Montgomery lifted the computer to follow his movement. A tinny voice came from the computer's speakers. "...Now we'll take a look at the brain and the three hearts." The scalpel was set down and another gloved hand reached in and peeled the mantle back, revealing the cephalopod's organs. One hand picked up the scalpel and prodded at a rounded organ buried behind viscera. "Notice how the brain is wrapped around the throat," the tinny voice continued.

"Recognize that voice?" Montgomery asked, unable to suppress a grin. "Keep watching."

Oliver, still rippling with sickly green, extended a tentacle to his voice keyboard. "Closer."

Before embarking on the *Shanklin,* Kyle Montgomery had done a deep search to find this particular video. He stepped closer to the glass and extended the computer toward Oliver.

On the screen the camera tilted up from the specimen on the table to reveal the lecturer. It was John Rauchenberg, several years younger but still recognizable. "Although this is the central processing unit," he continued calmly, "the majority of neurons are in the arms. What does that tell us about cognizance?"

"This is what they do to lab rats," Kyle said firmly. "And you are just a—"

Oliver's shot two tentacles from the tank and wrapped them around both of Montgomery's arms, knocking the computer from his grasp. Montgomery tried to pull away, but to no avail. "Let me go!" he shouted. The tentacles' grip only tightened. The octopus turned bright red, watching the struggling human impassively. Several seconds ticked by.

"Kigh-yull lies." The synthetic voice was flat but carried an undertone of anger.

"Let go!" Montgomery was frantic, his hands beginning to turn white as the circulation was cut off. Oliver released Kyle's arms and he stumbled backward. The octopus settled to the bottom of the tank.

"What's wrong with you?" Kyle demanded, scooping up his laptop computer.

"Kigh-yull lies," the cephalopod replied. "Kigh-yull is buggabugga."

Cursing roundly, Kyle Montgomery used a towel to wipe what water he could from his arms, then retrieved his computer and stormed out of the lab. Oliver pulsated a virulent red with yellow blotches as the company man shut the door behind him.

John stood at the back of the foredeck. Video monitors were set up and showed a raised platform on the main deck of the *Shanklin*. Rear Admiral Diaz, in full uniform, stepped onto the platform and faced the video camera.

"We gather this morning to pay our deepest respects to the six brave souls who gave their lives in an attempt to contact the aliens currently occupying Palmyra Atoll. With that I turn it over to Chaplain Burkin." The chaplain stepped to the mic and recited a few verses from the Bible, then solemnly spoke the names of each of the fallen. The last name was Lieutenant JG Norma Ellison. John felt a tear wander down his cheek. He made no move to stop it. The Chaplain strode to the rail and threw six makeshift wreaths into the sea. Taps were played and there was a twenty-one gun salute.

The admiral stepped back to the microphone. "May they rest in peace." He paused to let the moment sink in. "Now I have some good news. Washington has OK'd a show of force against the Krell." An excited murmur ran through the assemblies on both vessels. Diaz held his hands up for silence. "A *Los Angeles*-class submarine, the *USS Pendleton*, is on its way and will arrive in approximately forty hours. She will station herself ten miles offshore and three miles to our west and fire two Tomahawk missiles at the atoll. The missiles will carry conventional warheads and detonate above the central lagoon and over their spaceship at the west end of the atoll. Our aim is not to kill the aliens, but to let them know we mean business." A mumbling ruckus rose from the crowds on both ships. There were several shouts of "Nuke 'em!"

Admiral Diaz spoke forcefully into the microphone. "Quiet!" Both crowds quieted. "Washington has mandated that we try to make contact with the Krell a second time. The Tomahawks will be a shot across the bow to convince the aliens to meet with us. If they say 'no' we will send in a couple of bunker busters and detonate them underwater." A ragged cheer ran across the decks of both ships. "And if that doesn't complete the job, we'll call in the nukes." More cheering. "I expect you all to maintain secure-and-ready status. With the grace of God and a ready crew, we will prevail. Dismissed." The video feed switched to a U.S. Navy logo.

John ran into Larry and Barry in the hubbub, and they all hugged and clapped one another on the back and shared general attaboys. Heading down to his lab, he spotted Gina and raced to catch up with her.

"Diaz came through!" he exulted at her.

She beamed back at him, her smile like a hundred suns. "Who woulda thunk!"

"How about lunch?" John suggested.

"I need to check in on my pod," she replied. "I'll come pick you up when I'm done."

"Sounds great." John stopped at the door to his lab.

Gina continued down the hallway. She looked over her shoulder and waggled her fingers in a coquettish wave and gave John a coy smile. John floated into his lab on feather-light feet. Life was getting better. Something was going to be done about the Krell and he was going to have a celebratory lunch with a very smart and very gorgeous woman. Plus, she liked Oliver and Oliver liked her.

John went to the octopus tank and tapped on the glass. Time to share the good news. "Kisses!" he announced and plunged his arms into the chill water. The octopus did not come out of his rocky den. John frowned. Maybe Oliver was still in the funk from yesterday. He was about to offer Oliver a tasty treat when something out the corner of his eye caught his attention.

The porthole was open.

John had opened the porthole only a few times during the voyage, but definitely not recently, and here it stood open. Had somebody been messing around in his laboratory? He stepped around the tank to close it and froze in his tracks. A trail of water on the floor led to the bulkhead. The water trail continued up the wall, and he saw the faint imprint of sucker cups on the grey paint beneath the open window. Panic gripped his heart. John reached into the tank and tore the top off Oliver's lair. There was the TV and the remote and a small depression for Oliver to rest in, but no octopus.

Oliver was gone!

The panic in John's heart flared throughout his body. His arms and legs tingled, his heart ran wild, and his head swirled with bright confusion. He closed the porthole, then opened it again. He looked out at the rolling sea, then closed the porthole again, then opened it once more. He paced the small space between his equipment and Oliver's tank and pulled at his hair. What to do? What to do?

Gina appeared in the doorway. Her face was a mask of panic and agony. "The dolphins!" she wailed. "My whole pod is gone!"

# PART FOUR

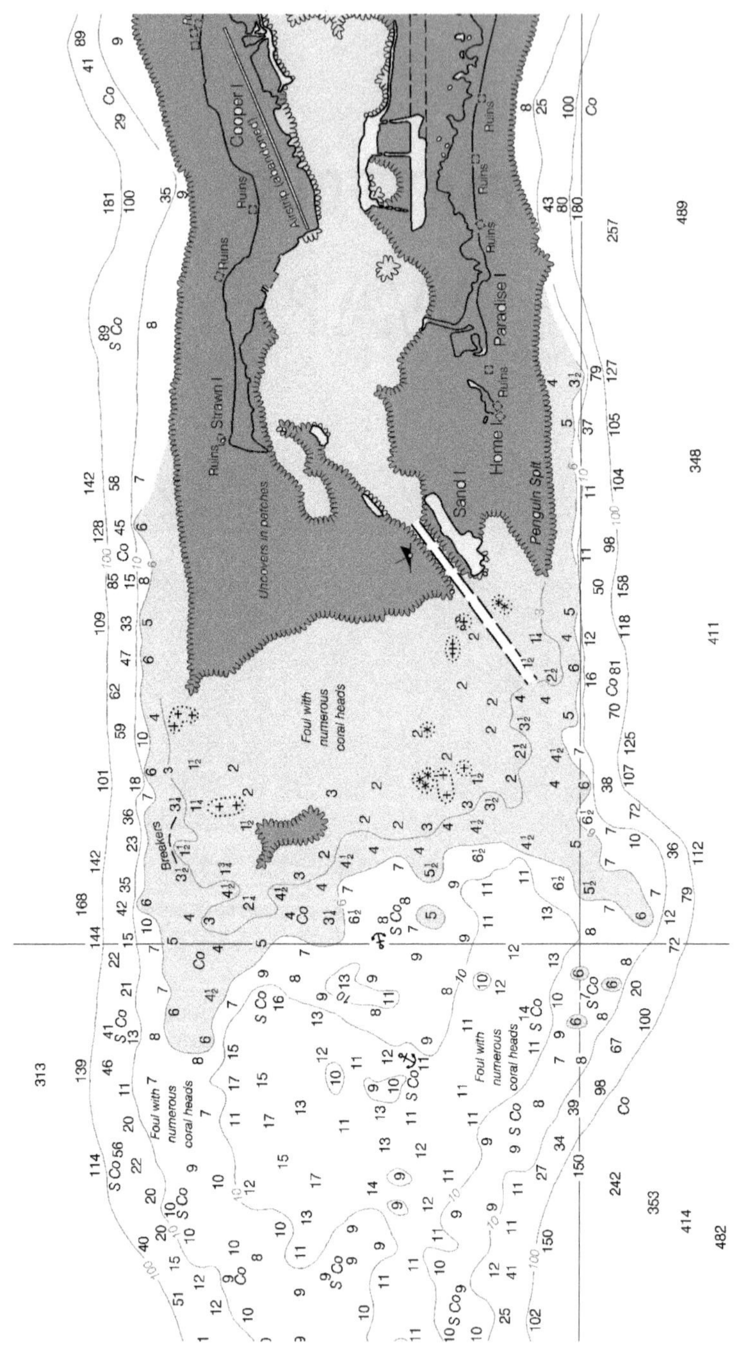

BATTLE THEATER AT WEST END OF PALMYRA ATOLL (ALL DEPTHS IN FATHOMS)

# CHAPTER TWELVE

The ocean felt big and wild when Oliver entered. His trek from the tank, across the floor, and up the wall to the round window had been strenuous. He had seen John open the window once, and his octopus mind remembered. The stiff handle yielded easily to Oliver's strength. He was well-wetted and could be out of his tank for several minutes, but it still felt uncomfortable, and he hungered for the touch of water. Oliver pulled the round window open and reveled in the cool breeze, soft on his skin and laden with comforting humidity. He oozed out the round opening, crawled a few yards down the side of the ship, then released his sucker cups and fell into the sea.

Oliver hung in the tropical warmth, feeling the surge of currents, the looming bulk of the ship he had just abandoned, the presence of other life in the oceanic immenseness. And something else. Something he could not wrap a tentacle around. Oliver liked adventures and outings, but this felt like neither. It felt wild and without form. He had sunk a bit and jetted himself up to a shallower depth. Oliver knew he could not stay at this shallow depth for very long; it took up too much of his energy and when his energy ran out he would sink to the abyssal depths and die. Oliver sensed the low pontoon raft nearby and swam over to it, tucking himself between two pontoons. Safely lodged, he let his mind spin up to speed.

The vastness of the water around him, and the darkness of the depths below, mirrored the strange ideas racing through Oliver's multivariate mind. The main brain encircling his throat and the eight other cognition sources in his arms tossed thoughts back and forth like a pack of cats playing with a mouse. He had been ruminating on the disturbing messages he had smelled on John and Gina the previous day, a bitter blend of doom, despair, and anger. Humans had in the past chemically communicated sadness, disgust, uncertainty and even fear to Oliver, but never anything as intense and desolate as what he had read from the two humans yesterday. His contact with Kyle had been almost as bad: a cold and lying heart empty of empathy. Oliver had tasted the camouflage that Kyle covered himself with and wondered what he was hiding. One thing for certain, though: Oliver was not a lab rat to John Rauchenberg; that was Kyle's manipulative lie.

Oliver put that thought aside. Here in the seemingly infinite ocean the water tasted of life and he felt an immenseness of being. Some ancestral voice had called to him in his comfortable tank and he heard it now, smelled it with his skin: an overwhelming need to merge into Mother Ocean. He had sensed this siren song on his foray to spy on the giant crabs; a sense of the vibration of life as a distant tingling taste. Now it came to him as an epiphany. All life. The world. And he knew that the world's cave was not safe. There was great danger. It jolted him into thoughts he had never had before.

Oliver curled into himself and let his thoughts run through his various synaptic centers. He had tasted a resoluteness on John and Gina, hidden deep in their anger. Plans and possibilities flashed through Oliver's neural network. He found the faintest whiff of something Gina had said in annoyance and homed in on the memory. He relaxed his mind, let the smell of the emotion and the taste of the words wash over him.

Oliver crawled out of his hiding place, up the side of a pontoon and laid three tentacles on the deck. He lifted himself out of the water and looked around. The thin air was uncomfortable on his eyes compared to the rich medium of saltwater, but he could make out something farther down the platform. He hoisted himself up onto the floating deck and began to undulate his way toward the object, his tentacles curling across the textured surface. Oliver's delicate sucker cups sensed a hodge-podge of tastes and smells.

Many feet had trod here, there was a presence of diesel exhaust, and a background sweetness of ocean salt. And very faintly, both John and Gina. It grew stronger as he approached his objective. Yes, they had definitely sat on the deck, John here and Gina next to him. And there was the object he sought. The octopus excitedly ran the tender tips of his tentacles over the keyboard, the wires, the small speaker.

The dolphin communicator was heavy, but Oliver was a strong creature and had no trouble wrapping his arms around the instrument and tumbling into the sea.

John found Rear Admiral Diaz in the briefing room next to his office aboard *Darwin's Dream*. The admiral, Lieutenant Commander Amundsen, Sergeant Davidson and several other officers were gathered around a map table when John burst in. Sergeant Davidson blocked him, scowling and holding up his hand. "You can't come in here," he said.

John ignored him, his eyes on Diaz. "Oliver's gone!" he blurted.

The rear admiral looked up from the map table, clearly short of patience. "Sad to hear that, son."

"We have to find him! You have to send out a search party or something!"

Admiral Diaz's patina of patience disappeared. "I don't *have* to do anything," he said. He did not raise his voice, yet the sharp steel underneath was evident. "And you have a lot of nerve coming in here and making demands."

"But Oliver is—"

"Your octopus's work is done," Diaz stated frostily. All the officers were now facing John. None were smiling. "Oliver is an interesting animal and he has been helpful, but his care is your problem, not ours. We have much more serious concerns right now than chasing after an escaped octopus."

"Gina's dolphins are gone, too," John said more calmly.

"I'm sure Ms. Martinelli will deal with it in her own way," Diaz replied with brittle patience. "And if she comes to me demanding a search party—as you have—my answer will again be 'no.' Now if you'll excuse me, I have a submarine arriving in forty hours." He returned his attention to the map table.

"You can't do nothing!" John exclaimed.

Admiral Diaz turned to him, thunderclouds behind his eyes. "A hundred-and-fifty years ago I could have had you keelhauled for your insubordination. You are dismissed, Mr. Rauchenberg." He turned back to the map table.

John opened his mouth to object, but the daggers Lieutenant Commander Amundsen stared at him made him think twice. Shoulders slumped, he turned and left.

His lab felt forlorn and empty, so he headed topside. He found Gina on the rear deck, leaning on the railing, gazing out to sea. John leaned next to her, not speaking. When Gina finally spoke, her voice trembled on the edge of tears.

"I've lost my pod. I don't know what I'm going to do."

John nodded soberly. "Me too. I've lost my best friend."

"I feel so alone." A tear ran down her cheek. She swiped at it with the back of her hand. John reached out to touch her shoulder, but she blocked his hand.

"Please. No." He withdrew his hand and she smiled shyly. "Thanks, though. I just … I have to…"

John smiled what he hoped was warmly. "Deal with it on your own? I know."

"Yeah. Something like that."

They turned and looked out at the sparkling ocean. A warm breeze blew on their faces, smelling of saltwater and steel. "At least they're going to hit back at the Krell," John offered.

"They're gonna bomb the hell outta those goddam Krell," Gina said. "That's a little poem I just made up." She tossed a weak smile at John. The smile faded, and the silence descended into melancholy.

The *USS Pendleton* did not arrive the next day. John and Gina passed the time moping around in their labs. When they tired of that they moped around on deck, burdened with great sadness. They had meals together, each recounting poignant anecdotes of pod and octopus. Time dragged on.

The *Pendleton* arrived just before eleven o'clock that night. Excitement spread like wildfire through the ships. John and Gina put their grief aside and joined Larry and Barry on the rear deck. Several other science and Navy techs were already there. John squinted into the darkness and saw a tiny bright light rapidly blinking some sort of code.

"They're identifying themselves," said one of the Navy techs. A few seconds later he added, "They say they are ready to commence." The blinking stopped. "We must be signaling back," the tech observed. Eventually the distant light blinked again briefly. "Roger wilco. One hour to launch. Message end."

Larry turned to the tech. "That was good! Where did you learn that?"

The tech grinned at him. "In the Navy, dummy."

People gradually drifted away until only John, Gina, Larry and Barry were left. Gina and Barry got a tray full of desserts from the mess hall and John helped Larry retrieve a bottle of Scotch that he had secreted aboard. They ate and drank themselves into a buzzy, sugary stupor by the end of an hour.

As the time neared, Rear Admiral Diaz got on the loudspeakers and gave a pep talk. Seven long minutes after he finished speaking, two streaks of flame rose from the distant ocean and shot across the water. Seconds later came the muted sound of rocket engines. Cheers and whistles burst from the decks of the research ship and the destroyer. The streaks of light stayed parallel to the horizon, traveling low.

"The Tomahawks cruise at about thirty meters above the deck," Larry said. "They'll get up to speed pretty quick and—"

Suddenly a bright red beam of light shot from over the horizon and the streaks of light on the horizon blossomed into small balls of fire. The cheers stopped.

"They've been intercepted!" Larry exclaimed loudly.

"And triangulated back to the launch point," Barry said. His voice was quiet, but everyone heard him in the sudden silence.

The ocean lit up crimson as a beam of red light shot underwater from the direction of the atoll. The *Shanklin* and *Darwin's Dream* were briefly lit from underneath, painting the grey hulls a dull pink. John happened to be looking in the direction of the *USS Pendleton* and saw the bolt of energy arc through the water and contact the submarine. In the distance, a plume of red-lit water geysered up out of the sea. Bone-shaking thunder hit seconds later, a concussion in the air, and the deck shuddered like a fevered dog. Against the light of destruction, John saw a wave coming at them, driven by the force of the explosion. It moved so fast that he barely had time to shout a warning before it hit.

Both ships were lifted and violently rocked by the shock wave. People and equipment went flying. Shouts filled the night air. Beneath his feet, John felt *Darwin's Dream* tremble and moan as if twisted by giant hands. He was thrown to the deck, and Gina landed on top of him. A small voice in the back of his head was calmly glad that he had cushioned her fall, while the loud voice in the front of his head gibbered with fear and panic.

And then the moment was over, and the ships rocked crazily in the choppy water.

# CHAPTER THIRTEEN

aptain Murphy aboard the *Shanklin* dispatched a rescue response team in two Zodiac rigid-hull inflatables to the *Pendleton's* position. Everyone was set to work to take their minds off the attack on the submarine. Even John and Gina were given clean-up tasks. No one said much and everyone avoided eye contact. They had all seen the destruction of the *Pendleton*. There was an unspoken agreement that humanity had lost. Lost the battle, lost lives, lost any hope of defeating the Krell.

The rescue crew returned as the sky was turning blue-grey with the coming sunrise. John woke from fitful sleep in his still-chaotic lab and made his way to the mess hall to listen to rumors over breakfast. Only two survivors, some said. Others said five, still others ten. This out of a crew of one hundred thirty. It was rumored that the ocean was littered with bodies, too many to bring back to the *Shanklin*. Emotions on *Darwin's Dream* ranged from rage to despair. John could only imagine what the mood was like on the *Shanklin*.

Later in the morning, General Diaz called an assembly. For a change, the crush of people was quiet, the mood solemn. Diaz stood on the main deck of the *Shanklin*, his image carried to video screens on *Darwin's Dream*.

"I'll get straight to it," he began. "The nuclear submarine *USS Pendleton* was destroyed last night by enemy fire of an unknown type just before oh one hundred hours. Our rescue crew found only seven survivors and ten bodies." He paused, clearing his throat. "The rest of the crew has been lost. They were our brothers and sisters in arms, our comrades and friends even though we never met. Their service has led them to the ultimate sacrifice. We will now pay honor to the fallen."

With that, he turned to face the open ocean. Seven sailors in full dress uniform fired three shots each into the sky, the smoke from their rifles dissipating slowly in the humid air. The chaplain said a prayer and spoke of the sacrifice of the dead, those recovered as well as those lost to the deep. A lone trumpeter played taps, the muted brass distant and haunting across the water. John was standing near Gina and glanced over at her. She was crying and trying not to look like it. John knew better than to intrude on her vulnerable mood. One by one, ten white linen cocoons were dropped into the sea where they sank from sight.

When the ceremony was over, Rear Admiral Diaz said a few more words for the departed, then announced that they would be shipping out at eleven hundred hours the next day.

John went to his lab and gloomily mopped up the spilled water from Oliver's tank. He had carefully rebuilt Oliver's lair and considered leaving the porthole open as a poetic gesture of hope that the missing octopus might return. They were leaving in the morning, his logical mind commented, so this would be a foolish act; he should close the porthole. But poetry won out over logic. John left the round window open and went to check on Gina.

She was still mopping up the water spilled from the large dolphin tank. He offered to help, and she handed him the mop. Gina turned on a shop vacuum to get the major puddles while John pulled up mopful after mopful of musty saltwater.

While she emptied the shop vac into the sink, John tried to make conversation. "We're pulling out in the morning. If the pod is coming back, they'll have a hard time catching up with us."

Gina stared blankly at the floor. "I know," she said with a small voice. She looked at John. "Any sign of Oliver?"

John worked at an errant puddle to hide his sadness. "No. He's gone."

"Maybe not," she offered. "Maybe he's at the atoll."

John shook his head. "He can't swim that far." He took a deep breath, trying to keep it together. "I just have to accept that he's gone. I, uh..." John's throat closed with grief and he concentrated on the act of mopping.

"I know," Gina said. "I know."

They worked silently, each lost in their own desolation. Buckets full, they dumped them down the sink. "I just want to do something," Gina said with grim determination. "But this isn't even a war. We're like ants to them. Anything we could do is meaningless."

John smiled ruefully. "Gandhi said something along the lines of 'anything you do is insignificant, yet it is important that you do it.'"

"Gandhi was talking about peaceful protest," she said. "He wasn't up against giant crabs with ray guns."

"He was up against an invasion by the British," John shot back. "And they had him outgunned six ways from Sunday."

Gina's features hardened. "We're all going to die anyway. The Krell are going to win. Maybe we should do something 'insignificant' instead of lying down and giving up."

"OK," John replied, "let's be insignificant. Meet me on the rear deck at two AM. Bring your scuba gear."

She perked up at this. "Really? What do you have in mind?"

"I don't know. Something. Anything. We'll make up a plan as we go."

"You're serious."

"Serious as a heart attack. I remember when my dad and I cornered a mouse in the backyard while we were moving a pile of brush. The little guy didn't curl up and quit. He stood up on his hind legs, let out as big a squeak as he could and attacked Dad."

"What did your father do?"

"He smashed it with a shovel. But that's not the point. The point is that the mouse didn't give up. And I won't either."

"Me neither," Gina said. She grabbed John's arm. "They can smash us with a shovel all they want. Let's do something insignificant."

He smiled a brave smile at her. "Two AM."

She returned his brave smile. "I'll be there."

*The Strategic Design headquarters sat atop a hill overlooking downtown Seattle and the expanse of Puget Sound. Manicured trees, graceful fountains and wide walkways fronted a gleaming slab of architecture. It was huge and impressive. Inside the atrium were displayed some of the company's most impressive weapons systems and support technology. There was a smiling receptionist, elevators, security guards, and people in suits moving about—all the trappings of a successful enterprise.*

*The dark soul of Strategic Design, though, lay deep underground, away from the busy offices. It was down there in the bunkers that the difficult strategies were concocted. Strategic Design had its fingers in everything from weapons design to electronics to missile guidance systems and communications. Such diversity needed the anonymity of darkness to do what had to be done in order to survive and thrive in the modern world.*

*A red-haired woman and two men in suits sat on one side of a tasteful oak table in a small room on level five. An untouched basket of fresh fruit and a pitcher of water graced the center of the table, an aquarium bubbled softly on a side table. The woman's face bore, in repose, the ghost of a wry smile. Across the table sat Kyle Montgomery, dressed in casual denim and a cotton shirt. His elbows were on the table, and he rested his chin on his clasped hands.*

*"Yes," Montgomery said calmly. "I can do it."*

*One of the men spoke up. "It's important that neither party bring back any alien tech. If the Navy gets it, we're screwed. They'll open it up for bids and we lose any advantage. If the Gershon Institute gets the alien tech, we're double-screwed. They'll be the lead dog and we'll go to the back of the line."*

*"I understand," Montgomery replied.*

*"And if you think for one moment that..."*

*The red-haired woman held up her hand, stopping the man's rant. "Enough, Robert. We all agree on the importance of Strategic Design's lead in this matter." She turned her attention to Kyle. "SD has always appreciated your work, Mr. Montgomery. Your methods are unconventional, to say the least. How much confidence do you have in this mission?"*

*Montgomery put his hands on the table and leaned forward ever so slightly. It was a calculated move. "Confidence is very high, Ms. Daniels. I'll be dealing with a bunch of scientists who are completely wrapped up in their work. Chaos is a ladder. It will be like stealing candy from a baby."*

*"Your sister-in-law, the captain of this ship you want us to arrange as an escort... you don't anticipate any problems?"*

*"Janet is a push-over. She'll be so excited to get her rusty tub out of museum duty she won't know what to do with herself. I'll bribe her with food and compliments. She won't be a problem."*

*The other man spoke, his voice a dark purr. "There is the matter of the smart octopus. How do you propose to deal with that?"*

*"The octopus has the mind of a child. It's just an experiment. It can barely put a sentence together and is still learning how to use a crescent wrench. I'll set up a little discord between it and its handler and let nature take its course. Trust me—this is my specialty."*

*Ms. Daniels nodded. "Your past efforts have been most impressive."*

*Kyle smiled his corporate smile. "Thank you. Besides," he continued, "you've seen the video. These aliens are giant crabs. Crabs and octopuses are mortal enemies."*

*"Bringing an element of unpredictability to the mission," one of the suited men stated.*

*"What about Rear Admiral Diaz?" Daniels said. "It was the death of his son that set all this in motion."*

"You've dealt with brass before. They're narrow thinkers. I don't see him as a problem either." Kyle Montgomery leaned back in his chair. "I'm the best you've got. Give me some trust."

Daniels sat back in her chair as well: a power move. "SD has a lot riding on this, Mr. Montgomery. Bring back any alien technology you can, make contact with the aliens if at all possible. We need to be the primary agent in the development of this new technology. We will provide you with any stealth equipment you may need."

"Thank you, ma'am."

"Bringing back samples of alien tech is the primary goal here. Communicating directly with the aliens and, if possible, forming some sort of liaison hold equal weight." She fixed her cold eyes on him. "Everything else—ships, personnel, your sister-in-law, everything—is expendable. Do I make myself clear, Mr. Montgomery?"

Kyle nodded solemnly. "Perfectly clear, ma'am. Perfectly clear."

# CHAPTER FOURTEEN

Gunnery Sergeant Davidson found Admiral Diaz by the railing on the foredeck, speaking with Lieutenant Commander Amundsen. They paused their conversation as Davidson approached and saluted.

"May I have a word with you, sir?" Davidson asked.

Amundsen took the opportunity to excuse herself. She gave the admiral a perfunctory salute, nodded to Davidson, and strode off. Diaz leaned on the railing and looked out to sea. "What's on your mind, Gunny?"

Davidson leaned on the railing next to him. "What happened to the *Pendleton*...it was terrible. I'm so sorry."

"We all are," Diaz replied.

"You and the Lieutenant Commander debriefed the survivors. I heard it was pretty bad."

The rear admiral sighed and rubbed the bridge of his nose. "The *Pendleton* was blown to pieces by the Krell. Our survivors were aft near the engine room and somehow managed to not get sucked down by the tail structure. One of them told me he saw pieces of the front of the sub, just pieces. And they were still glowing from the heat of whatever hellish force hit it. Pieces of bodies, too. His shipmates. Yeah, it was bad."

"Looks like we're doomed," Davidson said flatly.

"Looks like it."

They stood in silence for awhile, gazing out to sea. Davidson turned to Diaz.

"That's what I wanted to talk to you about, sir."

John stared into Oliver's empty tank for a long time. It was so still, so lifeless. He thought about how much he missed that damn octopus. So much loss in the world, and now the end of the human race. John realized that he had been crying and wiped his face with a towel that he would usually have used to dry his arms after kisses with Oliver. Hot anger rose in him. He had promised Gina some kind of nebulous revenge against the Krell. He hadn't the slightest idea of what that revenge would be, but it had to be done. A Pyrrhic victory at best. Bravery, John decided, is stupidity in the face of danger.

He double-checked his diving gear and topped off the tanks. On a whim he packed Oliver's underwater keyboard and bluetooth speaker into a dive bag. On an even whimmier whim he added the octopus's beloved tentacle-cranked car. John gazed at Oliver's empty tank again, fueling his resolve with anger and desperation.

Some part of John wanted to say goodbye to somebody. Larry and Barry would have read him like a book, so he sought out Dennis "The Menace" Harris, the bane of his institutional existence. Harris was in his cramped cabin staring at his laptop. John tapped softly at the open door and caught a glimpse of a picture of Harris's wife and daughter on his computer screen before the director snapped it shut. Shields up. All business.

"Mr. Rauchenberg. What can I do for you?"

"Looks like we're shipping out in the morning," John said.

"Eleven hundred hours. Maybe earlier."

"I just wanted to say that it's been an honor to work with you."

Harris smiled ruefully. "I doubt that, but it's nice of you to say."

"I've really enjoyed my time at the Institute."

"I'm sorry to hear about your octopus. Oliver was an amazing guy."

John was touched by the sentiment. "I guess we're all just saying goodbye," he said. "To our friends, to the world."

"They'll figure something out," Harris said, although John could tell he was just whistling past the graveyard. "We're not done fighting yet."

"I don't think there's much we can do."

He had never seen Director Harris exhibit anything but gruff command, so to see him on the verge of crestfallen was heartbreaking. "We had a good run, us humans," Harris said. "At least I won't have to put up with the cafeteria's lasagna anymore."

John smiled at his gallows humor. They spent the next ten minutes or so telling stories about bad food, covering their sadness with bravado.

John ate a forgettable meal alone in the mess hall and took a large cup of virulent Navy coffee back to his lab. He lay on his cot and thought about Oliver and his fate. Maybe Oliver wasn't dead at the bottom of the ocean. He was, after all, a very resourceful cephalopod. John drifted off to sleep chiding himself for having hope. Hope seemed, in those dark hours, to be merely another form of stupidity.

The alarm went off at one-thirty AM. and for a single sweet moment John thought he was back in California, ready for another day with the most intelligent octopus in the world. The slap of reality took care of that. He was sneaking out to meet certain doom, fighting for some shred of dignity against an alien adversary. The cold coffee washed away the grogginess and John grabbed his gear and left, easing the door shut behind him. In the darkened hallway he could hear the thrum and whisper of the sleeping ship. This was not a Navy vessel, so there was no night-watch. John again called himself a fool for engineering such a hare-brained, incoherent plan. But there was nothing else to do. Crawl back to the Institute and wait for God only knows what kind of fate when the giant space crabs took over? No thanks. Like the mouse John and his father had cornered, he summoned up his courage and strode forth.

John crept down the hallway and ghosted up the stairs to topside. The opening to the gangplank that led down to the pontoon deck was jet black against the faint image of the railing. John felt his way down to the raft, being as quiet as he could. A half-moon hung low in the sky behind a bank of clouds and the sea was sprinkled with its pewter light. Coming off the relative bright of the rear deck onto the dark gangplank, John was completely blind, depending on the railing to guide him. As he stepped onto the floating deck, three red flashlight beams were on him from the far end of the deck.

"Who goes there?" came a hoarse whisper. It was Sergeant Davidson.

"It's the octopus guy," came another whisper. John didn't recognize the voice. The third one, however, was a shock.

"Rauchenberg! What the hell are you doing here?"

John held his hand up to shield my eyes. "Director Harris?"

"Shhhh!" Sergeant Davidson commanded. "Come over here."

John carefully shuffled down the length of the pontoon deck to find seven figures gathered in a tight knot. He knew Dennis "The Menace" Harris and Sergeant Davidson, and recognized a couple of the others from seeing them around the ship. One figure turned toward him and John caught his breath as he recognized Lieutenant Commander Amundsen. She nodded curtly at him. All of them were in camouflage and heavily armed, their faces painted to match the camo. John looked past them to see the *Beagle* moored to the side of the deck and was amazed to see Barry grinning at him from the open hatch.

"What are you guys doing?" John stammered.

"I might ask you the same question," Davidson replied, staring at him with burning intensity.

"Um…I was going to take the, uh, submarine and go to the atoll and, uh, fight the Krell."

"You gonna bonk 'em with your scuba tank?" Davidson chided. "Slap 'em with your fins?"

John felt cowed and crushed under his logic. "Somebody has to do something. I thought…"

"He thought what the rest of us thought," Barry said from the submarine. "Time's wasting. Bring him along."

"There's one more!" John blurted out.

"Who?" Sergeant Davidson demanded.

"Me," came Gina's voice from the darkness. Davidson shone his red filtered flashlight on her and she shielded her eyes as she came clumping down the gangplank with her scuba gear and dive bag.

"You two shouldn't be here," Director Harris growled.

"But we are, Dennis!" Gina exclaimed. She stopped at the base of the gangplank, illuminated by the red flashlights, and regarded the group with cool eyes. "So what's the plan?"

"That's on a need-to-know basis," Sergeant Davidson said curtly.

Gina's eyes narrowed. "What am I gonna do? Turn my back on humanity and go tell the Krell?" Her tone was knives. "I think I have a need to know."

It was Dennis Harris who spoke. "We're going to assault the atoll," he said, not looking at her. "Try to get to the lagoon and sabotage whatever they're building in it."

"That's suicide!" she exclaimed.

Harris's face was rigid. "Do you really think anyone here expects to get out of this alive?" He held her gaze.

Barry broke the tense silence with his loud whisper. "Quit gabbing! Everybody on board now!"

Sergeant Davidson gestured at John and Gina. "What about them?"

Barry scowled at him. "Everybody."

Davidson nodded. The commandoes went first, wrestling themselves and their gear down the narrow hatchway. Gina went over to stand beside John.

"My hydrophones picked up dolphins," she said quietly.

John felt her hidden excitement. "Is it your pod?"

Her brow knitted ever so slightly. "Not sure. There's a lot of background noise and a lot of dolphins."

Sergeant Davidson had been listening. "Will they interfere with our Zodiac?"

"No, of course not."

"Then they're not my worry. We're a land assault."

Davidson turned to climb into the *Beagle*. Gina grabbed John's arm and spoke in an earnest whisper. "I'm getting whale song, too. I think it might be orcas."

"There's no orcas out here," John whispered back.

She squeezed his arm. "I know! New Zealand, Japan maybe, but not here."

"Weird," John said. It was all he could come up with.

"Yeah," she replied. "Weird."

They both ruminated on that for a few seconds until Davidson poked his head out of the conning tower and told them to hurry up.

"I have to hook something to the sub," John told him and started to put his scuba gear on. Gina wordlessly helped him while Davidson watched. John retrieved Oliver's underwater keyboard and speaker from his dive bag. Gina got a bulbous metal device the size of a baseball from her bag and handed it to him. She touched a switch and a green light came on.

"Hydrophone?"

"Try not to bump it." She smiled at him.

John sat on the edge of the dock and rolled backwards into the warm water. The immense quiet immediately grabbed him. Floating in infinite darkness, he felt the endless depth below. He turned his flashlight on and made his way to the stubby port wing, lashing Oliver's keyboard to the wing and making sure the Bluetooth connection was on. He then wrapped the hydrophone's strap around the wing, giving it a couple of feet of free cable. Both instruments secure, John fell back and looked at the submarine floating in the jet black sea. A calmness came over him, a deep moment effervescing with possibilities. He was running on hope and chutzpah. A chill passed over him and then the moment was gone.

Back on the pontoon deck, John shed his scuba gear and was alone on the dark raft, wrapped in night. He looked up at the hard, bright stars, smelled the cool tropical breeze redolent with the tang of ocean, and tasted the salt on his lips. *Here we go*, he thought to himself and clambered down the open hatchway.

John dogged the hatch closed behind him and gave the high sign to Larry and Barry. With the tiniest of jolts the *Beagle* began to dive, leveling out at fifteen meters in order to have better contact with Gina's dolphins. None of the "Yellow Submarine" antics this time. The vessel was crowded and everybody jostled for chairs or floor space, settling in for the voyage. Amundsen played a video game on her phone, her stony face aglow from the screen. Others read or played games or exchanged war stories in low voices. Gina plugged headphones into her computer and accessed the hydrophone. John looked over her shoulder. A 3D graphic of the underwater sound took up most of the screen; Gina was typing notes in the lower third. There appeared to be a lot of sound in the ocean. After a while she removed her headphones and turned to John.

"What?" she asked with mild annoyance.

John held up his hands. "Just looking is all. What are you finding?"

"Not much," she retorted. "A lot of cetacean location calls and name signatures. It's a noisy ocean."

"I'm worried about Oliver," John frowned.

"Understandable," Gina replied. Sensing his falling mood, she shook her fellow scientist's shoulder and put on a smile. "Hey! I took your advice and translated some more Krell. Take a look." She typed a few commands into her keyboard and the screen showed two different sound samples. The samples were short and simple and cycled on a loop through their spiky depictions.

"Cool," John said without much enthusiasm. "What do they sound like?"

"Sorta like dragging seashells across sandpaper and some fart sounds," she replied, "with a few marbles thrown against a window for good measure."

"Yeah," he grinned. "Foolish question. Better question is, what do they mean?"

Gina was in her element. "Aha, my dear Watson. Behold!" She tapped her cursor on the depiction of the alien sound and a video blossomed open at the top of the screen. It was a piece of Oliver's video of the Krell pathway. A giant crab was trying to push an errant box back onto a cart, but it was too ungainly. The display of the Krell word activated and another alien came to the first one's assistance. Gina was exultant. "See? That Krell asked for help and the other one came over to help him. So that's the Krell word for requesting help."

"As opposed to the verb form for 'help.'"

She poked him on the shoulder. "Assuming the human model for language is problematic. But yeah, you got it." She moved the cursor over to the other Krell word. "Take a look at this one."

The video at the top of the screen was a traveling shot from one of the dolphins as it arced around the Krell spacecraft. The shot digitally zoomed in, making the dim shot grainier. A Krell was carrying a large, wrapped object. The display of the Krell word activated and the package carrier turned toward a transport vehicle. Gina pursed her lips. "I figure it means 'over here' or 'this way.' I had a real hard time isolating it from the ambient noise, but there it is." She was obviously proud of herself.

"That's pretty impressive," John replied. "But what does—"

"Oh!" she interrupted. "Check this out!" She tapped on her keyboard and another Krell word display came up, this time with no video. "Remember the Krell word for 'hello?' Well I took another look at it. I assumed that the Krell were communicating in the high range the dolphins use, so that's where my thinking stopped." She used the cursor to circle high spikes scattered along the length of the word. "The word has really high overtones. I'm not even sure dolphins can sing that high. I didn't see it until I expanded my search." Her eyes lost their focus and the joy dropped from her face. "I found it too late. Too late for Norma."

John put his hand on her shoulder. "Not your fault, Gina. The Krell wouldn't have accepted Norma even if she was singing their national anthem. You know that."

Gina looked down at her lap. "Yeah. I know. Doesn't make it any less sad."

Kyle Montgomery listened intently to his earbuds. Gina the dolphin girl had also figured out the "hello" problem, albeit much later than his AI program had. He reflected again on how superior machines were to people, although both could be easily manipulated. She had ferreted out the "help" and "over here" words as well by using the clumsy tools of human observation and computer-aided sonic disassembly. Montgomery's AI had isolated those words as well; the Strategic Design cameras carried by the octopus and dolphins recorded sound well above the normal range, a secret carefully kept from their Defense Department buyers. Always keep an ace or three up your sleeve, Kyle smiled to himself. It was a lesson he had learned early on when he was running undercover operations for a street gang his older brother had introduced him to. Kyle had later used damning information against that same brother to compel the street gang to take punitive action, thereby elevating Kyle's value in the group. Ace well played. He paid full attention to his earbuds while simultaneously relaxing his body and preserving its *chi* as he had learned in his martial arts training. Ms. Martinelli had three Krell words; he had five…her three plus the command for "open" and a complex sound signature that had a reasonable probability of translating to "the time of hatching approaches." Kyle Montgomery was an information sponge, a master of strategy and manipulation, a cybernetic switchblade ready to open and take what was needed. Strategic Design would, no doubt, reward him handsomely.

John left Gina to her hydrophone and her sadness, giving her respectful distance. Instead, he brought up a Sherlock Holmes mystery on his phone, hoping it would draw him in. He spent the next hour trying to care about the Victorian detective's ruminations while being painfully aware that he was in a cramped metal tube on his way to certain danger and probable death. He still hadn't the slightest idea of how he was going to fight the Krell and Sherlock was no help whatsoever in that department. Eventually, Gina pulled her headphones off.

"Anything new?" John tried to not sound frantic.

"Just more location songs. Sorry. No mention of Ollie either."

Dennis Harris chimed in. "Nothing else? Just locations?"

"That's it. And some verbs for traveling. Sorry."

Harris frowned and nodded to her. They sat in glum silence. After a long while John turned to Director Harris. "I didn't know you were a gun guy."

"I was a Marine," Harris replied. "Re-upped twice. Couple of tours in Afghanistan. Part of the first wave in Malaysia. Bad stuff. Really bad." He grinned wickedly. "Where do you think I lost my sense of humor?"

"This is the realest I've ever seen you, Dennis," Gina commented.

Harris put on a poker face. "That's 'Director Harris' to you, young lady."

Gina giggled. Harris flashed her a grin and chortled. John laughed, too, and the three of them shared a tiny taste of levity as they cruised the dark depths. The laughter passed and the three exchanged faint smiles.

Emboldened, John turned to Sergeant Davidson. "Do you really think you're going to stop the Krell with your dinky Earthling pea shooters? They've got ray guns!"

Davidson gave him a "what-the-hell-do-you-know" frown. He reached into the duffle bag at his feet and pulled out the Krell ray gun. He grinned toothily. "So do we."

Gina and John were agog. "How did you smuggle that off the ship?" she asked.

"Who do you think they had guarding it?" he replied.

"Wow!" John said. "Something tells me Rear Admiral Diaz might have turned a blind eye."

"Something tells me you might be right." The toothy grin again.

"You realize," Gina said solemnly, "that those crab things probably have hundreds of ray guns to your one."

Davidson pursed his lips. "No guts, no glory, Ms. Martinelli. Everything is something."

"And there are always possibilities," she responded firmly. "I wish you luck." He nodded in response. She continued. "So in the spirit of openness, Sergeant Davidson, you always tell us to 'call you Dave,' but what is your real name?"

Davidson's mask did not slip. "It's David."

"Really?" John interjected.

Davidson turned to him. "Yes, really. David Allen Davidson. D.A.D. But only my kids get to call me Dad."

"I didn't know you had any kids."

At that moment Larry and Barry let out yells of surprise and the deck began to tilt. As Larry got control of the stick and the deck returned to level, John, Gina, and Sergeant Davidson crowded up behind the pilot's chair.

"What's wrong?" Davidson demanded.

"We just got buzzed by something really big. Swam across the bow."

"Turn the outside lights on," the sergeant said.

"But the Krell—"

Davidson was stern. "Lights on."

Barry flipped a switch and the outside lights came on full. There was something moving out beyond their reach—a large shape, definitely not mechanical. It dove below the beams of light, then swam up past the glass bubble. Close, not twenty meters away. It was a very large orca, its shape and black-and-white coloring unmistakable.

"Stop the sub!" Davidson barked. But Larry was already on it. The *Beagle* slowed and stopped, its motors whining through the hull. Everybody scrambled for a view out the front.

The orca, at least twelve meters long, swam lazily into view and hung before the submarine. John and Gina, the resident marine biologists, pressed their faces against the glass to get a better view. The whale's skin was mottled with what appeared to be scars. Strange scars, symmetrical, like misshapen asterisks.

"Oh my God!" John exclaimed. "It's covered with octopuses!"

The whale swam closer. A spatter pattern of octopuses dotted the cetacean's torso; large, small, and in between, all trying to emulate the whale's coloration. It gave the orca a mottled, almost pixelated look. A large specimen at the base of the dorsal fin detached itself and swam toward the *Beagle*. John pressed his face against the glass.

"It's Oliver!" he exclaimed. The cephalopod appeared to be wrapped around something bulky. Behind him he heard Gina's taut whisper.

"He has my dolphin communicator!"

Oliver landed on the glass front of the *Beagle*, his sucker cups holding him firm. John raised his hand and made the "kisses" sign. The octopus clinging to the outside of the glass bubble turned robin's egg blue. John put his hand against the glass and Oliver covered it with a blue tentacle. The moment lasted a couple of seconds until Sergeant Davidson cleared his throat.

"Looks like your little buddy came back." His tone was only slightly congratulatory.

"I gotta find out what's going on with him," John said to nobody in particular, not looking away from Oliver.

"No, you don't," Davidson said gruffly. "We need to get going."

Dennis Harris stood up. "No, Dave," he said, "we do not need to get going. John Rauchenberg needs to communicate with Oliver."

"You're not in charge," Davidson growled.

"Neither are you, 'Dave,'" Larry commented from the pilot's chair. "I think it's real heartening to see John's reunion with his pal."

"You can't—"

"Let it rest." Lieutenant Commander Amundsen's voice was low and calm. "We've got time."

Davidson rolled his eyes and sat down. None of the others said anything. Harris touched John's shoulder. "Go see what Oliver has to say, John."

John pulled his hand from the thick glass and pointed to the left. He made a typing gesture and pointed again. The large octopus released from the observation bubble and jetted out of sight. John stepped to his computer, the people parting to let him pass. He made sure the speakers were on, then sat on the edge of his chair. Barry activated an external camera and the video screens showed a view of the port wing. The room fell silent, save for the murmur of the *Beagle's* sleeping machinery. Oliver, still holding Gina's dolphin communicator with two tentacles, swam to the wing and latched on next to the keyboard. He tapped at the keys.

"John!" the speaker exclaimed, and everybody jumped. "John! John! John! Oliver wants kisses!"

"Kisses! Kisses!" John replied. "Oliver is very good. Oliver comes home."

Gina nudged John's shoulder. "I want my communicator back. Tell him that."

"Oliver," John said into the mic, "can you leave the dolphin talker with us?"

"Yes. Yes, please," the octopus replied.

"I'll open the specimen collection compartment," Barry interjected, jabbing at a few buttons on his console. "It's in front of the port wing. He should see it." The muted whir of an outside door opening came through the metal hull. John directed Oliver to the compartment and there was a light clunk as the machine was deposited, then another muted whir as the compartment closed. Gina patted John on the shoulder in a gesture of thanks as Oliver swam back into view and settled on the wing next to his keyboard.

"What have you been up to, Oliver?" John asked, trying to keep his tone light.

There was a pause at the other end. "Oliver has new friends."

"I see that. What's going on?"

"Buggabugga."

"Not acceptable. Try again." There was a long pause.

Gina whispered into John's ear, "Ask him about his new friends."

"Oliver," John said, "tell me about your new friends."

"Oliver is very smart."

"True, but how did you get new friends?"

"Oliver sees."

John sighed. More oblique statements from Oliver. "What do you mean? What do you see?"

"Octopus follows. Dolphin talker. Oliver sees lan-gwij."

"Very good, Oliver," John said. Another flash of the octopus's arcane intelligence. "How many new friends do you have?"

The synthetic voice was enthusiastic. "Oliver has many, many new friends! We are going hunting!"

# CHAPTER FIFTEEN

The *Beagle* got underway again, accelerating slowly so as not to dislodge the octopus clinging to the wing. The orca surfaced for a gulp of air, then returned to swim alongside the submarine. The next fifteen minutes were spent trying to understand what Oliver was up to and to coordinate Davidson's nebulous plans with the cephalopod's equally nebulous thought process. To Gina's delight, Gary, Sheila and Nancy found the submarine and joined in the conversation.

It boiled down to simple ideas, none of which were fully fleshed out. Nobody knew what advanced weapons the Krell had constructed in the depths of the central lagoon or what the combined forces of cephalopods, cetaceans and humans would face there. The seven members of the Navy contingent would be on their own in an overland assault to access the lagoon and sabotage whatever was in it. Meanwhile, the octopuses, dolphins and whales would stage an underwater assault of some sort. Oliver was not specific about his plans, perhaps because they were so unfocused and perhaps because he was an octopus and had a hard time putting his complex ideas into human speech. The word 'buggabugga' came up several times. Basically, the octopuses (Oliver could not provide a number, but John figured that there were probably hundreds) would blanket the reef at the west end of the atoll. They would destroy as many Krell and Krell eggs as possible. The dolphins would provide camouflage by employing the "curtain of bubbles" strategy they used to hem in schools of fish, as well as utilizing some shark-fighting techniques. Gina's dolphin pod indicated they would be coordinating that effort. Gina came up with the idea of the dolphins using her newly translated Krell words to distract and confuse the giant alien crabs. The role of the orcas was hazy, but it appeared that they would be attackers as well, ocean going tanks using their size and speed to kill as many Krell as they could.

Everyone knew that the ultimate key to this long-shot mission was to destroy or disable the Krell spaceship now embedded deep in the coral forest at the west end of the atoll. The humans aboard the submarine were at a loss about how to do this. Larry and Barry offered that perhaps the *Beagle* could be used as a battering ram to attack the alien craft. Unspoken was the fact that such action would be likely ineffective and definitely suicidal. Oliver indicated that he had a plan cooking in his blue-blooded brain. When pressed for details, the octopus replied with the cryptic phrase, "The Great Old One."

Gina pushed the mute button on John's microphone. "What the hell? Did you let him watch that H.P. Lovecraft special on PBS?"

"Yes, I did," John replied defensively. "It had an octopus."

"More like a squid," said Larry.

"A tentacle-faced demon," Barry chimed in. "Ol' Squid Lips."

"Not a standard demon," Amundsen said.

"You're a Lovecraft fan?" Barry asked incredulously.

"It's common knowledge that Great Cthulhu is, in fact, a transdimensional being," she replied with cool certainty. "With tentacles."

"Enough!" Sergeant Davidson barked. "We're wasting time. Move on."

Gina took her finger off the mute button and John continued. Oliver was pleased to hear that John had brought the crank car along and asked that it be delivered to the shallow reef at the west end of the atoll. John readily agreed, secretly hoping that he would be able to join in the actual battle. Gina would be riding along with the submarine to act as liaison and communication node for the dolphins. Everyone knew that they would be playing this mission by ear—or flipper, or tentacle. Sunrise was not far away and Oliver communicated that he had told all of his new friends, both tentacled and finned, that the operation would begin at false dawn. He turned a dull silver to show what the color of the water's surface would be at the appointed time.

Vague plans in place, Oliver swam back to join the large orca, flashing a red and blue ripple. John waved goodbye at the front glass wall, feeling silly when he realized how useless his gesture was. The *Beagle* cut its lights as the orca sped off into the darkness of the sea, leaving the inhabitants of the research submarine to await their arrival at the atoll.

John and Gina exchanged whispered conversation, talking about anything that came to mind. They spoke of family and dreams and the nature of intelligence. John smelled the ocean on Gina's skin overlaying the subtle scent of a woman and was pleased to be so near her. Eventually Barry turned around in his seat and said they had better suit up because they were only ten minutes out.

They helped each other don their tanks and used up the remaining time doing systems checks. John clipped a camera to the side of his mask. The submarine slowed and began to ascend. They were very close to the atoll, less than half a kilometer. Tension rippled through the air inside the submarine. This was it. D-Day. The real McCoy. The point of no return. The blackness outside the front glass barely lifted as the *Beagle* silently surfaced. Sergeant Davidson reminded his fighting force to let the two marine biologists set up the inflatable Zodiac before deploying.

Larry had decided that the waterlock made too much machine noise and told John and Gina to exit through the conning tower. John went up the ladder first, careful not to bang his tanks in the narrow passageway. Once outside, he knelt to give Gina a hand up onto the top of the *Beagle*.

John and Gina stood silently in the crisp quiet. The sky was still black, stars twinkling above. To the east, the horizon was a thin line of deep orange and red below an indigo blue that twisted up through deeper shades into blackness. The water was calm, small waves dim against the dark sea, their crests tipped with predawn light the color of tarnished copper. The atoll shore was only a few hundred meters away, its trees ebony cutouts against the stars.

John realized that they were holding hands. He turned to Gina. "I may never see you again," he said softly.

She looked up at him, her eyes soft and inviting. "I know," she said. "That would be a shame."

On impulse, John drew her to him and kissed her full on the mouth. She responded without hesitation, opening to him. They lingered in a deep, gentle kiss. He tasted her salt and sweetness, his spirit lifting in the bittersweet joyousness of the moment. When they broke apart, she held his gaze for several heartbeats before looking at her feet.

"I'm sorry I've been so mean to you," she said. "It's just that…I mean I have a bad history of, you know…" John could see her vulnerability.

"We all have our armor," he said. "When this is over we should go out for dinner and a movie and I could kiss you again."

"I'd like that," Gina said softly, a smile flitting across her lips. She donned a Cheshire cat grin and slapped him playfully on the arm. "Ever the optimist. You actually think we're going to get out of this alive."

"There are always possibilities."

"I like a man who quotes *Star Trek*. Let's do this thing."

They donned their fins and masks, clamping mouthpieces in their teeth. With no prompting they spontaneously joined hands, looking intently at each other through the glass of their face masks. John nodded to Gina and she returned the gesture. Her cheeks rose in a smile, impeded as it was by the breathing mechanism in her mouth, and winked at him. Together they fell backward into the sea.

In the dark of the ocean, John sensed that the *Beagle* was just a hundred meters or so from the sea mount's rise from the abyssal plain below. The two divers moved to the front of the submarine and watched the grappling arm underneath extend forward and release the deflated Zodiac. Working in unison as if they had been doing it forever, John and Gina unfolded the craft and activated compressed air tanks to inflate it, guiding the stiffening structure to the surface.

John had been ruminating about kissing Gina for several months. But when the moment had come at last and, as the cheesy romance novels say, "their lips met in ecstasy," it was very nice. Not fireworks, just warm and sweet. It was, after all, the end of the world and they were going off to die. It was a nice kiss, damn nice. Much nicer than the clumsy encounter he had had back in college with Laura Feldman out behind the Student Union after Invertebrate Biology lab, and worlds nicer than the dry little peck Becky Jones had given him in high school. The kiss John and Gina shared was wonderful and seemed so junior prom corny. *I don't care,* John said to himself. *Romantics are such dorks.*

They got the Zodiac inflated and tied off to the *Beagle's* conning tower, if you can call something that sticks just two feet out of the water a tower. They held the boat steady as the seven commandoes slipped silently aboard. One would think that with all the armaments, straps and bulging pockets they would be clumsy creatures. These were soldiers, though—strong and deadly and determined. A surge of throat-tightening pride welled up inside John. Insignificant as these warriors were against an obviously superior starfaring civilization, they made John proud to be human, proud to be a citizen of planet Earth, fierce of heart, the mouse standing brave against the shovel. Gladys Amundsen gave Gina and John a rare smile, and Dennis Harris gave them a grinning high five. Sergeant Davidson came last with an appreciative nod and a thumbs-up. Then the warriors paddled toward the atoll and were soon lost from view in the murky pre-dawn light.

John and Gina clung to handholds on the port wing as the *Beagle* dove to twelve meters and cruised silently toward the west end of the atoll. The Krell spaceship was there, and the entrance to the lagoon. John had brought a bag with him containing Oliver's crank car. He had given himself the task—the hope— of somehow finding Oliver in the Krell-infested reef and giving him his car. It felt like the right thing to do. Gina would be traveling farther west to contact her pod. She intended to put video cameras on the three dolphins so the *Beagle* could have some kind of view of whatever battle ensued. She was also going to impart to the dolphins the Krell words she had translated in hopes that the dolphins could use them to sow confusion among the aliens. Gina and John couldn't talk, but she put her hand on his and looked at him intently—more a need for human connection than anything romantic.

The submarine slowed and stopped. John made sure the bag with Oliver's crank car was snug to him, then kicked away from the *Beagle*, flipping over to look back at the submarine. Gina waved and he waved back. She put her hand over her heart. The simple gesture caught John by surprise. He returned the gesture and they held it for several heartbeats. It felt like goodbye. John took a deep breath through his mouthpiece to fight down the lump rising in his throat and waved again. He then swam vigorously toward the atoll's rising cliff of coral.

The sky above was the dull silver of false dawn. It was time to fight the Krell.

# CHAPTER SIXTEEN

O liver clung to the orca's dorsal fin, watching the dark cliff of the atoll speed by. Gary kept pace, and would sometimes come up to the octopus and make soothing dolphin noises. Oliver had difficulty hearing the dolphin because the register was a bit high for him. He missed the dolphin communication device that Gina had so fortuitously left on the floating dock; it had allowed for actual conversation. Oliver recognized a few dolphin words like "ready," "dolphin" and "orca." Oliver replied with a rippling blue of happiness and red flashes of excitement.

Above them the surface of the water had the muted shimmer of a fish's underside.

The octopus tapped the orca three times next to its blowhole. The whale surfaced and came to a halt, letting loose a long, warbling basso profundo note overlaid with ascending clicks. It made Oliver's skin vibrate. He heard the call answered far off several times. Gary squealed with excitement and sped away into the murky blue. Oliver released from the orca's dorsal fin, tapping with his tentacle tip a gentle pattern around the whale's blowhole, a little dance of "thank you." Oliver saw a myriad of other octopuses detach from the big orca. Big and small, they were camouflaging themselves as floating seaweed or blobs of moss. A few emulated sea snakes or lionfish. The cloud of blue-blooded warriors swam and jetted toward the atoll's shallow reef.

The bottom rose suddenly and the swarm of cephalopods disappeared into the jumble of coral. Oliver jetted to the top of a coral head and camouflaged into the splotchy jaggedness. He looked around. All quiet. His octopus companions drifted into the coral forest and also merged into the reef. Oliver caught movement off to the right and swam toward it, disguising himself as seaweed. Several octopuses followed, mimicking his camouflage. Oliver was not used to the company of other octopuses and it felt strange, but the burning importance of his mission overshadowed all else.

Two large Krell, both armed with ray guns, rounded a corner several yards away. Disguised as a piece of seaweed, Oliver jetted gently toward them, readying his attack. He headed toward the nearer one, aiming for the larger claw, the one holding the weapon. As the giant crab moved to brush the floating seaweed aside Oliver dropped his camouflage, wrapping his tentacles around the claw and the arm it was attached to. The Krell stopped and turned its eyestalks toward its claw. Oliver reached out a tentacle and grabbed one of the eyestalks. Several of the other octopuses were landing on the Krell, one following Oliver's lead and wrapping two of its tentacles around the other eyestalk. Oliver wrenched the eyestalk from the crab's carapace and the other octopus did the same. The huge crustacean began moving in jerky circles, snapping at the large claw with its smaller one. Another octopus grabbed the smaller arm and broke it off.

The other Krell froze in place. It raised its weapon toward its companion as two more octopuses, having learned from watching Oliver, landed on the giant crab and tore its eyestalks away. The Krell flailed wildly with its smaller claw at the offending creatures, grabbing one by an errant tentacle. All it got was a piece of the octopus's arm as the cephalopod jetted away in a cloud of ink.

Oliver saw the strangely human-looking third eye above the second alien's mouth fix on him and he knew that the giant crab would next raise its ray gun and shoot. Oliver ripped the claw he was holding from its arm. He remembered the briefing about these weapons and recognized the glowing blue trigger button near where the tip of the huge claw touched the ray gun. Oliver wrapped one of his arms around the claw while several other tentacles aimed the weapon at the Krell. *Like darts*, Oliver thought to himself, although not in human words. *Just aim.*

He squeezed the big claw, causing it to press the trigger, and a bolt of sizzling red energy tore the other giant crab in half, spewing alien innards into the clear tropical water. He then pressed the weapon against the top of the flailing Krell he was riding and pressed the trigger again. The shaft of red energy shot through the giant crab and it collapsed to the sandy bottom. The water tasted like burnt fish, a most unpleasant sensation. Oliver could tell the other octopuses tasted it, too.

Time to move on. He tore the ray gun from the dead Krell's large claw. Holding the weapon beneath him with two arms, a third tentacle poised over the glowing blue trigger, Oliver jetted further into the reef. Several octopuses followed while others, having learned from their observation of the Krell demise, swam off to find adventures of their own.

*One down, many to go* Oliver thought to himself, again not in human words.

Gina clung easily to the *Beagle's* port wing. Having few, if any, strategies to ponder, her mind darted through a labyrinth of thoughts. That this was a suicide mission was beyond question; she hoped she could make a brave showing. She recalled H. G. Wells' *War of The Worlds* and wished she was a deadly virus infiltrating the Krell to wipe them out. Thoughts of John kept popping up—his patience, his intelligence, his vulnerability. He had had the guts to finally kiss her and she re-lived the moment in small, warm flashes. Mostly she thought about her dolphins, what kind of plan they might have in mind and what she could do to help.

Looking back, she saw, dwindling behind them and silhouetted against the silvery ocean surface, a large orca stop, and a swarm of little blobby shapes detach from the whale. The sea was filled with the thunderous song of orcas. The hydrophone, slaved to her communication electronics, picked up Gary's excited squeal as he took off for the west end of the atoll. The *Beagle* had lost all pretense of sneakiness and sped after him.

Gina sent out a signal for her pod to meet up with her. She put it on a repeating loop with pauses for response. Nancy answered first, then Sheila. Gary sent a short burst of agreement as he swam swiftly west. "Find me," she told them.

The submarine's motors changed pitch as the vessel slowed, then turned to face into the current that followed the side of the atoll's sea mount. The sub gradually rose to a depth of eight meters and hovered there. Gina scanned the water, but it was dim and murky in the muted pre-dawn light. The ocean was full of dolphin songs, hundreds of them, yet her communicator was able to pick her pod's signals out of the cacophony. Nancy, Sheila and Gary approached in unison, rising for a breath of air then diving down to hang before her. She keyed joy into her keyboard and swam out to meet them. Nuzzling and rubbing and happy squeals ensued until she broke off the greeting ritual and got down to business.

"I want to help," she keyed into her communicator, which then sang the idea in Dolphin.

"Yes!" the dolphins squawked, and swam in circles.

"What do I do?" she keyed in, adding an interrogative. Dolphins seldom asked questions, but Gina had introduced her pod to the concept. It aided enormously in comprehension.

The dolphins continued swimming in excited circles, exchanging complex squeals and squawks and chitters that her computer could not keep up with. The two females raced to the surface for air, then came back to flank Gary.

"See the crabs, see the fish," Gary said. "We cannot see all."

*They want me to give them the big picture*, she thought to herself. She answered "yes, I am eyes." This was evidently what the dolphins wanted to hear. They chittered their happiness. She keyed in the signal to wait, then stroked and hugged each dolphin in turn before strapping cameras to their fins.

She turned her back to the *Beagle* and taught the dolphins the Krell words she had deciphered, making the dolphins repeat them several times to perfect their pronunciation. All three were proficient with "help" and "over here," but only Nancy, the smallest and youngest, could hit the high overtones necessary to correctly say the Krell recognition word. The dolphins were enthusiastic and at one point all three gestured at the *Beagle* and said the dolphin word for "strange fish."

Gina did not want the dolphins to lose focus. "Yes, it is a strange fish, but pay attention to me," she keyed. "The [dolphin word for alien] will want to kill you," she told them. This sobered them somewhat, but they still kept glancing at the *Beagle*. Gina brought them back to task, hammering them with the importance of the newly learned Krell words as a tool of distraction. "Yes," they replied, "we understand."

The lesson done, Gina's podmates gave her nuzzles and squeals of love as she sent them off to battle the Krell. She wished she could be with them, wished she could be a dolphin and fight these horrors from outer space, but instead she was relegated to the role of observer-slash-spotter. She looked back at the *Beagle*. Barry had said he would hold video screens to the front observation bubble to show that he was getting the dolphins' feed, but he was not there. She swam toward the submarine, hardened with determination to be the best eyes and ears she could be. But when she got there everything had changed.

Larry was adjusting the SQUID drive to keep the *Beagle* in place, so it was Barry who heard the subtle click and squeak from the rear of the submarine. He turned to see Kyle Montgomery emerge from an equipment locker. Kyle appeared to be holding a weapon. At Barry's short bark of surprise, Larry looked up from his controls just as Montgomery shot him.

It was a taser and the *bang* was loud as a gunshot in the enclosed space. Larry slipped out of his chair, screaming with pain, and had the presence of mind to turn and fall on his back so his body weight would not drive the taser barbs further into his chest. Kyle gave the submarine pilot an extra jolt of voltage, causing his body to twitch convulsively and his screams of pain to subside to moans. Meanwhile Barry had come up out of his chair and was advancing on Montgomery, his fists balled in fury. Kyle dropped the taser gun and stepped toward Barry with practiced ease. He grabbed the copilot's shirt and pulled him forward, slamming his elbow into the side of Barry's neck and knocking him to the floor. He whipped a stun gun from his pocket and pressed it to Barry's back. The stocky man convulsed as paralyzing voltage surged through his body. Montgomery reached over and tapped the stunner against Larry's chest, eliciting a twitch and low moan. He applied another shock to Barry, then stood to appreciate his work. The entire episode had taken less than fifteen seconds.

His impediments out of the way, the Strategic Design agent went to Larry's control board and typed in a ten digit code, then did the same thing to Barry's. The submarine was now his to command. He thought briefly about how to proceed. He could shut the machine down and blow the buoyancy tanks, relegating the research sub to a dark death in the abyssal depths. But practicality won out; the game was still in flux and he would need a means of escape. Montgomery finished Larry's instructions that would keep the *Beagle* in a stable position against the ocean current and hit the enter key.

Moving with efficiency, he retrieved two hanks of rope from the equipment locker and tied the two submarine technicians' hands. Barry tried to struggle against the binding and Kyle casually stunned him again, bringing forth a small cry of pain. He then gave Larry another jolt for good measure.

Kyle Montgomery retrieved his high-tech diving gear from the equipment locker and slipped into it. He could not resist a dark smirk as he nudged Larry's limp head.

"Thanks for the ride. I'll be back."

The company man glanced out the observation bubble and noted Gina several yards away, her back to the submarine as she communicated with her dolphins. Good. He looked at Larry and Barry and toyed with the idea of tormenting them a bit more, but there was important work to attend to and no time to waste. Kyle Montgomery was not one to wallow in self-congratulation, but in his emotionally detached way he was rather proud of how well his schemes had worked so far.

He donned his fins, put the breather mouthpiece between his lips, and climbed into the waterlock, glad that it faced away from the marine biologist and the dolphins. One minute forty-seven seconds had elapsed.

As John approached the steep face of the seamount that was Palmyra Atoll he tried to clear his mind of the poignant parting with Gina. He allowed himself to become awash with a sense of great peril, hoping that it would engender caution, not panic. He took deep, even breaths, feeling a forced calm flood through him. He was every superhero he had ever loved, every nerd he had ever encountered. The light brightened as he neared the surface, even though the sun was not quite up. The steep rise became less so and the amount of coral increased. He approached the atoll's shallows with renewed caution.

Coming up over the edge, the reef stretched out before him, a jumble of multi-colored corals with bright fish darting through the polyp labyrinth. Clumps of seaweed swayed in the gentle current. He ventured forward, moving slowly just off the bottom in hopes that it would make him less visible to the massive crablike invaders. He peeked around corners, ready to duck back at the slightest glimpse of any Krell. It occurred to John that for a smart guy he was pretty stupid: he had no weapon of any sort. True, there was the obligatory knife on his belt, but that would be useful only in close quarters and then only if he knew how to use it properly. The chances of getting close enough to use his knife on a ray gun-wielding giant space crab lay on the other side of impossible. Cold fear shot through his guts.

At that moment a Krell emerged from the coral not ten feet away. From his low perspective the alien looked massive. John tried to backtrack, but he was jammed up against a large block of coral. The huge crab saw him and raised its weapon. John knew he was dead.

Suddenly a dolphin sped by, followed by another, leaving a curtain of bubbles in their wake. The Krell turned, firing its weapon after them and missing. The water tingled with electricity. John silently thanked the departing dolphins for the brief reprieve from death, then steeled himself for the inevitable ray gun blast. But something astounding happened; two clumps of seaweed and a piece of coral morphed into octopuses and leaped onto the Krell. One wrapped its tentacles around the large claw holding the ray gun while another tore away the giant crab's eyestalks. John was stunned. But strangest of all, the third octopus—a medium size cephalopod with long, thin arms that his clinical mind recognized as *Thaumoctopus mimicus*—swam under the alien invader and pried at one of the crab's legs, obviously trying to open the softer connecting plates at the base. Without thinking, John darted forth, pushing against the huge crustacean's carapace, bracing his feet on the bottom and lifting. The Krell flipped onto its back, its legs frantically working. An octopus held the weapon claw immobile and a second octopus grabbed the Krell's smaller arm, trying to pull it loose. John put a flippered foot down on the leg the mimic octopus was trying to restrain, thereby forcing the crab's softer plates open. He had been acting on impulse in the mere seconds the attack had taken, but his mind recoiled in wonder and terror at what he saw next. A tiny octopus no bigger than the span of his hand detached itself from where it had been riding on the mimic octopus and jetted down onto the Krell's exposed leg joint. Rings on its skin pulsated a bright neon blue and John recognized it as *Hapalochaena lunulata*, the blue-ringed octopus, one of the deadliest creatures in the sea. Its bite could kill a grown human in under a minute. John's fear urged him to lift his foot from the giant crab's leg, but a calmer voice told him to hold the course. The blue-ringed octopus crawled onto the Krell's exposed leg joint and held still for a couple of heartbeats. John imagined that it was injecting its virulent poison into the alien. The tiny cephalopod then jetted back to the mimic octopus and settled onto its skin. The mimic octopus released the Krell's leg and jetted away to rest on a coral protrusion. John lifted his foot and backed off as rapidly as he could. The other two octopuses still clung to the struggling alien, restraining its claws as its flailing legs twitched slower and slower, finally stopping. A small plume of chunky brown matter seeped from the back of the giant crab and its legs relaxed in death.

The octopus holding the weapon claw cracked the appendage loose from its arm and jetted over to John. Standing on six legs, it held the Krell's claw aloft and presented it to the human. Having worked so closely with Oliver, John was only briefly shocked. He took the claw and its weapon and held it under his arm. Not quite knowing how to thank the cephalopod, he held out his hand for the octopus to smell, hoping his gratitude was readable in his skin chemicals. The octopus reached out a single tentacle and laid it on his palm, wrapping the tip around John's wrist. They held the pose for a few seconds, then the octopus flashed a mottled brown hunting color and jetted away to settle on the sandy bottom, watching John with unreadable eyes. *So far so good*, John thought, then turned his attention to prying the ray gun free from the giant crab claw.

Gunnery Sergeant David Allen Davidson and his fellow commandoes crouched low in the Zodiac, paddling as silently as possible toward the dark outline of the atoll. Starlight and a thin crescent moon gave scant illumination. Sunrise was just a rumor on the eastern horizon. They heard the waves breaking on the shore and slipped from the small boat. A beach of white sand stretched along the inner curve of a shallow inlet, the jungle coming down almost to the water on either side of the inlet. The water this close to shore was barely waist-deep and bathtub-warm. The commandoes stayed low, trying to blend in with the small waves. At the sergeant's signal, they split up and headed toward the jungle flanking both sides of the beach. Cradling the purloined Krell ray gun, Davidson remained hunkered behind the Zodiac, guiding it toward the shore and scanning the trees and underbrush for any sign of movement. When he felt the waves pulling the craft toward the beach, he activated the noisemaker Barry had concocted for him and gave the Zodiac a final shove. The noisemaker was a kludge of a gizmo designed to delay for about a minute, then make a clacking noise. Davidson sank down into the water and moved to his left toward the dense jungle touching the sea.

The inflatable boat washed up onto the shore, making a faint shoosh as it moved across the sand. Davidson was halfway to the cover of the jungle when the noisemaker went off. The rhythmic clacking was loud in the still morning air. He had barely moved another meter when a beam of crackling red energy from the jungle found the boat. The craft exploded with a resounding pop. Moments dragged by as Davidson made his way to where the jungle vegetation hung out over the water and nestled into the concealment. Two Krell emerged onto the beach, holding their ray guns at the ready. Davidson silently lifted his alien weapon and aimed it at the giant crabs. He had not fired the ray gun before—it had been fired just once off the aft deck of the *Shanklin*, and then only by remote control—but he had watched. It did not look difficult. Before he had a chance to depress the trigger, though, four shots rang out from the dense forest flanking the beach. The Krell received two rounds each, the depleted uranium hollow points blasting alien guts out large exit wounds. *Aim for the third eye*, he had instructed the commandoes, and their aim had proven true. Both giant crabs dropped to the sand, one still twitching and reaching for something on its upper carapace ridge. Another shot and the Krell stopped moving.

Davidson gave a low whistle. Soldiers from the left flank ran out onto the beach and retrieved the ray guns from the dead Krell. The pincers of the large claws had to be pried open to free the weapons and Davidson fretted over the delay. He climbed up into the vegetation and gave two more short whistles. The two soldiers raced to him; Lieutenant Commander Amundsen and a stoic man named Johnson who he had gone through Navy Seal training with, each holding one of the alien ray guns. Davidson gave them a thumbs up. Now they had three of the powerful weapons. The two commandoes from the other flank raced across the beach, staying low. The sky was getting brighter, although the sun had not yet cracked the horizon. The individual plants of the jungle were now discernible and Sergeant Davidson was pleased to see how well the members of the strike team blended into the underbrush. He crouched on the sandy jungle floor and unfolded a laminated map as the commandoes gathered around him.

"We are here," Davidson said quietly, tapping the northern shore of the main island. "The lagoon should be a little more than a quarter mile due south. We don't know if..." He paused, holding his hand up for silence. They all heard it: a crackling of shrubbery from the direction of the beach. Sergeant Davidson grabbed the ray gun by his side and crept to the edge of the forest.

An armed Krell emerged from the jungle above the beach and skittered over to the two fallen aliens. Its eyestalks swiveled madly, searching the surrounding vegetation, while the giant crab's smaller manipulating claw poked at the spattered remains of its comrades. It reached for a rectangular piece of technology clamped to its upper carapace.

Davidson saw the movement from his concealment. He raised the ray gun and fired, hitting the Krell just above its third eye and ripping a hole in the huge crustacean. But not before it had man-aged to activate the device attached to its shell. The metal square began to flash red and let out a piercing warble. Davidson took careful aim and pressed the trigger again, blowing the device from the dead alien's carapace ridge.

He gave the "gather and retreat" signal and dashed across the beach, the others close behind him. The soft sand slowed their progress, and they dove into the cover of the jungle as a beam of red energy from the ocean blew a palm tree apart halfway up its trunk. Davidson threw himself to the ground and aimed his ray gun at the beach. Two more Krell were emerging from the surf, skit-tering onto the beach in a weird, un-crablike way. He rolled aside and another bolt of red light took out a palm tree and pieces of underbrush, melting the sand in its wake. As he ducked behind a bush, answering fire from the jungle blew away the left half of the first giant crab in a nacreous spray of red light and green fluids. Davidson instinctively pulled off another shot, frying the other Krell as it rose up out of the water. He heard the crack of gunfire off to his right—three shots in rapid succession. A ray gun's red beam arced upward, slicing the top off a tree.

Davidson retreated into the jungle, seeing Amundsen and two other commandoes in the dense forest shadows. He found a clear-ing and gave the "come to me" whistle. He was relieved to see all six other commandoes emerge from the murky vegetation. They gathered round, watching the jungle and not each other. A band of searing gold sunlight touched the tops of the tallest palms.

"One came at me from the east," Harris rasped, *sotto voce.* "Took three rounds."

They stood frozen for several seconds, listening to a tropical breeze dance through the jungle. "There will be more," Davidson said. "We have to get to the lagoon."

They retrieved the ray guns from the dead Krell on the beach and crept through the tangled tropical undergrowth as silently as possible. At one point a dirt road cut through the jungle, hardly more than tire tracks with scruffy vegetation in the middle. They paused before venturing across the open space. And a good thing they did; a Krell came around a bend in the road, moving in that unnerving forward stride that the giant crabs were capable of. Other than a subtle scritch of sand, the alien made no noise. A square piece of technology clipped to the Krell's upper shell ridge like an earring flashed blue and a golf ball-size orb atop the illuminated block appeared to be slowly rotating. Davidson held up two fingers to Amundsen and made a low/high gesture. She nodded. They fired in unison, her bolt of angry red energy destroying the flashing square device and Davidson's ripping the alien in half.

Harris tapped the sergeant on the shoulder to get his attention and spoke in a whisper. "I think that round thing was a video camera. Definitely a signaling device."

Davidson nodded, his mouth grim. "The lagoon's not far. Get the gun."

Harris pried the alien weapon from the Krell's massive claw. He stowed his rifle across his back and cradled the newly acquired alien weapon as the group advanced cautiously through the jungle. The tree cover ended abruptly, giving way to sand and scrubby grass, but the commandoes stayed in the shadow of the jungle, observing the scene. The lagoon lay tranquil in the early morning light. The newly risen sun lit the top of the jungle across the wide water, the trees still black silhouettes against the sky. Shallow water, almost colorless, stretched before them for many yards before giving way to the dark blue of the deep caldera at the center of the atoll. To their left they could barely make out in the distance the shredded walls and burned dock of the ruins of the research colony.

The seven moved toward the beach and gathered behind some hillocks of dune grass. Everyone removed their backpacks, sighing with relief. Dalegowski, a big man with the largest pack, grouped them together, checking each one. Every commando had carried at least ten pounds of high explosives; the two biggest men, Dalegowski and Spinelli, each taking twenty.

"All here," Dalegowski said.

"How soon can you have them armed and ready?" Sergeant Davidson asked.

"Three minutes," Dalegowski said.

"Question is," injected Amundsen, "how are we going to deliver them to the middle of the damn lagoon? And without those freaking crabs seeing us."

Harris spoke up. "We can go to the dock, maybe there's a boat."

"The dock is burned to the water," Johnson said acidly.

"We could build a raft with the remains of the buildings," Harris suggested.

"We'll build a raft here," Davidson said. "Plenty of fallen trees and we'll have less chance of encountering Krell."

"Yo, Gunny!" Amundsen shouted, pointing at the lagoon. "The water!"

The shallow lagoon was no longer tranquil. The once still waters rippled over a wide swath, the ripples becoming larger. A low shape rose up out of the water, then another and another in rapid succession. And the Krell poured forth.

# CHAPTER SEVENTEEN

Barry rose painfully out of his stupor. He had been stunned, but not unconscious. In a dreamlike world of excruciating paralysis he had been aware of Montgomery moving around in the *Beagle*. He remembered the slight man striking him down, his emotionless face a center point of the recollection. He remembered being tied up. Even though he had been in agony from Montgomery's blow and the subsequent shock of the stun gun, Barry had remembered something about Harry Houdini. The famous escape artist would have volunteers tie him up and then slip easily out of the rope. The trick was to clench your hands and tense your wrists. This slightly expanded the hands and wrists so that when relaxed they would return to normal size and the rope would, theoretically, become loose. Barry tried to use that knowledge, hoping that the stun gun had left him with enough muscle control. He could tell from the way he was tied that Kyle Montgomery was an expert.

He rolled onto his side, finding himself pressed up against the back of the co-pilot's chair. The pain was slowly fading and he began to gain some control over his muscles. He flexed his wrists and wiggled his fingers. The Houdini trick had worked only partially. The bindings were not what one would call loose, but neither were they tight. Barry wriggled around on the deck until he was able to get the knot snagged on the chair's footrest. After much tugging and twisting he loosened the rope enough to pull a loop over his fingers and wriggle free. He pulled one hand free of the rope and sat up, working the other hand free. *One helluva binding job*, he commented to himself. He looked over at Larry. The submarine pilot lay on his back, his hands tied in front of him at the waist. Taser barbs protruded from his chest, their thin wires leading to the compact firing device. Larry's eyes were at half-mast and looked glazed.

"Larry," Barry said hoarsely. "You awake?"

Larry's gaze came into focus and he painstakingly turned his head to Barry. "That son of a bitch."

"I can think of a lot worse things to call him," Barry commented as he got on hands and knees. "But this is a family show." He crawled over to his friend. "I'm going to take the taser barbs out first. This might hurt some." With that he jerked a barb from Larry's chest and the submarine pilot howled in pain. Barry pulled the other one out, eliciting another yelp.

"That was worse than being shot!" Larry exclaimed.

Barry smiled. "Life is suffering, my friend."

He untied Larry and they both sat up, still feeling weak, and surveyed their surroundings. An equipment locker sat open at the rear of the *Beagle*, its contents strewn across the deck. Other than that the submarine was quiet, save for the ghostlike whisper of machinery.

"He was at your control panel, then mine," Barry said. "I'm sure he put in some kind of override code that you'll have to work around. Looks like you've got your work cut out for you."

"Me? What about you?"

Their bantering was interrupted by the sound of the waterlock's outer door closing and the water begin being pumped out of the chamber. They looked at each other with surprise. "He's coming back!" Barry hissed. He scrabbled over to the scattered items from the locker and plucked a metal rod from the litter, sliding it to Larry, then pointed at the taser. "Gimme that thing!" Larry accepted the metal bar and slid the taser to his co-pilot. Barry grabbed a taser cartridge from the detritus on the floor and inserted it into the weapon. The waterlock pump stopped and the handle of the door turned. Larry and Barry tensed up, bar raised and taser aimed.

The door opened and Gina stepped out.

The sub techs gave out cries of relief. Gina pulled the mask from her face and spit out her mouthpiece. "What's going on?" she asked, seeing their weapons.

"That Kyle Montgomery guy hid in one of the equipment lockers and knocked us out with a taser," Barry blurted. "Then he left."

"Kyle?" Gina was genuinely puzzled. "He's not the type."

"He's a corporate hit man," Larry replied. "It was written all over him."

"Don't hit men kill people? I mean...he seemed like a nice guy."

"Professional disguise," Barry countered. "Too nice, if you know what I mean."

"Where did he go?" Gina asked.

"Beats me," Larry said. "I was passed out on the floor."

Gina pulled her fins off. "That's what the dolphins meant about 'strange fish.' And I saw something swimming along the deep edge of the reef. Thought it was some kind of shark, but it must have been him. Let's go get him."

"Much as I'd like to, we stay here." Larry was firm.

"But...why?"

Barry spoke up. "We have a mission to fulfill. Your pod is out there, not to mention John and his octopus. We have to be here for them."

Larry nodded. "And 'here' means right here. Montgomery is one guy. How much harm can one guy do?"

Gina looked around the sub's interior. "Apparently, quite a lot."

But she had promised to be her pod's eyes. Barry set her up with four video screens, one for each of her dolphins and one for John. He tied her communicator into the hydrophone and an external speaker while Larry cursed and groaned over his keyboard as he tried to circumvent Montgomery's lockout. Gina hated being trapped in the submarine. She wanted to be out in the reef, making a last stand with her pod and the other cetaceans. And maybe even John. Meanwhile the rational woman in the back of her head reminded her that her role aboard the *Beagle* was important, but that did little to relieve her restlessness. The images on three of the video screens swirled and jounced, and it was almost impossible to grasp what was going on. John's camera was the exception, but he was laying low, doing guerilla marksmanship. He didn't move around much, but the dolphins did. She worried that the external speakers on the *Beagle* would not be able to handle the higher frequencies of dolphin language or that her pod could not hear her or that whatever paltry information she was able to pass on was of no use. And as for all the other dolphins' understanding her, for all she knew she could metaphorically be shouting in Swahili to an army of Hungarians. And she had no way to communicate with John.

It was agonizing.

The pod had broken up, the three enhanced dolphins each taking separate prongs of the attack. It was not an orderly approach such as humans would devise; the dolphins instead worked more as a guerilla force, using the tactics of conceal and attack, but in a random pattern. It worked corralling shoals of fish or going up against a school of sharks, and it worked pretty well against the giant crabs. The overall approach was disruption and destruction.

Sheila was smaller than Gary, but she was more agile and definitely bolder. She and Nancy led the attack on the Krell's supply chain that stretched from their ship buried in a deep coral forest to the mouth of the channel to the lagoon. They each worked with separate groups of pods, rallying them to follow as they crossed the line of crabs and machines, skimming across the sandy bottom and wildly weaving through the coral heads and Krell, all the while furiously exhaling bubbles. The two female dolphins kept repeating the alien "help" and "over here" sounds they had been taught. They added a Dolphin command for the other dolphins to learn and repeat, and the other pods started chiming in with the Krell words. More and more dolphins picked up on the two Krell words and the reef echoed with distracting sound. It worked amazingly well. The giant crabs would respond to the calls, breaking ranks and slowing the progression of the line. Nancy, Sheila and their followers worked in concert, crossing the Krell supply line in several places, trying to sow confusion. The bubble curtains dissipated rapidly, but more groups of dolphins followed in succession in an attempt to keep the confusion going. All the while, Sheila was guiding her fellow dolphins with squeals and chattering, exhorting them to see the pattern and work in unison. Nancy sang with her, creating complex harmonies to amplify the message.

This was only the first step. After crossing the line of Krell and exhausting their bubble making, the dolphins would double back suddenly and strike with their blunt, hard snouts at any giant crab they saw, then twist and turn toward the surface to fill their lungs again. They sang instructions and exhortations, their voices carrying through the water. Whole pods up and down the supply line struck at the hard shells of the giant crustaceans. Some bruised their snouts and shrieked their pain into the aqueous noise. Nancy's augmented intelligence helped her see the pattern first and shouted in Dolphin to use the tactic of multiple hits, Sheila taking up the song and singing harmony. The relentless cetacean attacks evolved; many crabs were split open, stumbling in their death throes and blocking the movement of other Krell toward the lagoon. Many more were knocked aside or thrown from the machines they were guiding.

Meanwhile the orcas lived up to their moniker as killer whales. While less agile than their dolphin cousins, they used their size and mass as hammer blows against the giant crabs. They would charge the stream of Krell, bashing aside the aliens' undersea tractors, crushing Krell in their jaws and hitting others with their tails as they barged across the supply line. One orca, an old and scarred male whose cetacean name translated loosely to Warrior With A Strong Tail And No Fear, attacked the Krell supply line directly. He dove straight into the column of vehicles and giant crabs, bashing and crushing as he went. He managed to tear through a hundred meters of Krell and their machinery before being brought down by alien ray gun blasts. He fought and thrashed to the last as coruscating bolts of energy tore through his flesh. And when he finally died, his body blocked the avenue, forcing the Krell line to splinter and expose themselves to attack as they moved around his corpse. The other orcas sang a song of grief and triumph, both lamentation and celebration, into the tropical waters. The dolphins picked it up and sang their variations of it, dedicating their efforts to Warrior With No Fear. The ocean rang with song.

The Krell fought back, of course. The water was electric with their ray gun blasts. The Krell were an organized and intelligent race, steeped in genetic memory such that they saw the marine mammals' strategy and counter-strategized accordingly. The massive crabs arranged themselves in circles of five to seven, forming defense and attack groups that could see in all directions. They shot wildly into the curtains of bubbles, hitting Krell and dolphin alike. They would answer the dolphin mimicking of Krell sounds with demands for response. The ruse began to lose its effectiveness and the tropical water ran murky with bits of blood and gore. Sheila saw how the giant crabs grouped and she shouted this information into the sea for others to hear. There did not appear to be any way to effectively attack the circles of crabs, though several pods tried. Bubbles were useless in confusing the aliens. Dolphins circling the Krell battle formations were easy targets and frontal attacks were suicidal. The circles of Krell fought efficiently, blasting at dolphins with their bolts of red energy, all the while edging toward and then into the line of giant space crabs making their way to the lagoon. The Krell were an ancient warrior race and their alien minds knew how to react to attacks, knew with thousands of years of genetic memory about forays and feints and fighting. They had seen many battles and were ready for the cetacean attacks.

What the Krell were not ready for were octopuses.

Time disappeared for John Rauchenberg. He was in a world of water, fighting with friendly aliens against enemy aliens. The reef, never deeper than six meters and often as shallow as two, brightened with the light of the oncoming day, but John barely noticed. All he saw were octopuses, hundreds of them. And alien crabs. Evidently many of the eggs had hatched and baby Krell were everywhere, scuttling among their oversize counterparts. Dolphins darted through the reef, spewing their curtains of bubbling confusion and filling the sea with their squeals and clicks. But John barely noticed them; he was in octopus heaven. Or hell. He was, after all, in the middle of battle and the water was strewn with blasted bits of Krell and dolphin and an occasional dead cephalopod. He saw more *Thaumoctopus mimicus*, some with their blue-ringed companions. He also spotted a great many *Octopus cyanea*, a Pacific reef dweller, as well as a lot of the smaller *Octopus vulgaris*.

What he did not see was any pattern of attack; no military formations or coordinated tactics. Two, three, sometimes five octopuses would attack a Krell. Sometimes the giant crab would prevail, shaking the cephalopods off, but usually the octopuses would triumph, tearing the big crustacean apart or forcing it open to receive octopus venom. Some octopuses gorged on tender young Krell, some clung to coral heads, sucking down the Krell eggs. Some disappeared into their camouflage, becoming rocks or blobs of coral, then jetting out to attack the invaders. The fact that the octopus attack was not organized was its strength. That and their sheer numbers. The Krell had no front to attack, no tactic to conquer. They could only try to dodge octopus or cetacean attacks. Many Krell joined the march into the lagoon while their the others protected the retreat.

John wondered how he was going to get Oliver's car to him. Between trying to stay alive, occasionally firing the clumsy alien ray gun, and marveling at the number and ferociousness of the cephalopods around him, he suspected that his chances of finding Oliver, minute as they were, would improve infinitesimally if he stayed in one place. So he backed himself up into a shallow niche in a wall of coral.

The water was becoming murky from the gore of battle, but John could see the Krell battle strategy evolving, the oversized crustaceans forming into defensive circles. He saw that this was definitely thwarting any frontal assault from the dolphins and octopuses. John abandoned the safety of his niche and positioned himself on top of his wall of coral. He lay prone and aimed his ray gun at a circle of Krell. He swept the destructive red beam across the crabs, cutting one in half and blowing others to pieces. Waiting octopuses used the opportunity to move into the center of the broken circle and attack en masse. Random dolphins raced between the reef and the alien crabs, leaving curtains of bubbles in their wake and battering the Krell. The giant crabs fired wildly at them, striking only a very few of the sea mammals. John waited for a wall of bubbles to disperse before turning his weapon on another circle of giant crabs, this one farther away. He moved the crimson destruction across the Krell and was rewarded to see more octopuses attack the giant crabs. But another group of Krell had pinpointed John's position and he barely escaped the sizzling bolt of energy that ripped through the reef not a meter to his left. He retreated back to his niche in the coral wall and watched the battle unfold.

John saw the octopuses observe and learn. When first they glommed onto a Krell ray gun and began shooting, the weapon fire was wild and often without target. But octopuses have an excellent learning curve. They watched each other's successes and failures. Soon there were octopuses camouflaged among the coral and seaweed, firing down on Krell circles. They learned that resting the ray guns on something solid improved their aim, learned how to change firing positions when the massive crabs fired back, learned to lie in wait and burst into the center of the Krell defensive circles. The fighting appeared to be about even; the Krell were hardened fighters, used to battle, while the ragtag octopus forces had no actual strategy and, not having skeletons, had a hard time with the bulky ray guns. More giant crabs melted into the well-protected line of aliens retreating into the lagoon.

At one point a dolphin flashed by John, then doubled back and stopped in front of him. The cetacean bombarded him with high pitched squeals and chitters, but it was the camera attached to its fin that drew John's attention. This was one from Gina's pod—his pod, too—although he could not tell which dolphin it was. He touched his hand to his chest, then reached out with that hand to the dolphin. The dolphin rubbed its snout against his hand, gave another squeal, then dashed away into the underwater melee, leaving John to wonder what to do next. He nestled back into the coral, ray gun at the ready.

After an interminable few minutes an octopus jetted from behind a nearby coral head and came toward him. A large octopus. It was holding a ray gun and blue ripples ran up and down its tentacles. John's heart was in his throat. He made the "kisses" sign as the cephalopod neared. The octopus darted forward and wrapped its arms around the marine biologist. John knew that nobody should ever get close to an octopus's mouth, that the beak could tear through flesh and inject poison, but this felt perfect. He relaxed into Oliver's embrace and filled his mind with love for his blue-blooded friend. Oliver's touch was firm yet gentle and John felt he could sense the octopus's delight. They did not hold the embrace for long. Oliver detached and sank to the bottom, reaching out an arm to touch the bag on John's back.

John untied the bag and removed the MIT crank car that Oliver had constructed back in California. At the sight of the rolling platform, the octopus turned fire engine red and yellow dots danced across his skin. He climbed onto the little car and settled the ray gun beside him. Oliver reached out two tentacles and wrapped them around John's shins. John reached down and gently ran his hand across Oliver's mantle. Cephalopods are not big on goodbyes. The octopus pulled his two tentacles in, turned the color of the sandy reef floor, and sped off.

Oliver was tired of swimming, happy to be at the helm of his rapid little crank car. Far less effort. He drove with a purpose. An idea had been gelling in his mind for some time, flashing like a shoal of fish in the sunlight, growing like the scent of prey in moving water: a plan to infiltrate the central lagoon.

The reef was a scattered landscape of broken coral and dead creatures. Most of them were the big crabs, but there were a lot of dolphins and blasted octopuses. Oliver remembered seeing a particular Krell casualty and used his octopusian memory to find it. The giant crab had been cut in half equatorially. The bottom half of the alien was a blasted splatter of chitin and greenish flesh against the coral, but the top half was pretty much intact, and the eyestalks had not been torn loose by some zealous cephalopod.

Oliver lifted one side of the carapace and slowly drove his car underneath. It took some adjusting, but quite soon Oliver had the upper portion of the Krell held up over his head and tilted back slightly so he could see out the front. The crab's shell was surprisingly light but front-heavy. Like an athlete, Oliver the octopus settled into a strength position, sitting on his ray gun to keep it from slipping off the car. Two arms cranked the car's drive, two arms steered, and four arms balanced the Krell's carapace.

Oliver cranked his vehicle at a moderate pace, getting used to the big clumsy shell he was holding up. He headed toward where he estimated the caravan of lagoon-bound giant crabs to be, careful not to catch the shell on the coral as he wound his way through the underwater battleground. Oliver assumed that the blurry moving line he was approaching was the path of the Krell. The smell of the water told him more. It was heavy with crab, but he also smelled their machines and sensed their movement through the feel of the sand under his wheeled platform.

A big Krell tractor growled by, its trailer piled high with packages. Oliver slipped in behind the trailer and in front of another tractor. He moved to the side of the trailer, obscuring the second tractor's view. The pace was brisk for Oliver, but not tiring. He watched the coral alongside the pathway rise up and suddenly he was in a channel cut from the living reef. It had been excavated by humans to allow boats to enter the lagoon, so the sides were rough and overgrown. But the bottom was coral and sand compressed almost to a tarmac by the passage of many Krell. Up ahead, a metal arch spanned the channel, blue lights on the front flashing every time a Krell passed under it. Oliver's instinct was to hesitate, but he dared not slacken his pace. A dolphin flashed under the arch, leaving a curtain of bubbles. The lights on the arch pulsed red and automatic weaponry shot at the departing cetacean, missing the twirling target. The next Krell passed under the arch and the light flashed blue. Then it was Oliver's turn.

Oliver did the octopus equivalent of holding his breath as he passed beneath the arch.

Blue light flashed overhead, tinting the pathway.

He was in.

# CHAPTER EIGHTEEN

Sergeant Davidson had lost three men to the Krell: Spinelli, the lanky ex-Seal recruited from kitchen duties; Miller, the weapons expert and excellent sniper; and Johnson, the sergeant's friend from their Seal training. The attack from the lagoon had been brutal. Dozens of giant crabs had come ashore, firing their deadly red bolts of energy. The commandoes had retreated to the jungle for cover. They did not dig in, but hurried from position to position in an effort to evade the weapons fire and confuse the Krell. A depleted uranium round or return fire from a captured alien weapon would cut down one of the massive crustaceans, and several would concentrate their fire on the area the humans had attacked from, only to be shot down with more DU rounds and bolts of energy from another location. Sometimes a Krell warrior would sweep the overgrown jungle forest with a coruscating beam of destruction, but the humans would have moved to a new location and would cut down the giant crab. Spinelli and Miller were both caught in the first few ray gun sweeps, sliced apart by the deadly red energy. Johnson was caught between two alien barrages, but managed to kill seven Krell before succumbing to crossfire. A furious Lieutenant Commander Amundsen immediately took out the remaining aliens by sweeping the shallow water with a sustained bolt from her ray gun. No more giant crabs came out of the lagoon. The four remaining commandoes scurried into the jungle.

They hunkered in the overgrown ruin of a World War Two airplane, its insignia long since given over to vegetation and rust. Speaking in furtive whispers, they concocted a plan: build a raft from three or four downed palm trees, take it out to the middle of the lagoon, and drop the explosives onto whatever thing the Krell were constructing out in the deep water. Pure suicide mission. Davidson and Harris would muscle the palm tree trunks, Amundsen would design and build paddles, and Dalegowski would look after the explosives and any captured ray guns. They crept from the wreckage and set to their tasks, aware that at any moment more killer crabs could emerge from the lagoon.

Harris had just finished helping Davidson drag a palm trunk down to the water's edge when Dalegowski called him over.

"You're good with tech," the big man said. "Check this out." Dalegowski took a ray gun from the pile of three in front of him and flipped it over. "There's this button here on the base." He indicated an unmarked depression on the underside of the weapon's stock. "I pushed it and nothing happens."

"Maybe it releases the ammunition or the power source or something," Harris replied.

"Nothing clicked or moved when I pushed it."

Harris bent in for a closer look. "Maybe it's meant to be used to give another control a secondary function."

"You're such a tech geek," Dalegowski smiled. "I love it." He depressed the button again and tried moving the firing trigger forward with no success. When he moved the firing trigger backwards, however, it gave a soft 'click' and began to blink red. He and Harris raised eyebrows at each other.

It was at that moment that Amundsen threw down the crude paddle she was fashioning and yelled, "Yo! Lagoon!"

The surface of the water began to ripple, heralding the arrival of more Krell fighters. Harris and Davidson followed Amundsen's lead and rained red beams of destruction on the Krell as they emerged from the water. Dalegowski, however, remained fixated on the flashing red trigger button of the ray gun he held in his lap. He muttered an expletive, then leapt to his feet and ran, cursing, onto the beach, holding the Krell ray gun by the barrel. "It's a bomb!" he yelled and threw the weapon overhand with all his strength. The ray gun spun end over end out over the water churning with Krell and disappeared into the lagoon with a disappointing splash.

Dalegowski paused to watch the weapon tumble to its rendezvous with the water. That was his fatal mistake. A giant crab rose from the water and cut him in half with a blast of crackling red light. The commandoes answered with furious fire, sweeping destructive energies across the attacking aliens before dodging for cover. It was a losing proposition; the shallow water was alive with big alien crabs. The three remaining human warriors skittered from dune to hummock, killing as many Krell as they could. But the giant crabs kept coming. Minutes dragged on seemingly forever.

Then, with a flash of bright light and the *whump* of a massive fist, the shallow waters of the lagoon shot up into the sky.

Oliver could not see much from under the carapace he held over his head for camouflage. But he saw the tractor he was traveling alongside reach the end of the man-made channel and turn left to descend down a ramp into deeper water. The concealed octopus veered to his right, following a secondary road on the shallow rim at the edge of the widening lagoon. A few Krell carrying items or pulling carts were also moving to the right and Oliver merged with the flow, hoping, in his cautious octopus way, not to be noticed. A shallow mount in the center of the widening channel was at the height of the coral rim and bristled with strange alien technology. He was again scanned and again passed muster. The path rounded a bulge in the side of the lagoon and the Krell security station fell out of sight. Oliver looked around for a place to ditch his camouflage.

A wide shelf on the edge of a drop-off into the lagoon presented itself. Packages were being off-loaded and sorted here before being taken to greater depths. A jumble of crumpled packaging and various detritus was piled away from the edge and Oliver insinuated the upper remains of the dead Krell under the mound of refuse. The octopus, feeling a bit worn from his efforts so far, treated himself to a few bites of delicious crab meat from the underside of the concealing carapace. He snugged his crank car into a niche in the reef. Leaving the ray gun behind, Oliver crept out onto the pile of discarded debris and took in the scene before him.

A huge tower of flattened spheres loomed in the center of the lagoon, gleaming with blue and red lights. Crablike machines, tiny at this distance, crawled over the outside. The edifice was still under construction. Krell and their machinery swam through the busy water, bringing parts to the upper floors.

Disguised as a crumpled piece of packaging, Oliver drifted out toward the center of the lagoon. The atoll was the weathered and coral-encrusted remains of a volcano, the central lagoon being its collapsed caldera. The bottom of the lagoon was thirty to sixty meters in places. He saw vague shapes down in the dim deep, large shapes, arranged in rows. War machines. Oliver lifted his gaze to the tower of flattened spheres in the center of the lagoon.

He jetted toward what seemed to be the main entrance, a wide opening shining with bluish light about fifteen meters below the surface of the water and connected to a bridge brimming with giant crabs coming and going. As he got closer, Oliver saw that the majority of them carried weapons. He tasted metal in the water and the electrical tang that came from the aliens' energy tools. The water was warmer than it should be at this depth and Oliver felt the rumble of machinery. He closed in on the large portal and attached himself to the hull of the structure just above the door, becoming the color of the metal. The surface had the chalky taste of an alien ray gun and it vibrated under him. Since he was basically a mass of intelligent gelatin, Oliver was able to insinuate just one eye over the top of the door and get a look into the fortress.

A long, straight, oval-shaped hallway led far into the structure. Krell flowed in on the right and out on the left. Oliver observed that many of the big crabs passing beneath him on the right were not armed. He watched the unarmed crabs scrabbling down the hall turn right into a doorway. Shadowy forms of giant crustaceans emerged from another doorway a few meters on, each now carrying a weapon, and joining their comrades on the left side of the hallway. *This*, he reasoned, *must be where they kept the ray guns.*

The deep bark of a distant explosion came through the water. Oliver quickly withdrew his eye from the doorway and flattened himself against the alien metal. A compression wave pushed against him, then was gone. The Krell went crazy, many turning toward the apparent explosion and pointing with their smaller claws, others hurrying about excitedly.

Octopuses may be cautious, but they are also immensely curious. The compression wave came from the north shore of the lagoon, the area where the humans had said they would attack. Oliver's curiosity led him in that direction.

The remaining three commandoes were drenched and the beach was littered with pieces of alien crab. Sergeant Davidson realized that they had a precious few minutes before the enemy could send in reinforcements. He hoped that Krell central command would assume the explosion killed the humans. Not likely, though. And they would inevitably be sending in more soldiers to investigate.

Davidson, Harris and Amundsen saw to their fallen comrades first. Each soldier carried a plastic poncho as part of the survival packet and they spread them out to receive the shattered remains of their comrades. They solemnly tied the bundles shut, not saying a word. Davidson rose to his feet.

"We go on with the mission." He paused to take in the moment. "I think Gladys and I can get a few logs together. Dennis, you're a techie guy. You've got ray gun duty." He clapped his hands. "Let's go!"

Davidson and Amundsen headed for the jungle while Harris went through the debris on the beach looking for undamaged ray guns. He found three and was down at the water's edge prying another loose when he saw a ripple near shore. He leapt to his feet, weapon at the ready. *Wait until they come up out of the water*, he told himself. *But don't wait too long.* What he saw next took several seconds to register. At first he thought it was a secondary ripple in the water, but then he recognized the tips of four tentacles waving above the lagoon's surface. *Could it be?* he asked himself. Harris advanced into the shallow water until it was just past his knees. He stuck a hand into the water, wiggling his fingers, and felt a light touch on the back of his hand, then a tentacle around his wrist. The urge to panic was overshadowed by his amazement. The top of a large octopus, its skin the color of sand, rose up out of the water and the cephalopod's cool eyes regarded him.

"Oliver?" Harris asked. "Is that you?"

He was answered with a pulsing squeeze of the tentacle on his wrist and the mantle of the octopus briefly rippled blue.

Extreme stress can lead to enhanced mental states. Standing knee deep in warm tropical water, fresh from intense, bloody fighting with inhuman alien invaders, and having just gathered the remains of his comrades in battle, Dennis Harris's mind rose into an epiphany. Here he was holding hands with an alien creature, but one that was a fellow Earthling, a fellow traveler on this beleaguered planet. He felt a deep connection with Oliver's intelligence and companionship. At this height of consciousness a plan of sorts sprang into Harris's mind.

"Oliver," he said solemnly. "I want to show you something. Do you understand? Teach." The octopus rippled blue again and gave a brief squeeze to Harris's wrist, then released his grip.

Harris displayed the Krell ray gun he still carried. "You know what this is, right?" Oliver flashed blue twice. Harris took that as a yes. He had watched Dalegowski earlier as he had fiddled with a ray gun. There was a small depression on the underside of the weapon's stock, a round inset without light or marking. In his fiddling, Dalegowski had pushed his finger into the inset and then slid the firing button backward, turning the ray gun into a bomb. It took about five to seven minutes to detonate.

Harris showed the procedure to Oliver, accompanying his explanation with mimed gestures and sound effects. He held up five fingers and said five minutes, hoping that the octopus knew the word "minutes." He repeated everything several times, then gazed intently at the unblinking eyes of the cephalopod, hoping that there had been understanding. Oliver digested what he had been shown for long seconds, then flashed blue twice. He took the weapon from Harris and mimed what he had learned, pointing at the inset on the weapon's underside and twirling a tentacle tip around the firing button, then shooting four tentacles straight up out of the water in an octopusian miming of an explosion.

Harris was awestruck. He had had a meeting of the minds with an octopus, an intelligence he had always discounted. The experience was both humbling and uplifting. Oliver held the ray gun out to Harris, who took the proffered weapon and mumbled a thank you. The octopus turned brick red, then disappeared under the water. Harris slogged back up onto the beach and took his pile of ray guns to the edge of the jungle where Davidson was helping Amundsen lash palm tree logs together.

"You wouldn't believe what just happened to me," Harris said. "We need to get out of here. Fast."

Sergeant Davidson was not having it. "We need to finish this damn raft and drop our explosives. Did you figure out how Dalegowski made the ray gun bomb?"

"Yes. And I taught it to Oliver the octopus."

Amundsen joined Davidson in giving Harris a quizzical look. He told them about his interaction with Oliver in the lagoon.

"So the octopus just took one of our ray guns and left?" Davidson asked.

"He gave the weapon back, Dave. I think we should let him do his thing."

"Whatever that is," Davidson snorted. "How many Krell guns do we have?"

"Altogether, seven. But we don't really know what's out there or if we have enough ordnance to make a difference. I think we should trust Oliver."

Davidson scowled. "You want me to trust a fish?"

"He's an octopus," Harris replied. "A very smart octopus. He figured a way to get into the lagoon. And he found us. Oliver's down there and he can see what's going on. I say we trust him."

"He's right," Amundsen said firmly. Davidson turned to face her, his brow still angry. "If we stay and finish the raft, we all die," she continued, her voice hardening "We have seven alien weapons that the Pentagon needs to see. The beach isn't far. I agree with Dennis: trust the octopus."

Sergeant Davidson looked from one to the other, then out at the lagoon. He nodded.

Gina was getting more and more restless. The video feeds from Nancy and Sheila were all but indecipherable. She tried to relay enemy positions as best she could in Dolphin, doubting that it was doing any good. She frowned and squirmed in her seat.

It was Gary's video feed that was the most troubling. He had positioned himself near the mouth of the man-made channel leading into the lagoon and was leading five octopuses in guerilla attacks on the Krell convoy. Their victories were hit and miss, mostly miss, but the effort did disrupt the flow of giant crabs into the lagoon. The video was choppy and confusing. Her heart was in her throat whenever she looked at Gary's screen.

Suddenly a giant crab loomed on Gary's video feed, there was a jumble of in-close wrestling, and the camera was torn loose from Gary's fin. It drifted downward and snagged on a branch of coral, aimed down at the sandy bottom. This was too much for Gina.

"I'm going out," she declared, rising from her seat. The look on her face was so dark and determined that neither Larry nor Barry said anything. They gave her the thumbs up. She gave them a nod, then stepped into the waterlock.

Frssk F'tig barely made it to the spaceship. Travelling through the coral was difficult at best. The True Race was falling behind in battle, and he knew that the ship must be readied. Red bolts from the True Race's *ardnls* filled the water, strange multi-armed creatures that seemed to come from nowhere tore members of the True Race apart, and there were many calls to come help, plus an occasional oddly accented recognition syllable. It was almost impossible to tell if the calls were from the True Race or the attacking oceanic animals. It was chaos, not warfare, and Frssk F'tig could find no corollary in his deep genetic memory. He met up with a few other warriors and they headed toward the deeper water where the spaceship was moored. They commandeered a cargo transport vehicle and were making good time when a huge whale smashed into the machine, throwing Frssk F'tig into the reef and crushing everyone on board. The sea rang with the animal's polysonic cacophony. Frssk F'tig held himself still amid the jagged coral heads until the whale departed, its tail brushing the smashed cargo transport aside. Frssk F'tig still held his *ardnl* in his fighting claw, but had not fired it. It was not cowardice—the True Race had no such emotion—it was just that Frssk F'tig had no strategy for a situation he found incomprehensible.

He scrabbled among the winding coral corridors paralleling the main road, avoiding any conflict. He encountered neither whales nor any of the multi-armed monstrosities. Getting to the spaceship was his overriding goal. From there he could fulfill his overview role and work toward some sort of counter-attack and/or departure. He detoured around the massive carcass of one of the attacking whales and ran as fast as his legs would carry him to the deeper bowl where the spaceship lay. He tapped the code to open the bay door and ducked in, hitting the "rapid shut" control just inside.

And he was in the ship. Frssk F'tig breathed the Krell equivalent of a sigh of relief. No time to waste, though. As one of the overview caste, Frssk F'tig was expected to take control in extreme situations. He headed to the control room and reached immediate consensus with the skeleton crew that they must ready the ship for takeoff. He sent two of the crew outside to release the anchors that held the ship to the sea floor. Others he set to awakening the flight engines and the stardrive algorithm. Two of the medical caste were onboard and Frssk F'tig gave them the task of bringing the flight crew out of stasis, a process that would take some time. He reported in to the headquarters structure in the lagoon and got only chaos on the radio. Frssk F'tig checked on the status of the war machines being assembled at the bottom of the lagoon. Two were fully operational and they were currently being powered up and assigned crews. Twenty-five more could be made operational by tomorrow and over two hundred others in the coming days. The fighting was not only disrupting the flow of supplies into the lagoon, but the sea creatures were actually beating the True Race. He communicated his concerns to headquarters, but again received no reply.

Oliver was excited and his blue blood pulsed with purpose. As he jetted rapidly toward the central megastructure, his myriad synapses sang in unison. An explosion! He knew what those were and regarded them with dread and fascination. Plans formed in his network of octopus brains. Bold plans. Plans that threw caution to the tide.

Many of the giant crabs were swimming toward the beach he had just left. Far below, the dim shapes at the bottom of the lagoon were beginning to show flashing lights. As he closed in on the entrance to the central structure, Oliver noted that the Krell moved with a new sense of urgency. He landed above the wide portal, again becoming the color of the metal, and peeked into the bustling hallway. Few Krell were scuttling into the tunnel, but many were coming out. He watched the doorway down the hallway on the right where he had seen the giant crabs go to get weapons. No crabs entered or exited as he watched. Oliver was intent on reaching that doorway; unfortunately, the smooth walls of the hallway offered no chance of concealment and there were no carts or machines entering for him to use as cover. He gathered his resolve, filled his mantle with water and jetted as fast as he could along the ceiling of the corridor, angling his siphon to jet himself through the desired doorway.

Oliver was, of course, noticed by the line of Krell he flew above. He released a cloud of ink just before he entered the weapons room, hoping to buy himself a few seconds. The chamber he found himself in was all that he had expected and more. The walls were lined two tiers high with the alien ray gun niches, half of them empty. At the far end, the chamber curved around to the left, no doubt leading to more weapons and the door he had seen armed Krell emerging from. Oliver jetted halfway down the narrow room and ducked into one of the empty niches. There he used every ounce of his mimicking magic to become one of the ray guns: he stuck his tentacles straight up and rested the big, blobby part of his mantle on the bottom of the niche. He turned the color of the alien metal, willing his skin to form faux controls on the stock.

A stream of armed Krell stormed through the weapons room, eyestalks swiveling, not noticing the camouflaged octopus in the weapons rack. After the last had passed, Oliver remained motionless. Finally, a very large alien, its carapace crest studded with much jewelry and tech, slowly walked through, eyestalks scanning the room. Its gaze passed right over Oliver-the-ray-gun, and the big crab trundled on. Oliver slid from his hiding place and hurried around the bend in the room. The long room was lined with more weapons.

The enhanced Giant Pacific Octopus pulled a ray gun from its niche and looked at it intently, letting his eight arms lightly touch the firing button and the depression on the bottom of the stock. His next actions would take concentration and he needed all his arms, all his brains, working in unison. He put the ray gun back in its niche and took the octopus equivalent of a deep breath.

Oliver stretched out all eight tentacles to four of the alien weapons, two tentacles to each ray gun. He hung there for a long second, spanning the corridor and feeling the controls on each of the four ray guns, summoning his muscle memory. The octopus simultaneously set all four to bomb mode. He jetted slightly forward and did the same to four more. Then four more. He was getting faster. He was just finishing arming the tenth set of four when he felt the hot sting of a blast of red energy ricocheting off the ceiling just over his head. The sizzling bolt caromed off the walls, striking a dormant ray gun and bursting the stock open. Dark green liquid swirled out of the ruptured weapon.

Oliver grabbed a ray gun. Without aiming he fired at the Krell crowding around the corner. Oliver swept them with a crimson beam of death. He jetted for the door, leaving a cloud of ink behind. Turning to the exit he saw a big Krell block the opening and begin lifting its weapon. But Oliver was faster, sending a blast straight through the giant crustacean. It collapsed, its corpse blocking almost the entire doorway. Under normal circumstances, like not being trapped in an alien fortress surrounded by hundreds of armed space crabs, it would have been easy for the octopus to slip out through pretty much any size opening. Oliver could have made it past the fallen crab, but the ray gun would not fit. Another two energy bolts hit the dead Krell and Oliver looked back down the narrow room. It was filled with huge crabs rushing toward him. The one in front fired its ray gun again and Oliver realized that they would tear him to pieces before he could slither through the jagged opening. In a flash, he made his decision.

He pointed the ray gun at the oncoming Krell and depressed the trigger. Then he used his powerful beak to bite his arm off. The tentacle continued firing at the advancing aliens, sticking with its powerful sucker cups to the shell of the dead Krell in the doorway as the rest of Oliver retreated. The severed appendage swept its weapon fire across the room as if it had a mind of its own, which it actually did, having been part of Oliver's networked brain. On its own, the tentacle could have been cogent in a reactive, octopusian sense for an hour or more. Its immediate life span was much shorter though. Slowing the Krell advance with its random fire while the rest of the octopus oozed over the giant dead space crab and out into the main corridor was a Pyrrhic victory for the brave tentacle. It was eventually blasted to pieces, all the while firing bolt after bolt of deadly red energy at its attackers.

Oliver did not see the fate of his sacrificed arm. He jetted down the corridor along the ceiling, trailing blue blood behind him. Already his musculature was rallying to cut off the leakage. The pain of his self-amputation put his entire system on high alert and he used the panic chemicals to propel himself down the metal corridor and out into the dimmer water of the lagoon. He brought his concentration to the fore and jetted with all his might toward the shelf where he had left his tentacle-cranked car. It was a long way and very tiring, but Oliver knew that the explosion would come soon. His survival reflexes kicked into overdrive.

Kyle Montgomery hugged the contour of the atoll's coral cliff, holding at a depth of twelve meters. It was a long swim to the deep coral bowl where the Krell ship was anchored. He had taken a booster pill, a methamphetamine analog that Strategic Design was experimenting with, before leaving the *Beagle*. The drug was much less jangling than the jagged little pill first invented by Nazi Germany. The methamphetamine analog gave him power and endurance, but he was careful to dole these assets out carefully on his way to the Krell ship. He saved his energies for whatever else might come his way.

Montgomery was guided by his intuition. He followed the old adage of planning an operation down to a fare-thee-well, then going forth and winging it. The diversion that the octopuses and dolphins and Navy goons were providing fit perfectly into his scheme. The Krell's attention would be focused on the shallow water conflict, leaving their spaceship relatively isolated. Find the ship, take photos, make contact with the alien crabs if possible, then get the hell out—with samples of Krell technology, if possible. Improvisation in dicey situations was Kyle's forte. He swam steadily on while whales and dolphins darted back and forth above him. Chunks of dead bodies, both alien and Terran, occasionally fell past him on their way to the ocean depths. The high-tech diving gear provided by Strategic Design pumped extra oxygen into his system. Kyle Montgomery felt exultant and scintillating, on his way to a grand meeting with Destiny.

The reef dipped down and Kyle saw the deeper blue of the edge of the bowl that held the spaceship. Turning on the low-light setting built into his mask, he swooped over the edge. The sides of the bowl sloped steeply downward. Kyle had memorized a map of the coral jungle at the bottom of the depression and swam in the direction he knew the spacecraft to be. Blue light shone dimly in the near distance. Montgomery slowed and approached cautiously. He came within several yards of the looming vessel and hid behind a mass of coral to assess the situation. He switched his breather mechanism over to internal so his diving gear would not release an incriminating column of bubbles.

A string of blue lights illuminated the lower part of the Krell spaceship, the trail of light disappearing around the curve of the ship in each direction. Directly in front of him was a large metal protrusion that dug down into the sea floor, anchoring the spaceship. He saw another anchor where the edge of the ship curved away to the right. Two Krell were working at un-deploying the nearest metal claw and wrestling it back into the body of the spaceship. Kyle took many pictures of the process, zooming in on the mechanism itself. He noticed that the alien crabs were not carrying ray guns, instead needing their larger claws for the heavy work. The

Krell workers got the first anchor out of the coral and back into its bay, closing a panel over it. Montgomery remembered that the dolphins' video had shown a large cargo door on the opposite side of the ship. A lot of light had poured out of that door but he did not see any such illumination now. Thc two giant alien crabs moved to the right toward the next anchor. Kyle swam left.

Oliver swooped up onto the shelf at the edge of the lagoon and dove into the pile of debris. Only one Krell on the cargo crew was armed and it fired wildly into the trash pile. Oliver found his crank car and settled onto it, two arms on the steering bar, two holding him to the floor, and the remaining three arms on the crank mechanism. Without hesitation he threw all his strength into turning the crank and the little platform burst from the trash and careened around the corner, evading the guard Krell's ray gun blasts. Not many of the giant crabs were coming along the path, and those that were, Oliver either avoided or knocked aside. He was racing headlong into the oncoming traffic. The lights on the security post in the middle of the wide channel went red as he sped by, but it did not fire on him. The dodging became easier when he reached the main channel, weaving his way among churning tractors and startled Krell. The traffic was much more sparse than when he had entered the lagoon. The entry arch loomed ahead. Red lights flashed and weaponry tried tracking him as he wove through the traffic. Oliver, acting on instinct, ducked beneath an oncoming trailer as the sentry weapons fired. The trailer was destroyed, but he managed to zig and zag through the light traffic and past the archway. Another bolt of crimson destruction took out a lone Krell he was going around.

The end of the channel was just ahead. Oliver hoped reef would shield him from the upcoming explosion.

John leaned back into his coral niche and checked his air; it was only half gone. He felt a need to join the battle, but the rational voice in his head told him that he was just a clumsy human with heavy scuba tanks and limited vision. John reminded himself that he had already killed nine giant space crabs and wounded at least a dozen more, and that maybe he should reward himself with some rest. Oliver had sped off on his crank car a few minutes ago, obviously on a mission. John was waiting to see what would happen next, trying to decide whether to ignore his fatigue and join the fight again.

As he wallowed in indecision, Gina showed up. She was on the back of a dolphin, holding onto its dorsal fin and carrying a ray gun in her right hand. She looked like Neptune's Amazon granddaughter. She was accompanied by another dolphin. John was able to maintain just enough awareness not to let his jaw drop open and lose his mouthpiece. The dolphin she was on reared up and chittered at him. The other dolphin—he assumed it was Sheila—positioned itself in front of him and made calm gurgling noises. Gina gestured at John to come out and grab the dolphin's dorsal fin. Which he did, remembering to bring his ray gun.

They took off at a breakneck speed and John almost lost his grip. The dolphins surfaced briefly for breath, then dove again to weave their way through the twisting avenues of coral, heading for the channel that led into the lagoon. They encountered a few giant alien crabs, but their numbers appeared to be dwindling. Gina blasted the first lone Krell they encountered and John took out one that came upon them suddenly from the left. They spotted a circle of armed crustaceans moving in the same direction, but many yards away. The Krell group noticed the humans as well but did not get a chance to attack because octopuses were suddenly springing from the coral and the sand to rip and tear at the frantic aliens. Gina and John raced on, Atlantean warriors riding their cetacean steeds.

They found Gary floating listlessly in a shallow coral bowl, struggling to keep his blowhole above water. He was surrounded by vigilant octopuses who reared up as John and Gina approached. A squeal from Gary calmed them. The two humans let go of their ocean steeds, and Sheila and Nancy immediately flanked Gary, speaking to him in their high-pitched dolphin language and supporting him at the surface so he could breathe. Gina dropped her weapon and swam to the wounded dolphin, touching him gently on his snout. Gary had gashes and cuts on his sides, some of them leaking blood into the tropical water. His left fin was the worst; half of it was gone. The edge of what remained of the fin was cauterized but still oozing blood. The wound was not mortal, but he needed medical care—and soon. Gina mimed carrying the wounded mammal to the submarine and John nodded his agreement. John laid his ray gun on the coral and held up a finger for "wait a sec." He swam over to the high edge that separated the coral bowl from the avenue into the lagoon and cautiously peeked over the jagged wall.

Traffic in the channel was sparse; only a few scrabbling Krell so intent on getting into the lagoon that they did not notice John. Suddenly, Oliver burst into view from the direction of the lagoon, his little car wildly careening among the giant crabs. The octopus leapt from his speeding vehicle and it continued on, crashing into the wall. He jetted toward John, flashing fire engine red, and trailed a tentacle tip across John's cheek as he sped toward Gina. Something was very urgent. She did not notice the octopus until he was upon her and reflexively held up her arm to shield herself. It was her left and Oliver grabbed at her forearm, frantically jabbing at the keyboard. Her rational mind kicked in and she relaxed, letting him work the communicator. The speaker on her shoulder squealed loudly, a penetrating sound, simple in structure. Gina looked at John, wide-eyed, and circled her forefinger over her head; the signal for retreat. John and Gina each put an arm under Gary and swam as fast as they could in the direction of the *Beagle*. Nancy and Sheila flanked them, cooing support to their injured podmate. Oliver flashed an array of colors to the guarding octopuses and they dispersed into the reef. The smartest octopus in the world retrieved John's dropped ray gun and followed the dolphins and humans.

Kyle Montgomery stood at the door to the alien spacecraft. It was three and a half meters tall and twice that wide and was shut tight. The cover of what appeared to be a control panel beside the door was also shut, but opened to Kyle's tug, revealing five large buttons sized to accommodate Krell claws. A strange keyboard, sized for the smaller manipulating claws, sat below the button array. The best find was a second door next to the control panel. Kyle had to figure out the Krell version of a door handle to open it. Inserting both hands into a rounded opening, again configured for Krell claws, he found a vertical bar. He turned it to the right and the panel opened easily, revealing a rack with seven ray guns. Kyle took one, leaving the door open. He cradled the weapon in the crook of his arm, its weight and feel odd and alien. With this piece of technology in hand he could make it back to the *Shanklin* and browbeat his sister-in-law into heading home. Mission accomplished. But an inner voice told him to stay. After all, he was standing next to a spaceship capable of interstellar travel. So much potential here.

He turned back to the open panel with the buttons and the strange keyboard and inspected it more closely. The alien version of a video screen was next to the keyboard. Montgomery reasoned that it would more likely be activated by one of the big buttons than a command typed in on the keyboard, so he tried the one closest to the panel door. Nothing happened. He pushed the one next to it and a faint glow came from the screen. So far so good. He took from his belt the sound generator he had pre-programmed and turned it to the "hello" setting. Holding it near the screen he activated the device. It emitted an alien screech. He tried it again. He counted to ten slowly, then played the screech again. After the tenth time, Kyle Montgomery was considering punching more buttons when the door slid open.

A giant alien crab stood in the doorway, its ray gun pointed at him.

Frustrated, Frssk F'tig roamed the ship, checking on progress. The engines were beginning to come on line, but the flight crew was still coming out of stasis sleep. He went to check on the two workers outside releasing the seafloor anchors. Plucking an *ardnl* from the rack as he passed by, he cradled it in his large claw, and proceeded to the cargo door. The video screen was flashing. Someone was outside punching the call button. The speaker kept repeating the True Race's recognition signal, but with a strange accent. Perplexed and worried that there might be a problem, Frssk F'tig touched the receive button.

The video showed one of the pink bipeds encumbered with primitive diving gear outside the door. And it was holding an *ardnl*.

Frssk F'tig jabbed a switch and the portal sprang open, revealing the pink biped. The two locked eyes. The pink biped held the ardnl in a lowered position. It had a device in one of its claws that emitted the recognition signal. There were only a few instances in Frssk F'tig's DNA memories that came anywhere near to matching this situation. A few of the encounters had proven beneficial for the True Race. He returned the recognition signal, adding an interrogation pulse on top of the word. The pink biped changed a setting on the device it held in its hand and the True Race word for help came out of it, although the particular case of the word indicated help with a physical object. Frssk F'tig's ancestral memory came up with an instance where the word had been copied without knowing the extent of its meaning and another where it could be interpreted as an offer to help. His caution kicked in and he raised his *ardnl*. At this the pink biped swam backwards rapidly, keeping its *ardnl* pointed downward. Frssk F'tig's deep memory told him that this usually meant submission. He decided not to fire on the biped as it disappeared around the curve of the hull. Something else had caught his eye.

Coming in low over the coral, two dolphins raced toward the spaceship, while a large whale dove downward from the surface. Frssk F'tig immediately saw it for what it was: a divert-and-attack scenario with the dolphins darting about to distract from the looming threat of the larger animal. What they hoped to do against the metal hull of an interstellar spacecraft he could not imagine, but it was definitely an attack. And he was standing in an open doorway. It could be bad if they got into the ship.

The dolphins twisted and turned, making them difficult targets. Frssk F'tig managed to hit one but the other kept coming, swimming wildly. He fired again, missing. The tactic was obvious; the dolphins were meant to distract him from the onslaught of the bigger and therefore more destructive whale. And the whale was closing in rapidly while the remaining dolphin headed for the cargo door, darting about erratically to evade Frssk F'tig's weapon fire. He could not fire on both at once and realized that their tactic might have some effectiveness. He fired at the dolphin, missing again.

Suddenly a bolt of red energy came from where the pink biped had hidden, striking the whale below its dorsal fin. Frssk F'tig's mind, capable through eons of genetic manipulation of holding two thoughts at once, fired his *ardnl* at the rapidly advancing dolphin, hitting it this time and reducing its head to a red pulp, while simultaneously realizing that the pink biped had acted in assistance to the True Race. Frssk F'tig turned his fire to the whale, striking its underside. The hidden biped pumped shot after shot into the head of the whale, finally landing one into its eye. The huge cetacean flailed and died. Its mangled body drifted down to join its two companions on the jagged coral.

Frssk F'tig made the daring move of stepping out of the cargo door, his *ardnl* held high and pointed upward. He fired a shot straight up, in the True Race's gesture for success through cooperation. He reasoned that the pink biped, obviously sympathetic to the True Race, would likely interpret it as such. Sure enough, the badly accented word for "help" came from the nearby coral jungle. Frssk F'tig replied with the correct version of 'help' and the biped responded with "help" and "over here." Frssk F'tig decided that this turn of events might be beneficial to the True Race and took another cautious step away from the ship.

That was when the shock wave hit.

Palmyra Atoll was shaken to its core. The forty Krell weapons that Oliver had converted to bombs went off in rapid succession, the pressure of their explosions jolting nearby weapons to explode. (The total count of exploded alien ray guns, had that been possible, was three hundred and sixty-two.) The destruction of the alien battle station was total, the concussive force of the blast killing every living thing in the lagoon. The hammer blow of the massive explosion, focused to an even greater force as it made its way down the lagoon's access channel, turned the shallow ditch through the reef into the barrel of a shotgun, shattering whatever Krell and their machines were caught in the passageway. The bowl of the extinct caldera aimed a lot of the force upward and outward, spewing the chaff of destruction into the sky. The wide, shallow ground surrounding the central lagoon is how the animals and humans and Krell in the reef at the west end of the atoll survived.

Far more impactful, though, was the effect the explosion's pressure wave had on the two hundred forty-three nearly finished war machines at the bottom of the lagoon. The power sources for the instruments of warfare had been installed and activated in preparation for the armada's completion. The massive force wave from above not only caused all the power sources to explode, it focused their energy release downward into the dormant heart of the extinct volcano. The ancient, sleeping giant towered almost three thousand feet from the abyssal plain to the surface of the ocean and the volcano's roots reached deep into the crust of the Earth. The fury of the war machines' simultaneous explosions sent shock waves down the volcano's lithic pathways and tectonic stress faults, into the very heart of Hell. Slowly, the mountain began to awaken.

John and Gina had managed to carry Gary a couple of hundred meters when the shock wave hit them. A giant fist punched John in the chest and he felt his legs bash into the coral. It was as if the entire atoll had been slammed down onto some giant's floor, cracking the reef itself and breaking coral heads apart. The calm voice in John's head noted that there had been a very large explosion in the central lagoon and that this was undoubtedly what had driven Oliver's panic. The animal part of John's brain screamed at him to run away, while the scientific observer part couldn't resist looking back over his shoulder to see the effects of the blast. A high pressure stream of shattered Krell and broken machinery shot out of the channel, spewing debris out onto the reef. The water roiled and frothed from the immense force.

But there was no time for gawking. Flanked by the two female dolphins, John and Gina swam with frantic new energy through the rollicking water toward the north edge of the atoll, where they hoped the *Beagle* still waited. Debris blasted from the lagoon began to fall around them: water and coral and twisted pieces of metal and many chunks of dead Krell. Humans and dolphins pushed diligently on, pulling the big injured dolphin through the shallow water while dodging the debris that rained down on the reef. A mass exodus of octopuses and dolphins was racing toward the edge of the atoll as well.

The darker blue of the open ocean came into view ahead. Orcas hovered out over the deep water while swarms of octopuses jetted frantically toward them. Dolphins streamed out into the blue. John was watching the exodus and telling himself that they had made it, when a large Krell stepped around a wall of coral. Its madly swiveling eyestalks fixed on the approaching group and it raised its ray gun. John let go of the injured dolphin and reached for his weapon, only to remember that Oliver now had it The octopus swam up beside John, angling to get a good shot, but Gary and Gina were in his way. Sheila and Nancy closed in to attack. The giant crab fired at Sheila and missed.

Gary acted as the leader of his pod. He shook Gina free and surged toward the enormous crab, swooping upward to catch the edge of its carapace and knocking it onto its back legs, exposing the underside. But the Krell was also fast. It pressed its weapon to Gary's ribcage and blasted a jagged hole the size of a grapefruit through the big dolphin, blowing him aside. Oliver jetted in and ran a coruscating beam of deadly red energy up the Krell's exposed underside, slicing the alien crustacean in two. The octopus, his skin a furious red, perched on the torn carapace and proceeded to cut the giant crab's corpse into pieces.

Sheila and Nancy hovered over Gary's torn body, keening a song of grief. The song was echoed from other distant dolphins along with the accompaniment of the orcas. Gina clung to Gary and cried into her mask. She trembled with unheard sobs and she did not shake John off when he squeezed her shoulder. Oliver came over and laid a tentacle across the fallen dolphin. John put his arms around Gary and, ignoring the gore coming from the hole blown in his side, swam north again. Gina took hold as well, and they moved solemnly toward the edge of the atoll. Oliver came up beside them and put out an arm to help carry his fallen friend. Nancy and Sheila swam alongside, still keening.

The *Beagle* was waiting for them out over the abyssal depths. John rapped on the observation bubble and both Larry and Barry pressed their faces up against the glass. Two dolphins, two humans, and one octopus held out Gary's corpse. Barry turned to a control panel and a specimen repository door opened near the back of the submarine. The fit was tight and the big dolphin's tail had to be angled down a bit, but they placed their friend's body as gently as possible into the storage compartment. Oliver then climbed into his transport box, Sheila and Nancy went to the surface, and John and Gina cycled through the waterlock and into the *Beagle*.

The bedraggled humans looked at one another. Gina and John slumped with grief while the sub techs looked beat up. Stress was heavy in the air.

"We've been monitoring your video," Larry said solemnly. "We're so sorry. Gary was..." Here the lanky tech paused, at a loss for words.

"Special," John offered.

"Dear to my heart," Gina said, her voice husky and tears rolling down her cheeks.

They stood in silence for a while, heads bowed. When the spell of mourning broke, Larry and Barry each went to their consoles. Their faces were grim and humorless. Gina sat on the deck, arms around her knees and her back to the others. The three men knew to leave her to her sorrow.

Davidson, Amundsen, and Harris were just stepping onto the beach when the lagoon exploded.

Harris and Amundsen each carried the remains of one of their comrades and two Krell ray guns. Davidson, being the biggest, carried two of the fallen and three ray guns. The going was rough. They were exhausted and shaken, the palm forest was thick with undergrowth, and their loads were heavy. When they came to the dirt road, they knew they were about halfway and slogged on. Eventually they could hear through the trees the breakers on the beach up ahead. Then the wide, bright beach revealed itself and the ocean beyond, deceptively calm.

Three steps out onto the sand, the earth jerked beneath them and they heard a deep boom from below, like a door slamming in the depths of Hell. Then a concussion wave ripped through the jungle and knocked them to the sand. There was a sound so loud it was felt mostly in their bones, followed by another pressure wave, this one heavy with high velocity water. Having been thrown onto his back, Harris was looking at the jungle and saw the second compression wave coming, flattening trees and tearing at the undergrowth. The water droplets mostly passed over him, but the water that hit his hands and face stung like buckshot. Stunned, staring up at the sky, Harris watched a plume of dirty water cover the tropical blue. It geysered upward as if in slow motion, flecked with debris. *That is mighty damn high*, Harris thought to himself as he rolled over and struggled to his knees. The first drops of water from the sky fell on him and he had the presence of mind to point upward and shout at the other two, "Watch out! There's gonna be a lot of crap coming down!" although they were all deaf from the sound of the explosion. Harris glanced up; the specks of debris were getting bigger and the dirty lagoon water was turning into a steady rain. He went to Amundsen and helped her to her feet. She held her hands up over her head in instinctive protection.

Harris had just turned to Davidson and called out to him when the first pieces of shattered debris began to shower the beach: a rain of coral and rock of all sizes—first rubble, then the larger pieces, heavy and undeterred by air resistance. A coral-encrusted boulder the size of a horse landed within feet of Davidson, spraying him with sand where he lay face down. Harris and Amundsen rushed to him and turned him over as more detritus fell around them. She brushed sand from Davidson's face, clearing his nose and mouth and shaking him, shouting his name. Harris looked up again, trying to judge the falling pieces of destruction. Plant matter, sometimes entire trees, swirled far above and more coral and rocks speckled the dirty backdrop of descending water. He noticed for the first time what had to be chunks of alien metal, light grey against the darker sooty grey of the lagoon's water. Some fluttered like tissue paper in the sky while other, darker pieces fell straight down among the pulverized chunks of Palmyra Atoll.

The first piece of Krell technology, a broken mass of wires and dull metal, thudded into the sand nearby. They were still deaf from the concussive sound of the explosion. Davidson opened his eyes and blinked up at Amundsen, mouthing the word, "Gladys." She smiled at him, then looked at Harris, fear in her eyes. He nodded at her, a soldier's way of saying, we are in this together. And the rain of debris began in earnest.

They were pelted with rocks and water and broken metal and irregular pieces of shattered alien technology. A sharp shard of metal cut Davidson on his cheek and he rolled over onto his front, shielding the back of his neck with his hands. Lieutenant Commander Amundsen was showered with shredded metal, one fragment slicing through her sleeve and into her forearm. She cried out in pain, unheard in the lingering deafness. A large sheet of light-colored metal slammed onto the beach just yards away. Harris ran to it and pulled it from the sand, hurriedly dragging it to where Amundsen knelt over Davidson. He propped one end on the nearby boulder, making a crude lean-to. Squeezing himself under the cover, he helped the other two curl up beneath the protection. The debris rained down around them with unceasing intensity. Mostly water, a lot of broken pieces of the Krell stronghold, and a great deal of coral and rock beating a tattoo on the metal above their heads. Shattered pieces of alien crab littered the beach. A chunk of something heavy smashed into the protecting plate and Harris, his strength magnified with fear and adrenaline, struggled to keep the upper end on the boulder. The vegetation was the last to come down. They saw an entire palm tree fall on the sand mere feet away from their lean-to, followed by a steady stream of ferns and underbrush. The deluge of detritus was relatively short lived, not more than a couple of minutes, but it felt like forever to the three huddled humans.

The hammering and thudding on their protective cover lessened, then stopped. Harris pushed aside wads of wet vegetation and crawled out, giving a hand to Amundsen, then Davidson. Davidson shook his head and dragged his fingers through his hair, then helped Amundsen pull the metal shard from her arm. She winced and clapped her hand over the wound, dark blood slowly staining the fabric of her blouse.

The scene around them was utter chaos. Rocks, trees, and shredded ferns littered everything in sight, all covered with the torn and twisted remnants of whatever alien technology had been in the lagoon. And dead Krell—lots of them—ripped to pieces by the force of the blast. Harris thought he saw an intact alien move, but it was just the upper carapace of a giant crab answering the call of gravity to flop down on a pile of broken vegetation and smashed metal. Some trees still stood, though they leaned crazily away from the center of the blast. The rest had been blown down and covered with debris from the sky. It was a desolate scene.

Hearing began to return and they assured each other that they were OK. Harris got his first aid kit out of a zippered pocket and dressed Amundsen's wound. The cut was not deep. It had missed both bone and major blood vessels. He and Davidson wound it tight with gauze.

"I've always wanted to be stranded on a desert island with two handsome men," Lieutenant Commander Amundsen quipped. Gallows humor. Both men hugged her.

"Do you have an emergency beacon?" Harris asked Davidson.

The sergeant nodded and took a small black cylinder from an inside pocket. He flipped a cover open and pressed a button. A bright light began to flash on top of the cylinder. Davidson propped it up in the sand. "Let's hope somebody hears us."

"I guess we got 'em," Amundsen said wearily. "It's over."

"Not really," Harris replied. "There's still the mother ship."

Beneath their feet the ground rumbled.

# CHAPTER NINETEEN

The subtle whir of the *Beagle's* SQUID drive came to life and the submarine began to move forward.

"What's up?" John asked. "Are we going back to the *Darwin*?"

Larry's voice was grim. "There's still the Krell spaceship. We have to stop it."

"You're going to attack it?"

"Somebody has to," Barry replied.

Oliver's speaker blared to life. "No! No! No!" John glanced at the screen and saw that Oliver had come out of his box and was pulsating red and black as he jabbed at his keyboard. The speaker kept shouting "No!"

"Shut that thing off," Larry commanded.

John turned the sound down, but not off. "We should listen to him."

"He's an octopus," Larry said. "I know he's smart, but—"

"Damn it, he was the one who planned this whole thing!" John interrupted. He clicked the microphone to the octopus. "Oliver!" No response. "Oliver, stop!" The cephalopod lifted his tentacles from the keyboard.

"Why do you say no?" John asked. "Do you know where we are going?"

Oliver's tentacle tips flashed over the keyboard. "Home cave of crab!" the synthetic voice shouted. "No! No! Wrong!"

"Why is it wrong?"

Usually "why" questions would make Oliver pause to cogitate before answering. This time the response was immediate. "Great Old One has crab!"

"Oh, for Pete's sake!" Larry exploded. "Not that Lovecraft garbage again!"

"Look, I'm just as confused as you guys, but I think we should—"

"Why should we trust the word of a glorified garden snail?" Barry said. "Especially one who is in love with an early twentieth century horror writer."

John was miffed. "We've trusted him so far and done OK."

"You really think so?" Larry's face was flushed.

John had just opened his mouth for an angry reply when Gina leapt to her feet, fists clenched. "Stop it! Just stop it!" she shouted. "Look at you guys! Bicker, bicker, bicker! Ollie could be right! Stop the sub!"

"No!" Larry shouted back.

"Then I will!" She stomped forward two steps. Larry gripped the controls tighter and Barry was poised to leave his chair.

John felt an electric jolt of resolve and rose to his feet. He spoke with the heaviness of command. "Stop the submarine! Otherwise we've got a mutiny. We *have* to talk."

His tone and volume halted the argument. Larry pulled back on the controls and the engines quieted to a soft whisper. John put his hand on Gina's shoulder. She glared briefly at Larry and Barry, then took a seat. Larry frowned at John. "What do you have in mind?"

"I say we give Oliver a chance," John said.

"I agree," Gina added solemnly.

"He's done a bang-up job so far," John continued. "Let's see what he has in mind. Give this some time and see where it goes. If it doesn't work we'll go with your plan."

Larry and Barry exchanged dark looks. "I'll give him ten minutes," Larry scowled.

John sighed and spoke into the mic. "OK, Oliver. Now what?"

At the octopus's direction, the *Beagle* advanced to the west end of the reef near the edge of the deeper coral bowl where the Krell spaceship lay. The submarine stopped, holding its position out over the deep water, and Oliver jetted into the abyss. Soon Oliver was lost to sight in the dark temple of the sea. They waited.

After a bit Barry asked sarcastically, "That's it?"

"He has six minutes and twenty-three seconds left," Larry intoned icily.

Time dragged by. At John's urging, Larry brought the submarine up to ten meters. They could see the edge of the dropoff into the bowl where the spaceship lay, but could not see the alien craft.

"Shut the lights off," Gina suggested. Larry killed the cabin and outside lights and dimmed the computer screens to a deep red. They waited in the crimson dimness, the water outside sapphire from the morning sun. "Two minutes fifteen seconds."

Out in the dark water a silver light flashed several times, then paused and flashed again.

"Do you think that's Ollie?" Gina whispered.

"A minute forty-two."

"Stop the clock," John said.

The distant mote of light went through its flashing sequence again. "I'll give you another ten minutes," Larry said. "Then we're going in."

"Whatever," John replied absent mindedly. He was gazing intently out the observation bubble. Time crawled by. John thought he saw something moving.

"Eight minutes, ten seconds."

Gina slapped Larry on the arm. It was not a playful slap. "Stop it!"

The moving dot was Oliver, resolving from a wriggling splotch against the blue into an actual octopus, his arms trailing behind as he jetted toward the *Beagle*. John could tell from the way Oliver's mantle contracted as he swam that he was tired. He settled onto the sub's wing, his color a dirty beige. John stepped to the microphone.

"What do we do now?"

The octopus poked listlessly at a key and the synthetic voice was dull. "OK."

"OK, what?" John asked, but Oliver made no reply. He turned to the others. "We wait, I guess."

"Anybody want to know how much time we have left to waste on this octopus plan?" Larry asked.

"Not really," Gina said acidly.

They floated in the semi-darkness, the time seemingly interminable. Then there came a faint flash from the dark water of the deep. It was a silvery flash like the one Oliver had made. It flashed again, slightly bigger as whatever was flashing approached the shallower water. Another flash; a silver circle with lines radiating outward like a pictograph of the sun. Then another silver circle flash, bigger still, and they saw that the lines were waving like seaweed. With no point of reference it was impossible to judge the distance to the lights, but it seemed far off. A few more seconds dragged by without any more flashing circles.

"What the hell is it?" Barry whispered.

Suddenly the darkness was lit with flashing blue and silver and red. And they saw it.

There are legends of creatures that attack from the deep, written in the histories of Herodotus, the legend of the Kraken, Viking tales, and so forth. Modern science has since identified *Architeuthis*, the famed giant squid known to dwell in the hyperabyssal depths of the ocean. Dead and decaying specimens have been collected from beaches and fishing nets, the biggest measuring over eighteen meters in length.

But there have been indications of even larger ones.

There emerged from the deep a squid of god-like proportions, its skin rippling with flashing colors, black and silver against waves of red. The creature was not a hundred meters from the submarine as it swam over the edge of the reef and down into the bowl where the Krell spacecraft lay. As it slid by, the light show on its skin ceased and the monster turned all black. Its unblinking eye stood out stark white against the dark pigmentation and the top of the gigantic cephalopod's mantle came less than a meter from the ocean surface. It slid silently past the stunned humans for a long time. First came the massive palps, each the size of a Sherman tank and lined with clawed sucker cups at the ends of the squid's extendable gripping tentacles. Then came the eight undulating arms surrounding the giant's beak, the huge eye just behind that, and finally the long parade of the mantle, its side fins rippling in the water. The last of the enormous squid's tail disappeared into the sunken reef and there was a shocked silence in the submarine.

"My God!" Larry exclaimed. "That thing was at least a hundred fifty meters long!"

"Score one for Ollie," Gina smiled.

John glanced at the camera feed of Oliver's transport box. The door stood open. "Speaking of which, where is he?"

"There he is!" Barry exclaimed, pointing at the lip of the coral basin. The octopus, now the color of the reef, was almost invisible at this distance. The tiny undulating blob disappeared into the basin.

John pressed his face against the glass. "What the hell is he doing?"

"We'd better get out of here," Larry said, turning to his controls.

Barry put a hand on his arm. His voice was stern. "No. We wait here."

John and Gina nodded in unison. "We wait," she said.

"Yes," John echoed. "We wait here for Oliver."

The shock wave from the central lagoon's destruction threw Kyle Montgomery against the coral head he had been hiding behind, cutting his arms and legs and banging his compact scuba apparatus against the hard wall. The accelerant in his bloodstream gave his reflexes the quickness needed to turn his face away from the jagged coral. Only the right side of his head sustained any scraping. During the shake-up, he saw the Krell warrior who had hailed him scurry back into the spaceship and close the door behind him.

Montgomery did not take the time to speculate on what had caused the shock wave. He only saw a trove of alien technology shut tight before him. Driven by his mission, he swam to the cargo bay door and pushed the large button that had previously summoned the alien. He keyed his communication device to repeat the Krell recognition signal and the alien word for "help." Nothing happened. He added the phrase that supposedly meant "the time of hatching approaches" into the mix. Still nothing. He punched all the buttons on the control panel repeatedly but to no avail. The drug he had taken earlier boiled up into anger and he struggled to keep it in check. He picked up a piece of coral, intending to beat it against the metal cargo door.

Then it began to rain debris.

Rocks and pieces of coral came first, followed by broken bits of giant crabs and shards of their technology. Kyle looked up and saw the surface of the water above him crazed with the impacts of various debris. His racing mind deduced that there had been an explosive incident, most probably in the lagoon itself, and that the heavier, most aerodynamic pieces of debris were the first to come down around him. The water slowed their fall, robbing them of their projectile deadliness. He reasoned that the lighter pieces with more air resistance would be coming down last, a rain of precious alien technology. The explosion had caused havoc, but a lot of the falling technology might be intact, or not too damaged to be useful. The cargo door in the Krell vessel was unlikely to open, but the cascade of pieces of their technology floating down into the coral bowl was like manna from heaven.

He dropped the piece of coral and opened the compartment containing the remaining six ray guns. He filled his arms with the weapons, able to carry only three, and, dodging the larger detritus, swam back to his hiding spot behind a wall of coral. Dumping the ray guns on the sandy bottom, he returned for the remaining three and stashed those with the others. Montgomery then turned his hyperattention to what was coming down around him. Among the shredded pieces of giant crabs and tangled vegetation were plenty of only partially destroyed machine parts, and glittering metal things. He wove through the falling debris, gathering what looked useful and interesting and stashing it with the purloined ray guns. Any liaison with the aliens now seemed extremely doubtful, but raining from above was treasure that would ensure Kyle Montgomery's gloriously bright future.

Frrsk F'tig was blown back by the shock wave, but managed to dig his legs into the sea bottom to keep from being tossed up against the ship. Instances of underwater explosions rippled up from his genetic memory. This one was bad. He darted into the open cargo bay, slapped the door shut, and scurried up to the command deck. Communications personnel informed him that there had been a very large explosion in the lagoon. A flash from a remote camera showed the bright destruction of the central headquarters structure.

Frrsk F'tig ordered the engines immediately brought to working status. Even though they were not yet warmed up enough for interstellar or even interplanetary travel, they could at least get the spacecraft away from the atoll and into orbit. From there they could send a message to the home planet and do what they could to salvage the mission. He asked for a status report from the two workers releasing the anchors holding the ship to the sea floor. Seven anchors had been stowed, but three remained. He ordered the two outside workers to redouble their efforts and blast the anchors loose if need be. The workers reported that they had left their *ardnls* in the cargo bay. Frrsk F'tig sent up a curse to the strange crab god the True Race worshipped. He could not spare any more personnel to go outside and help with the anchor release, and the exterior compartment with spare *ardnls* was on the opposite side of the ship from the release workers. More curses. He noted that the pink biped that had helped kill the attacking whale briefly again tried to get in the cargo door, bleating the word "help" or extolling the glory of hatchlings from the device in one of its claws. It gave up as debris from the lagoon's demise began to drift down around the ship. *Good riddance, weak biped*, Frrsk F'tig said to himself. His full attention turned to freeing the spacecraft.

As Kyle Montgomery swam to his stash point to deposit another armful of scavenged alien technology pieces, his back was to the north side of the coral basin. Suddenly he got the feeling that something was behind him. He looked over his shoulder and saw, coming up over the rim of the basin, an enormous squid, its colors shifting from red and silver to black. Cold electricity ran through him. He had been trained to ignore fear, to deny its debilitating shock, but the sight of the immensely huge squid jolted him into panic. He dropped his armful of tech bits and swam like a frightened fish to his stash point behind a wall of coral.

His training kicked in and he controlled his breath, forcing calm on himself. Peeking up over the coral he watched the enormous cephalopod approach the spaceship. Kyle's rational mind was back on line and he noted details: the squid was well over a hundred meters long, its skin was iridescent even in its blackness and bore many scars. It moved with massive grace, the grasping tentacles with their oversized palps pointed forward, the eight central arms writhing menacingly. He postulated that this was the animal's attack stance. Kyle watched as the giant squid reached out to the alien spacecraft with its grasping tentacles.

The two Krell working to release the ship's anchors did not see their doom until it was upon them. The looming monster rushing toward the spaceship, a circle of undulating black tentacles against the dim coral, did not register at first in their consciousness as anything recognizable. It was only when one of the giant squid's grasping tentacles, as big around as a pine tree, shot out toward the ship that the alien crustaceans took action, scurrying away and jabbering warnings into the communicators attached to their shells. The elongated tentacle wrapped around the spaceship, its massive palp clamping to the surface, the clawed sucker cups digging into the metal. The two worker crabs scurried for the cargo bay only to find the door covered by the thick, black tentacle. The gigantic cephalopod stretched out its other grasping tentacle, wrapping the alien vessel from the other direction and crushing the worker crabs against the hull. The squid then pulled at the ship the way it always did to bring its prey to it. But the spacecraft, still partly anchored to the sea floor, moved only slightly.

Inside, the Krell were in panic mode. Frrsk F'tig watched the approaching monster on the video screens, saw the unsettling movement of the massive squid's central arms, and watched as the grasping arms shot out toward the spacecraft. The sight triggered a deep memory in him, a terror reaching far back in his ancestral memory. The deck shook as one of the cephalopod's giant palps slammed onto the side of the ship, followed moments later by the shuddering impact of another grasping palp on the other side of the spacecraft. The floor tilted and rocked as the monster pulled at the ship. Frrsk F'tig ordered whatever engines were available to be ready to fire on his order.

One Krell had the presence of mind to deploy the large *ardnl'kssk* on top of the ship and fire at the giant squid. The weapon managed to rip away one of the eight writhing tentacles. This only served to infuriate the giant of the deep. Its black coloration flared bright red and silver and in a flash it pulled itself to the Krell ship, wrapping its remaining seven arms around the spacecraft. The enormous strength of the immense cephalopod, amplified by its rage, wrenched the half-buried craft from the reef like a rotten tooth. The big ray gun fired again, this time only singeing one of the grasping tentacles and maddening the giant squid even more.

Angrily flashing its battle colors, the massive monster of the deep squeezed the spaceship and the metal began to buckle under the pressure. Frrsk F'tig gave the order to fire the engines.

Montgomery watched as the huge cephalopod attacked the Krell spaceship. His mind raced to find a way to turn the situation to his advantage. Helping the aliens was the obvious solution, and, in his experience, violence was usually the most effective tool. He picked up one of the alien ray guns and edged out from his hiding place. A bigger version of the weapon he was holding unfolded from the top of the spaceship and fired at the giant squid, slicing off one of its eight central arms. The severed appendage, as long as three semis and still wriggling, sank slowly to the sea floor where it lashed about among the coral corridors. The large gun fired again, this time only nicking one of the grasping tentacles. The huge squid quickly pulled itself to the spacecraft, wrapping its remaining arms around the vessel. This brought the squid's enormous eye even with Kyle and he found himself being observed by an angry animal the size of an ocean liner. Montgomery watched as the huge cephalopod ripped the Krell ship from the sea floor. His clinical mind noted that there had been half again as much buried below the sea floor as had been above it and that there appeared to be an array of hexagonal nozzles on the underside of the vessel. Two of the hexagons at the center of the ship lit up with actinic fire and the craft began to rise, albeit at an angle, dragging the squid with it. The massive cephalopod pulled at the spacecraft and the tug of war appeared evenly matched.

Kyle Montgomery decided that now was the time to act. He raised his ray gun and aimed it at the center of the giant squid's eye. Perfect kill shot. The eye turned its attention from the spacecraft and focused directly on Montgomery. Kyle felt fear and triumph in equal parts pour through his veins. He placed his finger over the glowing blue trigger.

A clump of coral broke loose from the reef and became an octopus. It shot forward, grabbing his arm and pulling it upward.

Oliver had spotted Kyle near the alien spaceship and waited nearby in case the company man caused any trouble. When Kyle aimed the ray gun at the Great Old One, Oliver burst into action. He jetted to Montgomery and pulled the weapon from his grip. The red bolt from the ray gun fired harmlessly past the enormous squid and destroyed a metal panel drifting down through the water. Kyle grabbed a knife from his waist belt and, reaching back over his shoulder, drove it into one of Oliver's arms. Panicked and furious, Oliver pulled himself tightly to the human and bit him on the shoulder. Bit him hard, injecting as much poison as he could.

Kyle, the dangerous human who had lied to Oliver, spasmed backward, his spine clenching into an arc of pain. He fell to the sand. Two of Oliver's arms pulled the knife from his flesh, letting it fall to the debris-covered bottom. Blue blood shot forth into the turbulent water from the wound on his tentacle. The octopus retrieved the alien ray gun and jetted to the top of a coral head. He had, by dint of battle, become a pretty good shot. Gripping the coral head with four arms, he used his remaining three to cradle and aim the weapon. Looking up, he could see scalding energy pouring from the nozzles on the underside of the craft and felt hot turbulence in the water. Oliver poured a sustained beam of searing red energy on the central engine. The metal began to glow and distort. Then something popped and the engine nozzle flashed and died.

The Great Old One, feeling the loss of power in the spacecraft, poured all its fury into its tentacles. Oliver turned the ray gun on the other blazing nozzle on the ship's underside until it, too, flared and died. The metal buckled and screamed as the starfaring vessel crumpled in the cephalopod's grip. Flashes of green fire sparked from the broken metal. Oliver dropped the energy weapon and hunkered tighter down onto the coral head as he saw the huge cephalopod inhale water into its mantle in preparation for jetting away.

Inside the Krell spaceship the video screens went blank and the lights went out. Frrsk F'tig and the rest of the Krell onboard felt, for the first time in their lives, the chill grip of fear. It was a genetic memory buried so deep that it almost never came to the surface. The giant crabs were frozen with terror as the ship groaned and shrieked under the massive squid's crushing embrace. They did not drown as air-breathing human sailors would have, but were instead trapped in the mangled darkness of their interstellar coffin as the stardrive flashed its death and the power systems shorted out. Then the ship tilted and began to move.

Kyle Montgomery lay twitching on the sand, feeling the octopus's neurotoxin sap strength and control from his muscles. The pain was excruciating, his body burning with fire. Any movement brought on new pain and he could not stop his body's involuntary clenching. But in spite of the agony, his consciousness was untouched. He watched clearly and calmly as the octopus that had attacked him—he was sure it was Oliver—picked up the ray gun and fired on the Krell spaceship, knocking out its central engines. The cool part of Montgomery's mind witnessed the unimaginably huge squid squeeze the life out of the spacecraft, hearing the skreek and scream of metal being crushed. Green fire flashed from the underside of the broken spacecraft.

The giant squid's enormous eye came level with Montgomery and he felt its attention turn to him. *Please go*, the company man silently begged. *Let me die here*. He looked up at Oliver perched on the coral above him. Struggling through the pain, the company man touched his hand to his heart, then extended that hand toward the octopus. Oliver turned black and squirted a cloud of ink at Montgomery.

One of the giant squid's tentacles, silver ripples running up and down its length, undulated over to Montgomery. The very tip of the arm felt Kyle's twitching legs, then ran up the length of his abdomen, gently exploring the company man's body. The tentacle wrapped itself around Kyle Montgomery and lifted him from the sand. Then the giant squid shot a powerful jet of water from its siphon and exited the coral bowl.

Oliver's seven arms clung tightly to the coral. Even the stump of his eighth arm, the one he had bitten off, gripped the rough surface with its scant remaining sucker cups. The water pushed out of the Great Old One's siphon sent strong swirling currents through the coral basin that would have spun Oliver through the forest of sharp coral had he not been holding on firmly. Fish, sand, and pieces of debris danced around him in the swirling water. The gigantic body of the Great Old One picked up speed and gracefully jetted up and over the edge of the coral declivity, still holding the sparking ruin of the spaceship. One tentacle held the struggling form of Kyle Montgomery. In spite of the neurotoxin Oliver had injected him with, Montgomery beat frantically at the encircling arm. A little snack for the Great Old One's journey home, Oliver thought to himself. The octopus's skin turned green with purple circles. Checkmate.

The enormous squid disappeared from view and the water calmed. Oliver felt an overwhelming fatigue. He released from the coral and painfully filled his mantle with water. Pushing it out as a jet was difficult, his muscles aching with weariness. Though not far, the trek back to the submarine felt like the longest journey of his life.

# CHAPTER TWENTY

The people on board the *Beagle* watched the enormous squid exit the reef: first its tail, then the rest of the body with its huge staring eye, and lastly the tentacles gripping the mangled Krell spaceship. Gina gasped as she spied the struggling form of Kyle Montgomery clasped in one of the monstrous squid's arms. The cephalopod moved with astonishing speed, flashing silver and bits of deep blue as it slid past their view. Green fire flashed from the bottom of the alien spacecraft clutched in its arms. Then the enormous beast angled downward and disappeared into the deep, its captured prize trailing sparks.

In the stunned silence that followed, Barry whispered, "Cthulhu fhtagn R'lyeh."

"Stop that," Gina chided, slapping his shoulder, this time playfully.

When they turned the radio on they picked up the commandoes' distress call. By the time the *Beagle* got to the designated beach, tremors from the island were buffeting the submarine and a plume of steam rose above the center of the atoll as the water that rushed in to fill the lagoon was boiled away by the awakening volcano. The remains of the four fallen soldiers were transported to the *Beagle* first and carefully placed in a storage locker. John and Gina helped Harris and Amundsen, who were each carrying two ray guns, swim out to the submarine. Sergeant Davidson was the last to make the crossing, bringing the remaining three. There were hugs and tears aboard the *Beagle* and a few brief recaps during their return trip to *Darwin's Dream* and the *Shanklin*. Oliver rested in his box on the sub's left wing, a trailing tentacle dull ocher with fatigue, and Sheila and Nancy paced the submarine. Mostly the trip was silent. They all knew there would be time to tell their stories.

The five heroes were buried at sea, given over to the rolling deep with highest honors. Rear Admiral Diaz stood at the aft of the *Shanklin* and spoke eloquently of the honor and sacrifice of the fallen warriors. Davidson, Amundsen, and Harris stood behind him, their faces grim. The Chaplain praised the brave spirits and read a verse from the Bible. Every person on both ships stood silently as seven rifles fired a twenty-one gun salute. A bugle sounded taps, and the remains of those who fought and died were commended to the sea; first Spinelli, then Miller, Johnson, and Dalegowski, and lastly Gary. The soldiers' weighted shrouds, an American flag sewn on each one, disappeared beneath the waves.

Gina thought she had cried herself out, but silent tears ran down her cheeks during the ceremony. She had placed Gary's favorite toy, a short hank of rope knotted at both ends, in his shroud. Director Harris had cut the Gershon Oceanographic Institute banner from one of his T-shirts and helped her sew it onto the dolphin's shroud. As Gary's body slipped into the sea, Nancy and Sheila's keening song of grief quivered at the edges of Sheila's heart. She glanced over at John and saw tears on his cheeks, too. He reached out and took her hand.

It was a long, somber voyage back to American shores.

The eruption of Palmyra Atoll—or simply Palmyra as it came to be known after the obliteration of its atoll—barely made it into the top ten volcanic events of all time, being a mere third of a Krakatoa. Nonetheless, the spectacular reawakening of the Palmyra volcano from its ancient sleep was on every screen on the planet. The explosion that had cleaned out Palmyra Atoll's central lagoon opened the way for a magma outpouring of epic proportions. Seawater flowing back into the caldera flash boiled into steam. Then the Earth cleared her throat, shooting gobbets of molten magma thousands of feet into the air. Glowing lava fell into the sea like a fiery necklace surrounding the atoll. Wild winds ripped away the steam and smoke. A fissure opened at the bottom of the caldera, the Earth coughed again, magma pouring forth in a never-ending torrent. Molten rock flowed into the sea, hiding the fractured atoll behind a curtain of steam. But not all the magma flowed into the water. A cone quickly began to form; rising to forty meters the first day, adding another twenty-eight the next, and more thereafter. Seismic monitors around the world jumped and jittered.

The eruption was shown on live television, with video from the International Space Station and spectacular images from weather satellites. It went super-viral on social media. The Weather Channel featured it 24/7. There was initial fear of a tsunami, but Samoa got only a few meter-tall waves and Hawaii and Fiji barely half that. The viewing public watched a mountain form before their very eyes. The Palmyra volcano was a boiling maelstrom during the day and a demonic lightshow at night. Volcanic soot made for spectacular sunsets throughout Asia, Australia, and the western parts of the Americas. Air traffic was diverted, causing massive delays. In a week it was all but over, with the newly birthed volcano blurping out smaller and smaller streams of magma. A massive mound of steaming lava towered out of the ocean where there had recently been a tranquil tropical paradise. Then the news cycle turned to something else, and everybody went back to watching reality TV.

Digital information, especially video, is like helium; it is almost impossible to contain, and a story such as the incident at Palmyra was definitely uncontainable. The tabloids and the internet had a field day. The government did its best to control the narrative. Press releases said that a virus from a meteor strike caused mutations in a few sea creatures, but that there was no chance of the virus spreading. The meteorite had set off the volcano; and the *USS Pendleton* had been sent to investigate but there had been an unfortunate accident with the nuclear reactor. The Navy was conducting an inquiry and the area was off limits for the foreseeable future. All other information was classified. End of discussion.

In Washington, D.C., a private ceremony took place in the depths of the Pentagon. The Secretary of the Navy and the Secretary of Defense were there, as well as the head of the Marine Corps. Rear Admiral Diaz was given the Department of Defense Distinguished Service Medal and a third star was added to his epaulets. Lieutenant Commander Amundsen was given the Navy Cross for extraordinary heroism in combat by the Secretary of the Navy, and the head of the Marine Corps laid the same medal around the necks of Dennis Harris and Gunnery Sergeant Davidson. The Secretary of Defense presented both John and Gina with the Navy Distinguished Service Medal, the highest honor the Navy can bestow on a civilian. The president called on a secure line to give the group her congratulations. It was a solemn affair.

Afterwards, they all went out for sushi and drinks to celebrate. Admiral Diaz, once he loosened up, did an excellent imitation of Patrick Stewart, and Gladys Amundsen and Dave Davidson rocked the room with their soulful karaoke rendition of "Stand By Me." John and Gina slow danced to the music, and in the taxi on the way back to the hotel, he kissed her again.

Back at the Gershon Oceanographic Institute, John took his medal off its satin ribbon and gave it to Oliver. He rambled on for a bit about bravery and cleverness and how smart Oliver was and this and that, then leaned the medal against a rock next to the octopus's lair. With the tip of a tentacle, Oliver touched the medal and its bas relief of an eagle. When John dumped a congratulatory crab into the tank, the commendation was forgotten. The next day, though, John peeked into Oliver's little cave and saw that the medal was propped up on a decorative pebble, the eagle facing the TV. John smiled. He knew Oliver liked it.

Gina gave her medal to her pod. The ceremony was more raucous than the one John had with Oliver, but the sentiment was the same. The pod sang a song of mourning for Gary, Gina chiming in on her keyboard and speaker. Unlike John, she left the medal on its satin ribbon and the dolphins tossed it from snout to snout, carrying the dangling piece of metal around the big tank while the others sang of Gary's prowess. It was their way to mourn, and Gina joined in the play. The Navy Distinguished Public Service Medal ended up hanging by its ribbon on a coral outcropping at the back of the tank. Almost no one noticed it, and the few who did thought the eagle was a mermaid.

# EPILOGUE

The wedding took place in the atrium of the Gershon Oceanographic Institute in front of the dolphin tank. Rear Admiral Diaz and Lieutenant Commander Amundsen took John aside before the ceremony and gave him an update on The Palmyra Incident. The volcano had completely covered the atoll with a thick coating of lava, destroying all evidence of the Krell. The Navy had scoured the deep ocean around the atoll with remote submersibles, but found only scattered, broken pieces of their tech. Some pieces, though, were relatively intact. Amundsen brought up the possibility of investing in tech stocks.

Diaz changed the subject. "How is Oliver doing?" he asked.

"Real good," John replied. "His wound is healed, his tentacle is almost completely grown back, and he's his old, feisty self again. I'm teaching him ping-pong."

The admiral thought about this for a few seconds. "I imagine he's pretty good."

John nodded. "Scary good."

"Give him my best regards. He's an amazing guy, for an octopus."

"I'll pass on your sentiments. He's the ring bearer, you know."

Diaz laughed. "You are a strange cookie, John. I found working with you to be fascinating."

"I hear Sergeant Davidson is your best man," Amundsen commented.

"Yes, ma'am. He helped me pick out the tux. Been giving me a lot of pointers."

Diaz chuckled. "You couldn't hope for a better best man. After all, he's been married three times."

"So where are you guys honeymooning?" Amundsen asked. "Hawaii? Tahiti? Bali?"

"Switzerland," John replied. "Far away from any ocean."

Lieutenant Commander Amundsen put on a serious face. "You realize, do you not," she intoned with knotted brow, "that at one time Switzerland had the eighth largest submarine fleet in the world. Just behind Disneyland."

"We will avoid anything aquatic," John replied with mock solemnity. Both Diaz and Amundsen gave him their best wishes and went to their seats.

Suddenly, John found himself standing on a raised platform in front of the glass wall of the main tank as the dolphins raced back and forth, laughing and chattering. Nancy and Sheila and the rest of the pod were leaning over the top and giving a running commentary. John glanced down at the bucket beside him. Oliver was a relaxed beige. All good.

The organist launched into the opening chords of the Wedding March and the dolphins sang along. It was otherworldly. The organist had been warned that this would probably happen and she was a real trooper, even throwing in some high notes to harmonize. Larry and Barry howled along like wolves with the tune and merely grinned at John when he gave them the hairy eyeball. Gina stepped through a flowered arch, beaming on her father's arm, the sun pouring through the skylight making her white dress glow like holy fire. John grinned like an idiot and thought he might faint. "Hang in there," Davidson whispered to him. Gina stepped up beside him and they shared a private smile. The minister led them through the vows.

Then it was time for the rings. Gina and John stood facing each other on either side of Oliver's bucket. John and Oliver had gone through the routine many times, John promising the octopus triple crabs if he did a good job. It had come off flawlessly at the rehearsal.

John tapped the side of the bucket twice with his shoe, the agreed-upon signal. Oliver was supposed to just place the rings in

Gina and John's outstretched hands and then settle back into his bucket.

But not this octopus.

To the delight of the gathering, two sinuous tentacles came swaying up out of the water like snakes rising from a basket. Oliver was a bright shade of green that John had never seen before. Weaving his tentacles through the air to whatever strange music was flitting around in his array of cephalopod brains, Oliver rolled the gold rings up and down his rows of sucker cups, eliciting gasps from the audience. As he did so, he slowly rose above the rim of the bucket and wrapped two more arms around Gina and John's legs. Gina looked at John questioningly but he merely shrugged and kept his hand out. Then, in a beautifully executed gymnastic move achievable only with boneless limbs, Oliver wrapped his dancing tentacles around Gina and John's outstretched wrists and, using his delicate tentacle tips, deftly slipped the rings onto their fingers. It was beautiful. It was magical.

"I now pronounce you man and wife," the minister smiled.

Oliver squirted all three of them with water, his skin rippling blue and purple with laughter.

The mind of an octopus is a curious thing.

# ACKNOWLEDGMENTS

First and foremost I want to thank Sy Montgomery—author of *The Soul Of An Octopus*—for her inspiration, encouragement, and delight in the finished book. The amazing Michael Mayhew cheered me on and helped hone the ideas, then edited the cumbersome manuscript. I cannot thank him enough. The insights and acumen of Alyson Kuhn buffed the novel to a high sheen. Her guidance has been fabulously invaluable. Many thanks as well to Tex Thompson for her support and encouragement, Larry Nicholson for Navy advice, Sam Marshall for her unflagging friendship, and Walt Disney for introducing me to the power and mystery of cephalopods.

# THE SCIENCE

I have endeavored to make the science in *Eight Arms To Hold Me* accurate regarding the strange, almost alien physiology of octopuses—their intelligence, their ability to change the color and texture of their skin, etc. Although Giant Pacific Octopuses are not capable of the wide variety of colorations that Oliver displays, in this telling, his DNA contains elements from several species of octopus, allowing him the increased spectrum. The correct nomenclature for an octopus's eight appendages is 'arms,' not 'tentacles.' Unlike standard cephalopod arms, tentacles have sucker cups with claws on the end and are extendable. The public at large, though, thinks of octopuses as having tentacles, therefore I have used both 'arms' and 'tentacles.' Oliver doesn't mind, and you shouldn't either.

I have taken several storytelling liberties and beg to invoke the power of my poetic license. The awakening of the ancient Palmyra volcano is geologically improbable. Not impossible, but improbable. My notions of the dolphin language are informed speculation. Scientists are only now delving into the rich and complex language of dolphins, and cetaceans in general. And yes, I know that it is 'the far side of the moon,' not 'the dark side of the moon,' but if Pink Floyd can get away with it, I figure I can too.

# ABOUT THE AUTHOR

JOSHUA MERTZ has a degree in film from USC, which is where he learned how to tell a story. He became a mellifluous radio deejay before finding his calling as a teleprompter in Hollywood—helping stars express themselves with fluidity—for over 20 years. His cyberpunk novel, *Machine Dreams*, was published in 2000. His short stories have appeared in *Amazing Stories*, *Aboriginal Science Fiction*, *New Maps*, and the Halloween anthology *Harvest Tales & Midnight Revels*. He is oddly compelled to compose—and recite—limericks.